I0755793

LEAVES
FROM A
FAMILY JOURNAL
BY
EMILE SOUVESTRE.
NEW-YORK:
D. APPLETON & CO.

LEAVES

FROM

A FAMILY JOURNAL.

FROM THE FRENCH

OF

EMILE SOUVESTRE,

AUTHOR OF "THE ATTIC PHILOSOPHER IN PARIS."

NEW YORK:
D. APPLETON & COMPANY,
346 & 348 BROADWAY.
MDCCC LV.

To the Memory

OF HIM WHOSE TONE OF FEELING FIRST SUGGESTED,

AND WHOSE FRIENDLY

INTERCOURSE AFTERWARDS ENCOURAGED MY LABOURS,

THIS TRANSLATION OF HIS WORK IS DEDICATED,

WITH FEELINGS OF MELANCHOLY REGRET THAT THE PEN

WHICH KNEW SO WELL

HOW TO TOUCH THE TRUTHS OF OUR COMMON NATURE

IS NOW LAID ASIDE FOR EVER.

E. M. H.

CONTENTS.

CHAPTER VII.

CHAPTER VIII.

CHAPTER IX.

CHAPTER X.

CHAPTER XI.

CHAPTER XII.

CHAPTER XIII.

CHAPTER XIV.

CHAPTER XV.

CHAPTER XVI.

CHAPTER XVII.

CHAPTER XVIII.

CHAPTER XIX.

CHAPTER XX.

LEAVES

FROM

A FAMILY JOURNAL.

CHAPTER I.

HOME.

Our Married Life had commenced, and this was Home. As I opened my eyes in our new abode, the rays of the morning sun were penetrating the muslin curtains, the air was filled with the fragrance of mignionette, and in the adjoining room I heard a loved voice warbling my favorite air.

On the different articles of furniture lay a hundred things to remind me of the change which had taken place in my mode of life. There lay the bouquet of orange-flowers worn by Marcelle on our wedding-day; here stood her work-basket; a little further on, and my eye fell on her small bookcase, ornamented with her school prizes and several other volumes, recent offerings from myself. Thus all my surroundings indicated that I was no longer alone. Till then in my independence I had merely skirted the great army of humanity, measuring all things with regard to my own strength only. I had now entered its ranks, accompanied by a fellow-traveller, whose powers and feelings must be consulted, and whose tenderness must be equalled by the protecting love shed around her. A few weeks ago, and I should have fallen unnoticed and left no void, henceforward my lot lay bound in that of others. I had taken root in life, and for the future must fortify and strengthen myself for the protection of the nests which would in time be formed beneath my shade.

Sweet sense of responsibility, which elevated without alarming me! What had Marcelle and I to fear? Was not our departure on the voyage of life like that of Athenian Theori for the island of Delos, sailing to the sound of harps and songs while crowned with flowers? Did not our hearts beat responsive to the chorus of youth's protecting genii?

Strength said, "What matters the task? Feel you not that to you it will all be easy? It is the weak alone who weigh the burden. Atlas smiled, though he bore the world on his shoulders."

Faith added, "Have confidence, and the mountains which obstruct your path shall vanish like clouds, the sea shall bear you up, and the rainbow shall become a bridge for your feet."

Hope whispered, "Behold, before you lies repose after fatigue, plenty will follow after scarcity. On, on, for the desert leads to the promised land."

And lastly, a voice more fascinating than any, added, "Love one another; there is not on earth a surer talisman; it is the 'Open Sesame' which will put you in possession of all the treasures of creation."

Why not listen to these sweet assurances? "Cherished companions of our opening career, my faith in you is strong; you, who like unto the military music which animates the soldier's courage, lead us, intoxicated by your melody, on to the battle-field of life." What can I fear from a life through which I shall pass with Marcelle's arm entwined in mine? The sun shines on the commencement of our journey; forward over flowery fields, by hedges alive with song, through ever-verdant forests! Let one horizon succeed another! The day is so lovely, and the night yet so distant!

Whilst thus occupied with my new-born happiness, I had risen and joined Marcelle, who had already taken possession of her domestic kingdom.

Every thing must be visited with her; her precocious housewifery must be admired; her arrangements must be applauded. First she showed me the little "salle à manger," dedicated to the meals which would unite us in the intervals of business; to this cause it owed the air of opulence and brightness which Marcelle had carefully striven to impart to it. China, silver, and glass sparkled on the shelves. Here, lay rich fruits half-hidden in moss; there, stood freshly-gathered flowers—every thing spoke of the reign of grace and plenty. From thence we passed into the salon, the closed curtains of which admitted only a soft and subdued light, which fell on statuettes ornamenting the consoles, and the gilt frames on the walls; on the tables lay scattered in graceful negligence, albums, elegancies of papier-maché, and carved ivory; precious nothings which had constituted the young girl's treasures. At the further end the folds of a heavy curtain concealed the bower, sacred to the lady of the castle. Here admittance was at first denied me, and I was obliged to have recourse to entreaty before the drapery was raised for our entrance.

The cabinet was lighted by a small window, over which hung a blind representing a gothic casement of painted glass, the bright colors of which were now rendered more brilliant by the sunlight which streamed through. The principal furniture consisted of a pretty lounging chair and the work-table, near which I had so often seen Marcelle seated with her embroidery when I passed under her aunt's window. Her pretty flower-stand, gay with her favorite flowers, occupied the window in which hung a gilt-wire cage, the melodious prison-house of her pet bird; and lastly, there stood, fronting the window, the bureau, consecrated since her school-days to her intimate correspondence.

She showed it to me with an almost tearful gravity. Every thing it contained was a relic, or souvenir. That agate inkstand had belonged to her elder sister, who died just when Marcelle was old enough to know and love her; this mother-of-pearl paper-cutter was a present to her from her aunt, before she became her adopted child; this seal had belonged to her father! She half opened the different drawers, for me to peep at the treasures they contained. In one were the letters of her dearest school-friend, now married, gone abroad, and therefore lost to her; in another were family papers; further down, her certificates for the performance of religious obligations, prizes obtained, and examinations passed—the young girl's humble patent of nobility!—and last of all, in the most secret corner, lay some faded flowers, and the correspondence which, with the consent of her Aunt Roubert, we had interchanged when absent from each other.

In the contents of this bureau, were united all the touching and pleasing reminiscences of her former life; they formed Marcelle's poetic archives, whither she often retired in her hours of solitude. Often, on my return from business, I found her here, smiling, and seemingly perfumed by memories of the past.

Ah! thought I, why have not men also some spot thus consecrated to like holy and sweet remembrances, a sanctuary replete with tokens of family affection, and relics of youth's enthusiasm? Our ancestors, in their pride, cut out of the granite rock safe depositories for the proofs of their empty titles and long pedigrees; is it impossible for us to devote some obscure corner to the annals of the heart, to all that recalls to us our former noble aspirations and generous hopes?

Time has torn from the walls the genealogical trees of noble families, but he has left space for those of the soul. Let us seek the origin of our decisions, our sympathies, our repugnances, and our hopes, and we shall ever find that they spring from some circumstance of bygone days. The present is rooted in the past. Who has met by chance with some relic of earlier years, and has not been touched by the remembrances called forth? It is by looking back to the starting point, that we can best calculate the distance traversed; it is in so doing that we feel either pleasure or alarm. Truly happy is the man who after gazing on the portrait of his youth, can turn towards the original and find it unimpaired by age!

These reflections were interrupted by the sound of my father's voice, which brought us out of Marcelle's retreat to welcome him. He came to see our new abode, and add his satisfaction to our happiness. He was a gentle stoic, whose courage had ever served as a bulwark to the weak, and whose inflexibility was but another name for entire self-abnegation; he was indulgent to all, because he never forgave himself, and ever veiled severity in gentleness. His wisdom partook neither of arrogance nor passion; it descended to the level of your comprehension, and while pointing upwards, led you by the hand, and guided the ascent. It was a mother who instructed, never a judge who condemned.

Though pleased with my choice, and happy at seeing us united, he had nevertheless refused a place at our fireside. "These first hours of youth are especially your own," he had said to me with a paternal embrace: "an old man would throw a shadow over the meridian sunshine of your joy. It is better that you should regret my absence, than for one moment feel my presence a restraint. Besides, solitude is necessary to you, as well as to me—for *you* to talk of your hopes for the future, for *me* to recall remembrances of the past. Some time hence, when my strength is failing, I will come to you, and close my eyes in the shadow of your prosperity."

And all my entreaties had been unavailing; the separation was unavoidable. Now, however, Marcelle sprang forward to meet him, and led him triumphantly across the room, to begin a re-examination of its treasures. My father listened to all, replied to all, and smiled at all. He lent himself to our dreams of happiness, pausing before each new phase, to point out a hope overlooked before, or a joy forgotten. Whilst thus pleasantly occupied, time slipped away unnoticed, until Marcelle's aunt arrived.

Who was there in our native town that did not know Aunt Roubert? The very mention of her name was sufficient to make one gay. Left a widow in early life, and in involved circumstances, she had, by dint of activity, order, and economy, entirely extricated herself from pecuniary difficulty. Of *her* might be said with truth, that "sa part d'esprit lui avait été donnée en bon sens." Taking reality for her guide, she had followed in the beaten track of life, carefully avoiding the many sharp flints which caprice scatters in the way. Always on the move, alternately setting people to rights, and grumbling at either them or herself, she yet found time to manage well her own affairs, and to improve those of others, a faculty which had obtained for her the name of "La Femme de ménage de la Providence." Vulgar in appearance, she was practical in the extreme, and results generally proved her in the right. Her nature was made up of the prose of life, but a prose so clear, so consistent, that, but for its simplicity, it would have been profound.

Aunt Roubert arrived, according to custom, a large umbrella in hand, while her arm was loaded with an immense horse-hair bag. She entered the little cabinet, where we were seated, like a shower of hail:—"Here you are at last," she exclaimed; "I have been into every room in search of you. Do you know, my dear, that the chests of linen are arrived?"

"Very well, I will go and see after it," said Marcelle, who, with one hand in my father's, and the other in mine, seemed in no hurry to stir.

"You will go and see after it," repeated Aunt Roubert; "that will be very useless, for you will find no place to put it in; I have been over your abode, my poor child, and instead of a home I find a 'salon de theâtre.'"

"Why aunt," exclaimed Marcelle, "how can you say so! Remi and his father have just been through the rooms, and are delighted with them!"

"Don't talk of men and housekeeping in the same breath," replied Madame, in her most peremptory tone; "see that they are provided with a pair of snuffers and a boot-jack, and they will not discover the want of any thing else; but I, dear friend, know what a house should be. In entering the lobby, just now, I looked about for a hook, on which to hang my cloak, and could find nothing but flowering stocks! My dear, flowers form the principal part of your furniture!"

Marcelle endeavored to protest against the assertion by enumerating our stock of valuables, but she was interrupted by her aunt.

"I am not talking of what you have, but of what you

have not," she said; "I certainly saw in your salon some little bronze marmozettes."

"Marmozettes!" I cried, "you mean statuettes of Schiller and Rousseau."

"Possibly," Aunt Roubert quietly replied, "they may at a push serve as match-holders; but, dear friend, in the fire-place of your office below, I could see neither tongs nor shovel. On opening the sideboard, I found a charming little silver-gilt service, but no soup-ladle, so one can only suppose that you mean to live on sweetmeats; and lastly, though the 'salle à manger' is ornamented with beautifully gilt porcelain, the kitchen unfortunately is minus both roasting-jack and frying-pan! Good heavens, these are most unromantic details, are they not?" added she, noticing the gesture of annoyance which we were unable altogether to repress; "but as you will be obliged to descend to them whenever you want a roast or an omelette, it would perhaps be as well to provide for them."

"You are right!" I replied, a little out of humor, for I had noticed Marcelle's confusion, "but such omissions are easily rectified when their need is felt."

"That is to say, you will wait until bedtime to order the mattress," replied Aunt Roubert; "well, well, my children, as you will, but now your attendance is required on your linen, which awaits you in the lobby; I suppose my niece does not propose to arrange it in her bird-cage, or flower-stand: can she show me the place destined for it?"

Marcelle had colored to the roots of her hair, and stood twisting and untwisting her apron string.

"Ah well! I see you have not thought of that," said the old aunt, "but never mind, we will find some place to put it in after breakfast; you know we are to breakfast together?"

This was a point Marcelle had not forgotten, and she forthwith led the way to her breakfast table.

At the sight of it my father gave a start of pleased surprise. In the centre stood a basket of fruit, flowers, and moss, round which were arranged all our favorite dainties; each could recognize the dish prepared to suit his taste. After having given a rapid glance round, Madame Roubert cried out:

"And the bread, my child?"

Marcelle uttered a cry of consternation.

"You have none," said her aunt, quietly, "send your servant for some." Then lowering her voice, she added, "As she will pass by my door, she can at the same time tell Baptiste to bring the large easy chair for your father, and I hope you will keep it. Your Gothic chairs are very pretty to look at, but when one is old or invalided, what one likes best in a chair, is a comfortable seat."

While awaiting the servant's return, Madame Roubert accompanied Marcelle in a tour round our abode. She pointed out what had been forgotten, remedied the inconvenience of several arrangements, or superseded them with better, doing it all with the utmost cheerful simplicity. Her hints never bordered on criticisms; she showed the error without astonishment at its having been committed, and without priding herself on its discovery.

When she had completed her examination, she took her niece aside with her accounts. Marcelle fetched the little rosewood case which served her as cash-box, and sat down to calculate the expenses of the past week. But her efforts to produce a satisfactory balance, seemed useless. It was in vain that she added and subtracted, and counted piece by piece her remaining money, the deficit never varied. Astounded at such a result, and at the amount spent, she began to examine the lock of her box, and to ask herself how its contents could have so rapidly disappeared, when Aunt Roubert interrupted her.

"Take care," she said in one of her most serious tones. "See, how from want of careful account keeping you already suspect others; before this evening is here you will be ready to accuse them. It always is so. The want of order engenders suspicion, and it is easier to doubt the probity of others than one's own memory. No lock can prevent that, my child, because none can shelter you from the results of your own miscalculations. There is no safeguard for the woman at the head of a household, like a housekeeping book, which serves to warn her day by day, and bears faithful witness at the end of the month. I have brought you such a one as your uncle used to give me."

She drew it from her bag, and presented it to Marcelle.

It was an account-book bound in parchment, the cover of which was separated like a portfolio into three pockets, destined for receipts, bills, and memoranda. The book itself was divided into several parts, distinguished one from the other by markers corresponding to the different species of receipts or expenditure, so that a glance was sufficient to form an estimate, not only of the sum total, but also of the amount of expenditure in each separate branch. The whole formed a domestic budget as clear as it was complete, in which each portion of the government service had its open account regulated by the supreme comptroller.

M. Roubert, who had been during his life a species of unknown Franklin, solely occupied in the endeavor to make business and opinions agree with good sense, had written above each chapter a borrowed or unpublished maxim, to serve as warning to its possessor. At the beginning of the book the following words were traced in red ink:

"*Economy is the true source of independence and liberality.*"

Further on, at the head of the division destined to expenses of the table:

"*A wise man has always three cooks who season the simplest food, 'Sobriety, Exercise, and Content.'*"

Above the chapter devoted to benevolence:

"*Give as thou hast received.*"

And lastly, on the page destined to receive the amount of each month's savings, he had copied this saying of a Chinese philosopher:

"*Time and patience convert the mulberry leaf into satin.*"

After having given us time to look over the book, and

read its wise counsels, Aunt Roubert explained to Marcelle the particulars of its use, and endeavored to initiate her in domestic book-keeping.

While they were conversing, my father took me by the arm, and drew me gently into the window recess.

"Thanks to Madame Roubert, your house will be perfectly ordered," he said to me; "the spirit of arithmetic herself will hold the pen, and will become the faithful biographer of your outward life; but who will regulate your spiritual and mental career? The columns of this account-book will notify the amount of your losses and gains; it will lead you to increase or diminish your expenses, and by it you will regulate your habits; it will put you 'au fait' as to your pecuniary interests; but will you as clearly understand your mental position? Where will you find the journal of the thoughts which have occupied your mind, your moments of vacillating purpose, the crisises of joy and sorrow, which will in turn disturb your soul? What will be the subject for your reflections? Will there not be portions of your experience requiring justification? If daily notes are indispensable to form an accurate reckoning of money expenditure, are they less necessary to note the employ of your faculties? Think you that it is more difficult to maintain order in a money-box, than in a conscience? How many errors, aye, how many vices even, have, unknown to us, become engrafted on our nature from this heedlessness! It is the same with the soul as with the body: an attitude taken in negligence, and persevered in through inattention, results in deformity. Avoid this evil, let light into your souls, study their movements, and note down what you see. Whilst Marcelle balances the family accounts, do you write the moral history of that family; her pen will trace a chronicle of events, yours one of thoughts and feelings."

I pressed my father's hand, promising to follow his advice, and it was in fulfilment of my word that this Journal was written.

CHAPTER II.

WE ARE LEFT TO OURSELVES.

AUNT ROUBERT's lessons to her niece were far from being yet completed; they were renewed each day at every false calculation, or neglected duty. Marcelle, accustomed to profit by forethought, about which she had never troubled herself, and who had enjoyed the results of excellent order, without being called upon to preserve it, was rather surprised to find how much care and attention it requires to maintain the humblest household in order and comfort. Until now, a mere passenger on life's vessel, she knew neither how to trim the sails, nor steer her course across the deep. Her aunt hastened to her assistance at each false manœuvre, and was ever at hand to point out the right thing to do; but at last this constant watchfulness began to annoy me; I should have preferred to endure the consequences of the mistake, rather than submit to all the vexations incurred in its reparation, and I could not help thinking this housekeeping talent very dearly purchased at the cost of these weary lessons. Without diminution of respect or regard for Madame Roubert, I yet dreaded her visits, and felt her departure a species of deliverance.

My father noticed this, and warned me.

"You are quite right," I replied, "but I am oppressed by this constant recurrence to small realities; they are forever presenting themselves on the frontiers of the region of ideality, like some rude vulgar neighbor perpetually meditating an intrusion. Shall I confess it? that so much time and attention being given to the useful, makes me begin to feel a stupid sort of hatred of it."

"And in fact makes you unwilling to do justice to her who wishes to render you assistance," interrupted my father: "it is a very common sin. Fond of what pleases us, we despise that which is useful to us. We prefer the poet who sings of harvest to the laborer who has sown it. Our gratitude for the service overflows, not in proportion to its value, but according to the gratification we derive from it. The useful man is a grim physician, to be repulsed as soon as he has ensured our safety. You are irritated to-day at the minute instructions Marcelle receives, and when she has gained ample profit from them, when order, comfort, and plenty surround you, you will enjoy them as carelessly as the light of day, without remembering to whom you owe them. How many there are who thus devote their existence to making life more easy to others, receiving indifference as their sole reward! Others may talk of the world's injustice towards genius, my sympathies belong to you, humble soldiers of necessity, forgotten by the world, and yet indispensable to all."

I understood and approved of my father's reasoning, but the feeling was too strong. I was too young to have already fully recognized the truth, that true wisdom ever makes the ideal subordinate to reality; and I had yet to learn from experience, what genius once revealed to a great thinker—that as the world of reality is limited, while that of the imagination is infinite, the only chance for repose lies in the contraction of the one, the other being incapable of enlargement.

Besides, this apprenticeship to practical realities deprived me of much of Marcelle's society; and in these first happy days of domestic intercourse, I was indignant at every thing that sundered us from one another. Since our marriage, I had neglected my old friends, forgotten my benefactors, and had very impatiently rendered the attentions due to my relatives. Forever longing for the "tête-à-tête" solitude, the joys of which seemed to me inexhaustible, I would willingly have erected an impassable barrier between the world and our fireside; I would fain have lived imprisoned in the circle of our own thoughts and emotions, deaf to all sounds beyond.

Unfortunately, the nature of my profession obliged me to be much absent from Marcelle during the week. Sunday was the only day I could call my own, and that was too often occupied in receiving visits from friends or relations, or in satisfying the demands of society; whilst Aunt Roubert was forever recollecting some forgotten duty. Many a time did we determine to go off early in the morning, and make a holiday of the whole day, but April showers had always kept us at home. At last, one Sunday the sun rose unobscured by a single cloud. The bullfinches were chirping on the lilac-trees in the court-yard, and when I opened the window, the breeze which entered, laden with the aromatic odor of the rising sap, seemed the harbinger of spring.

"Quick, quick, Marcelle," I cried, "your straw bonnet, your parasol, and let us go!"

"To what country?"

"To the land of liberty! The woods will sigh our welcome, the primroses call us, and soft mossy seats await us. Do you not hear the sweet voice of nature crying 'come, come?' Our visitors will seek us in vain to-day; they will find the cage empty, and the birds flown!"

Marcelle, delighted with the idea, clapped her hands, and was ready directly, with some fruit in her little Indian basket, while I provided myself with a volume of my favorite author. One more glance at the skies, which are blue as the forget-me-not, and we take each other by the hand, like two children escaped from school, and turn to depart.

At this instant the door-bell rings; we utter an exclamation; the door opens; it is my father! We stand motionless with disappointment. Marcelle does not advance to embrace him, and I forget to offer my hand. He comprehends matters at a glance.

"You are going out?" he gently asks.

"Now, that you are come, we shall remain," Marcelle says with a forced smile.

But he refuses; he had but looked in, in passing, to ask me for a book which he points out to me: I remind him that he has already read it.

"I know that," he replies cheerfully, "but I would wish to read it again. I have nothing to do to-day; I shall therefore spend it in studying the poet, in sounding the depths of his inspiration, in seeking where lays the secret of his fascination. Until now, I have been content to like him; I am determined now to know him."

He has taken the volume, and has wished us a pleasant walk. This time, I have pressed his hand, and Marcelle has offered him her cheek. He is gone! We do not delay an instant longer; the danger we have so narrowly escaped hurries us the more quickly forward. We all but run through the streets, and do not slacken our speed until we have lost sight of the steeple of the town-hall.

At last, the country lay before us; she was our own. The shackles of worldly life, housekeeping responsibilities, all were left at home; escaped from the weary round of vulgar duties, we wing our way into solitude.

It seemed to us at first a delicious sort of intoxication. We skirted the woods of oak and horse-chestnut, whose buds were peeping from out their blushing coverings. The sound of our footsteps was lost on the soft grass; we heard nothing but the murmur instinct with life, that always accompanies awakening nature.

We were then at last masters of our actions, of our words, of our thoughts; free from witnesses or interlopers. We could exchange our thoughts and feelings, remark upon them, and follow them up.

Nature is one vast mirror, the rays of which find their focus in every human soul; it matters not which seizes our eye, we are sure, in tracing its course, to be brought back to ourselves; what meets our eye without, leads us insensibly to look within.

We presently began to exchange our most secret

thoughts. Together we traced to their source our opinions and sentiments, and freely confessed the romance that till then each had separately made up. Our dreams of the future were altered, and rearranged a thousand times, to suit each other's fancy. Now, they consisted of unexpected successes—fortune, power, or fame—whom we imagined knocking at our door, and demanding admittance; then it was a modest, unpretending destiny, fulfilled in some unknown retreat, in which life would glide away, like the limpid stream which ripples past the woodland bower; then again, instead of pleasures to be enjoyed, our visions turned towards duties to be performed; and in the fulness of our happiness, every thing looked easy to us; no task seemed too great for our strength, no burden too heavy for us to bear. We formed for ourselves a truly Stoic code, every article of which we greeted with the courage that happiness gives.

These mutual confessions were only dropped to be as frequently resumed; for a long time, something remained to be said, some hidden corner of the heart or mind to be unveiled. At last, towards the middle of the day, when the fatigue of walking began to make itself felt, our conversation slackened, and then ceased entirely.

I was the first to remark the silence of Marcelle, and gently reproached her for it; but she vainly endeavored to resume her former strain, and I myself could find nothing new to say. We had nothing more to learn of each other,—the book was known to the last page. A species of apathy had succeeded the tender and joyous excitement in which the first few hours had passed. Each attempt to renew the conversation was succeeded by a fresh pause; and sometimes, whether from some fresh mental condition, or that words inadequately expressed our thoughts, we felt that we did not so perfectly understand each other as before. Different shades of opinion began to appear; every concord being exhausted, discords made themselves heard, and insensibly we became absent and embarrassed.

Abstractedly we quitted the charming glade in which we had seated ourselves, and our feet, of their own accord, struck into the path leading to the town. The excitement in which our flight towards solitude had commenced, had given place to languor. The sight, in returning, of the turret of the town-hall, gave me nearly as much pleasure as I had experienced a few hours before in its disappearance.

On reaching home, we found my father awaiting us there. He could not have failed to perceive the expression of our faces, but he said nothing of it.

"Ah! here you are at last!" he cried, holding out his hands to us; "thank goodness, I was getting very tired of my solitude."

I pointed to the volume of poetry open before him. "Have you not had your favorite companion?" I asked.

"Yes, certainly," he replied with a smile: "I shall astonish you, my friend, with what I am going to say, but by dint of turning over the leaves, reading over and over the choice pieces, I grow too familiar with them, I know them by heart. The charm of any human individuality has its limits, and is diminished with too great acquaintance; repetitions are then remarked, and faults of detail are noticed. I have, for the first time, discovered some badly constructed verses in my favorite poet. See the danger of excess even in reading; until now, I have never laid down the volume without regret, this evening I quit it only too willingly. Remember this, dear children, it is as necessary to curb the appetite of the heart and mind as that of the stomach; better remain but partially satisfied, than experience the disagreeables of aftertaste and satiety."

Whether the lesson were intended or unintentional, it was so much to the point, that Marcelle and I exchanged a furtive glance, immediately withdrawn in embarrassment at finding each other's feelings so mutually understood. Since then, we have made it a rule to observe some discretion in our intercourse one with the other, depriving neither our duties, nor our friends of that portion of our life which belongs to them. Our hours of companionship, from being less frequent, are all the sweeter; and when we do meet there is so much to say on what has occurred during our separation, that instead of forming a mere continuation of the daily routine, the "tête-à-tête" to which our leisure moments are devoted, is become the happiest period in our domestic life, and the recompense for our daily trials.

CHAPTER III.

THE GARDEN—ACQUAINTANCES—A FRIEND.

WE found our lodging extremely inconvenient, as Madame Roubert had foreseen, and requiring a large amount of management to make it at all comfortable. Marcelle's aunt excelled in finding a place for every thing, but that once accomplished, the disciple of order was satisfied. It was then that my father came to our aid, with some expedient ever at hand to transform inconveniences into comforts, and irregularities into graceful whims. Thanks to him, our dwelling assumed, at very little cost, a most original aspect, which occupied the mind and amused the eye. Aunt Roubert was at first scandalized at his boldness, but ended in approving his contrivances.

"Your father would make a bedroom in an egg-shell," she said to me; "invention costs him less than imitation does us. If all the world were like him, it would be with dwellings as it is with men, each would have its own peculiar physiognomy."

"Madame Roubert understands the matter," observed my father, when I repeated her words to him. "Men should arrange their houses according to their wants, and they would then necessarily reflect something of their owners. I do not like that want of interest in one's surroundings, the lack of endeavor in the possessor to make his abode suit his particular wants. It is the most natural field for the exercise of his energies in his leisure hours. If he neglect to embellish his dwelling, to remedy its inconveniences as far as thought and contrivance can do so, and thus render his outward life more easy, he recedes a step towards the savage, who lives content with an apron of leaves and a hammock of bark.

"The increase of domestic comforts is one of the strongest evidences of man's civilization. It proves his attachment to his home and family, the existence of daily duties, and the need felt for innocent pleasures. 'The badly-built nest,' says the Chinese proverb, 'indicates the migratory bird.'"

"Agreed," I replied, "but to arrange things as you have done, needs such an imagination as yours."

"There is far more of memory than imagination here," said my father. "Whenever I have seen an ingenious contrivance I have taken a note of it, and have thus compiled a repertory of domestic arrangements, from which you have profited. We too generally neglect to notice these details. It is all very well for the rich to depend upon the taste of their architects and upholsterers, nothing hinders them; they can if they choose throw down a wall, by way of altering a hanging. But for us who must content ourselves with things as they are, who must surmount, instead of remove, the obstacle, and disguise its deformity, observation and memory prove valuable auxiliaries. Each difficulty is set aside by some expedient remarked elsewhere, until our dwelling is adorned by degrees with scraps of everybody's genius. Never despair of improvement. By infusing something of ourselves into our surroundings, we become more strongly attached to them. Our abode thus becomes a sort of record in which are inscribed our habits, our preferences, and we love it not only as our shelter, but as our own work."

I approved of these ideas of my father's, and did my best to put them into practice. I was seldom without saw or hammer in hand completing some contrivance; until after a time every thing was so thoroughly arranged, that unless I undid, there was nothing more to be done. I was falling into unwilling idleness when I heard that the little garden at the end of the court-yard was to let.

Many a time had Marcelle and I, whilst leaning from the window, and looking down on its flower-beds and linden bowers, envied the possession of this spot of verdure, removed from the noisy streets, and enlivened by the song of birds. On hearing that it was to let, our first impulse was to hasten to the proprietor, but reflection came in time to arrest us. Our household accounts could only be made to balance by strict economy. Ours was that small competency which the slightest stumble would convert into poverty. It was in vain for Marcelle to re-add the column of figures, propose reforms, or encroachment on our tiny capital—the proposed expense always destroyed the equilibrium.

We were obliged to give it up!

But many times during that day I saw her turn towards the window which overlooked the oasis of leaves and flowers, and after a sad glance, return to her needle with a sigh.

My inability to satisfy this natural wish gave me acute pain, and I in my turn began to calculate, but without arriving at a more favorable result. I at last reached the stage of discouragement which precedes the renouncement of all hope of success, and was mechanically turning over the leaves of Aunt Roubert's account-book, in which all our expenses were noted down, when my eye fell on an item.

It was like a sudden illumination.

I rapidly turned over the leaves of the register, seeking several other articles connected with the first. I took a pen, drew up a statement, went over it carefully a second time, and rising with an exclamation of joy—

"My hat, Marcelle!" I cried; "quick, quick: we will rent the garden!"

"Are you serious?" she asked.

"Quite serious," I replied, while looking for my gloves.

"But reflect; it will cost us 150 francs."

"I will economize 170."

"How?"

"Listen."

And taking up my newly-made account, I read aloud—

Amount of my smoking expenses:

	f.	c.
Three cigars a day, costing per annum,	164	25
Four packets of allumettes per annum,	0	20
One cigar case,	2	0
Scented waters for the mouth,	4	0
TOTAL,	170	45

Without taking account of burnt clothes, lost time, and injured teeth! The rent of the garden paid, there will still remain 20 francs 45 centimes for the purchase of seeds and roots, and this will all be gained by the sacrifice of a bad habit. Quick, bring me my hat; I tremble lest somebody should be before us.

A quarter of an hour after I returned with the lease in my pocket, and Marcelle and I forthwith took possession of the little garden.

Never did new-made lord survey his new domains with such joy as we did ours.

Each tuft of verdure, each flowering shrub, elicited an exclamation. Marcelle discovered some violets growing at the foot of the bower, and I gathered her a mountain strawberry which had ripened in the shade.

Acquaintance must be made with every tree, the fruit must be counted, the rose-trees must be trimmed, and a plan be drawn out of the work to be done during the season. I gravely took out my note-book, that nothing might be forgotten.

We decided that the flower-baskets should be filled with geraniums, that mignionette must be sown, that the honeysuckle should be transplanted during the coming autumn, and that I should immediately re-gravel the paths.

The borders round the garden required alteration also: two trees were chosen from which to suspend the Indian hammock given to us by my brother; and places were marked out for some more shrubs. These important arrangements occupied us during several evenings; ten times was the garden planted and replanted in imagination, before I had thought of taking up either spade or rake. I set to work in earnest at last, and ever found, in my garden, a pleasant relaxation from mental occupation, as well as healthy exercise. There was always some bed to weed, flowers to tie up, or digging to do, and whilst thus employed, Marcelle sat with her work in the arbor, and encouraged me in my labor with her voice and smiles.

Aunt Roubert, from the moment of our possessing the garden, had been anxious to plant my borders with cabbages and lettuces, and, after defending them foot by foot I was at last compelled to relinquish the lower part of the garden to her management entirely; but not satisfied with that, she was continually invading my domains with her rows of onions and parsley; and I found that the only means of preventing still further encroachments, was to plant a strong boundary line of sorrel, which was to be recognized by both as the limit of our territories. My father and Marcelle decided where it should be; but even then, Aunt Roubert managed to appropriate a few more inches than belonged to her, and I did not always deny myself the pleasure of encroaching a little upon her rows of cress and chervil. But we reciprocally forgave these invasions, unavoidable between two such active and ambitious neighbors.

My father heartily approved of my new occupation. "The earth," he often said to me, "is our first friend; it is on her lap that each community has been fostered. Every production of hers either supplies our wants, or enchants our eye; her every phase carries with it a perpetual charm to man. Whether he gaze on waving corn-fields, the towering forest, or the perfumed flower, his heart swells in presence of this gigantic cornucopia, whence so unceasingly flows all that can charm and enrich mankind. History confirms the fact, that those races occupied in agricultural employments have ever been of gentle manners, and given to hospitality; and this they mainly owe to nature's softening influence, who, by her constant munificence, keeps up in the human soul a species of inward content and vague feeling of gratitude. The man who labors in the open fields, under the glorious sky, breathing freely the fresh invigorating air, with the thousand prodigalities of nature spread before his eyes, knows nothing of the troubles which embitter the life of the worker in cities. His existence is free as the mountain air, and flows as peacefully as the waters of the gentle streamlet; and country life, the starting-point of all communities, is still the hope and aim of every worn-out citizen. Satiated with honors and pleasures, we depart, like Abdalonymus, the descendant of kings, to cultivate a field, and watch the ripening fruit, far removed from the world in which we reigned."

The garden supplied me with occupation for my leisure-hours, but I could not always have the pruning-knife or spade in my hand; besides, this mere manual labor was insufficient for me: I felt the need of mental relaxation and a communion of sentiment. The difference of age and opinion prevented my enjoying this with my father, who, having reached the mountain's summit, nearly freed from human passions, and purified by life's ordeal, looked down on the world from his calm, clear atmosphere, while I, enveloped in the mists of the valley, could as yet barely distinguish the reality of the clouds. What I needed was a companion for my ignorance, a believer in my Utopia, to whom I should dare confide all my thoughts, and who would reclaim me from error by the confession of his own.

Marcelle could not be this friend. Solely occupied in loving, and being happy, she, in common with other women, possessed the wisdom that is content to be ignorant—the wisdom alike of the simple and the genius. She understood nothing of the preoccupations of a mind always in quest of some chimerical ideality; in her I possessed a sister and a friend—all that I needed was an interlocutor.

Unfortunately our family connections and neighbors seemed unable to supply this want. All those whom chance had made our friends belonged to the genus *monochord*—men whose minds could produce but one sound Yoked to one idea, like a horse in a mill, they undeviatingly trod the same circle.

First on the list came Captain Le Sur, a first-rate soldier, who had travelled all over Europe without having perceived it, who had gained forty victories without knowing how, and who detested a civilian without knowing why.

This hatred of everybody and every thing, to which I however formed an exception, thanks to my father having served, combined with the cultivation of an acre of land outside the town, constituted the sole occupations of the retired hero. Besides this, he was in possession of a dozen anecdotes of bivouac life, in each of which the civilian made but a sorry figure, and with these he never failed to regale us at each visit, till at length Marcelle began to call them "*the twelve labors of Captain Le Sur.*"

Monochord the second was an old tradesman, who, after having passed forty years of his life in measuring cloth, devoted his old age to picquet and the rearing of rabbits. Every evening as the clock struck seven, the card-table in his little salon was brought forward; little baskets of ivory fish were placed at each side of the green cloth; the cards, wrapped in a leaf of some old ledger, were laid in readiness, and the usual party assembled for their daily game. Then followed the customary conversation on the price of provisions, the hours of departure of the diligences, the state of their neighbors' health; interspersed with two or three everlasting puns on hearts and diamonds from M. Duplessis, which had never failed to elicit a laugh from his companions on each evening since the fall of the empire.

Among these was old Richard, formerly a tax-collector, but now pensioned. His individual peculiarity was punctuality. For thirty years he had done the same things, and uttered the same phrases, at the same hour of each day. His watch regulated at noon by a neighbor's sun-dial, formed his supreme code; he consulted it to ascertain if he had an appetite, or was sleepy; whether he should walk, or go to bed. He imagined he had found the true aim of this life, for the right employment of which God has given us a heart and intelligence, in being, like the hero of the epigram, the man of all France *who best knew what o'clock it was.* But the greater part of our neighbors, relations, or acquaintances, had not even *such* an amusing peculiarity.

Striking blindly against events, whilst borne onward by the great current of existence, they reminded one of the smooth ocean pebbles, which differ from one another in color and size alone. In vain did I seek for character among them; the wear and tear of the world had effaced all impression from this human coin.

I one day expressed to my father my extreme annoyance at being thus surrounded by a crowd without a feature. "Because they have the power of locomotion they think they live," said I, "but look into their eyes, and you will see no spark of enthusiasm; listen to what they say, and you will find it mere repetition; they fancy themselves men, whilst they are only automatons; theirs is a living death! How am I to find amongst these speaking images a being who can understand and answer me? What have I in common with them?"

"Humanity!" my father replied: "it is because you expect too much, that every thing around you seems miserable; the ideal renders you unjust to the reality. You imagine want of sense in that which is only common-place. Search more deeply, and in every one of these beings whom you compare to statues, you will find a spark of living fire.

"Not one among them but has inherited some qualities which link him with his fellow-men. This one has order, that one contentment, the other courage. You see these qualities in a distorted light, owing to their insolation, and consequent want of equilibrium; but Aunt Roubert would tell you, in her practical morality, borrowed from Sancho Panza, 'that there is no mill too old to produce some meal;' she would counsel you to learn perseverance from the captain; how to refresh your mind by the various combinations of the games which make us again children, from the old merchant; and from old Richard how to regulate the external actions of life, and the art of attaching the leaden sandals of habit to the feet of fancy! I would add that you expect too much, and claim from acquaintances what you should only look for in a friend.

"With the latter you may hope for the communion of mind which heals and strengthens; from the former you should merely expect the kindliness of feeling which refreshes us. Both one and the other are necessary in different degrees; but *acquaintances* are thrown in your way by chance; *friends* will be the reward of your devotion.

"Put your heart into the search for one, freely offer assistance to any of the crowd who need it, and sooner or later you will find a hand outstretched towards yours, and your soul will meet its likeness. Do not imitate those who, shut up in their individuality as in a citadel, indifferent to all passers by, yet send forth on the four winds of heaven the melancholy cry, 'there are no friends!' They do exist, be sure of it; but only for those who seek, for those deeply interested in the search, and for those who do not remain content to spin out the thread of life in a corner, like a spider's web, intended to catch happiness."

My father's words brought conviction to me, but gave me

neither the courage to seek, nor the patience to wait. I grumbled at the smallness of my native town, every inhabitant of which I believed I knew, and none of whom answered my expectations as a friend. The novelty of my domestic happiness having worn off, I felt a void in the social circle, and like the Sybarite, I found this crumpled rose-leaf insupportable.

The opposite side of the court in which we lived, was occupied by a pile of buildings of considerable size, inhabited by several families, with whom we had, until then, held but little intercourse. We had merely interchanged a bow, a few words in passing, and the little services required of every good neighbor. The third floor was occupied by a junior clerk, who had only lately arrived with his young wife and one child. M. and Madame Hubert were evidently on the brink of poverty, and it would have been difficult to say whether their mute resignation was the result of courage or languor. Never did the sound of voice or song issue from their humble abode; the windows were always closed; the husband might be seen going to, and returning from the office; the wife fetching water from the well, walking with her child, and bringing home the necessary provisions; but all in silence. They were ever polite to their neighbors, responding to their smiles and salutations; calm in appearance, but a calmness veiled by a cloud.

Marcelle and I had from the first noticed these two shadows, melancholy, rather sorrowful, and had taken a lively interest in their doings, though this instinctive inclination towards them had not led to more than the bestowal of a few caresses on the child, and the exchange of some friendly words, until an accidental circumstance brought us into closer connection.

Marcelle used often to sit with her work in the arbor, during my absence at the office; and one evening having forgotten her embroidery, she returned to fetch it, leaving the garden gate half open. Having finished business sooner than usual, I entered as she was coming down stairs, and taking me by the hand she led me off, to show me a cluster of snowdrops which had just blossomed.

They were my favorite flowers; the plants had been sent me from Paris, by a friend, and I waited their flowering with impatience.

We hastened to the garden, Marcelle a little in advance, that she might have the pleasure of serving as guide. We had nearly reached the spot, when she suddenly stopped short with a half-repressed cry, and following her glance, I in my turn stood motionless.

Before the flower-basket stood Madame Hubert's little girl, with her apron full of the snowdrops she had just gathered; the plants were stripped, and nothing remained in the plundered basket, save shrivelled leaves and broken stems; her mother, who, while occupied in hanging out her linen in the court, had not noticed her child's absence, hastened to the spot, and stood in consternation on beholding the work of destruction.

When she perceived us, she turned very pale, and clasping her hands, stammered forth some forlorn excuse.

My first emotion of vexation could not withstand this

humility. Marcelle, however, better able to appreciate the young mother's painful embarrassment, did not content herself with the appearance of resignation, she knew how to pardon gracefully, and advancing smilingly towards her neighbor:

"It is nothing," she said;—"a few flowers which two or three sunny days will replace: I am alone to blame. I should have closed the door on going away, or rather I ought to have opened it long since to your little girl, in order that she might learn to be careful of the flowers."

And kneeling before the child, she took her in her arms.

"I am sure, Renée, that you will never again pick the flowers, if I ask you not to do so," she said.

The little girl looked at her, her large eyes full of tears, and shook her head.

"And you will be content to play on the paths, and to walk on the grass, without breaking the plants?"

Renée made another affirmative movement.

"Well! I want to see if you know how to keep your promises," Marcelle replied, while embracing her; "we will begin from to-day. I shall beg your mamma to send you to play for a couple of hours under our linden-trees, unless she would like better to accompany you herself."

All this was said with such free, good-humored gayety, that Madame Hubert regained her composure, warmly thanked her, and consented to make the tour of the garden, to which she was a stranger.

I was struck with the sweetness of her voice, by the elegance of her language, and the reserved delicacy of her manners. Without being pretty, she possessed that charm which seems to emanate from within and illuminate the exterior. She did not accept Marcelle's invitation to Renée, until insisted upon by me, and then only came at far-distant intervals for a very short time. At length Marcelle's ever-friendly reception made her more familiar; the child served as a connecting-link between the two women; the caresses bestowed on her little one won the mother's heart, and little by little we learnt her history.

Poor, and an orphan, Madame Hubert had been brought up at a boarding-school, paying for its advantages, at first by successful displays calculated to recommend the establishment, and in the end by the devotion of her whole time. Bound down by a seeming obligation, on which speculation had made a capital rate of interest, she had borne every thing uncomplainingly, until a young relative, isolated like herself, had made her acquaintance, and finally united his fate with hers. Both had been so long accustomed to the galling fetters of patronage, that they had not yet dared to assume an erect attitude: theirs was a timid happiness, that feared to be noisy; the effort employed by most in seeking to attract notice, was spent by them in the endeavor to avoid it.

It was only by slow degrees and happy chances that we succeeded in penetrating this closed existence, and in discovering its hidden treasures. We had been acquainted with Madame Laura Hubert for some months, when one day on entering Marcelle's room, she mechanically passed her hand over the open piano, and elicited a modulation so distinct and so sweet, that we both raised our heads at the same moment. The young woman blushed, but it was too late; she had betrayed herself. We obliged her to seat herself at the instrument, and our little dwelling was soon inundated with a flood of harmony.

M. Hubert was master of several languages, had read much, and reflected still more, and possessed one of those choice intellects, in which the silent process of germination is succeeded by luxuriant and overflowing harvests.

Content to receive their bread day by day, celebrating their fêtes in their own hearts, and together mounting the Jacob's ladder, of which each round is an idea, the young couple lived unknown, and without a desire ungratified.

"We have all that is necessary," said Hubert to me one day. "What would be the use of enlarging our possessions? we have an unlimited kingdom at our command—that of thought. Is it not there that man's true dominion lies? Once certain of the needful supplies for his daily life, and having satisfied the demands of reality, what better occupation can he find than in studying the world's progress—in applauding its advance? Which is the nobler, worthier character think you, that of the man, who finds his happiness in gazing on his riches, heaped up in his own individual corner, or that man's who seeks and finds it among the riches distributed abroad for the benefit of all? At which should we the most rejoice, at a gratification attained, or at the circulation of a useful idea through the world? at a legacy which adds another dish to our table, or at a discovery which increases the supply of bread to the famished? Our individual life is but a necessity; the true interest lies in the general life of humanity."

I repeated these words to my father.

"Here is the interlocutor of whom you are in search," he said. "Aunt Roubert and I have initiated you in practical life; Marcelle has opened to you the world of the affections; you needed a friend to unlock that of reflection, and fortune has granted you one. You are now in possession of all that can assist in the development of your being, and in the completion of your mortal education. The rest depends upon God and yourself."

CHAPTER IV.

MANKIND—COUNTRY AND FAMILY—WOMAN'S INFLUENCE—THE FIRST ACT OF BENEVOLENCE.

Our friendship with M. and Madame Hubert filled up the void in our existence. However pleasant the home-circle may be, none can with impunity remain shut up in it. The vision which dwells constantly on a contracted horizon, becomes shortened; the air gets thickened in this narrow inclosure from the world; and the mind, which shuns all other contact, insensibly tends towards, and ends in crochetiness. Besides home affections which fully develop individuality, it is well for us when chosen friendships connect us with the world and prevent our estrangement from it.

My father had frequently warned me against this voluntary seclusion, which transforms home into a convent, and withdraws us from earth, not for pious meditation, but for the sole and entire contemplation of ourselves.

"Beware," he constantly said to me, "of those hermitages built entirely of your own happiness, and to which you retire, like the rat of La Fontaine into his cheese—indifferent to all that passes on the outside. Keep at least one friend who will bring you a little of the outer air. In these modern days, men are too dependent on one another to make entire detachment from the rest—a safe experiment for any one, for in their dependence lies their strength. The blow struck, however distant, will at length reach you, as the wave which leaves America in time washes the shore of France. It will never do to imitate in act the speech of the egotistical clown: 'What signifies the deluge to me? If it inundate Lorraine, I shall take the diligence for Franche Comté!' The embankment once levelled, the torrent flows on till all is flooded."

Our new friend was of all others the most suitable to encourage this feeling of community with our fellow-creatures. An orphan from an early age, he had had teachers, but no parents; and sentiment was less developed in him than ideas. Straightforward and simple-hearted, though resolute, he had from early youth sought consolation in the lap of morality, and had, to use his own expression, been brought up at its knees. The human race was his family, and all who bore the form of man were dear and sacred to him as members of that family; nothing could root out this strong instinct of universal fraternity: he was the Abel of the human race.

With more limited sympathies myself, I often found it difficult to reconcile our feelings and opinions; from this numerous debates resulted, the traces of which I find scattered through the notes of my journal, and of which I will give a specimen.

Tuesday.—We were seated for some time under the lime-trees. Justin (M. Hubert) had brought me the works of Anastasius Grün, and I read aloud, translating for Marcelle's benefit, one of the German poet's songs, which is as follows:

"An old and hoary rock reared itself in the midst of the waves, and I admired its solitary strength.

"A tree grew on the hoary rock, where it partly raised its crest, and I admired it, so solitary, yet so verdant.

"A swift-winged swallow sang on the tree on the rock, and I thought her happy in her solitary joy.

"But I no longer envy your destiny, O tree, rock, and swallow! for see, a storm has arisen, and the *solitary* tree is overthrown.

"The weary swallow has sunk into the waves, ere her sisters can succor her, and the solitary rock is engulfed in the waters.

"O poets of Germany, the rock, tree, and swallow, bring you to my remembrance, who think to gather your laurels apart from your brethren.

"With aspiring souls ye look to the north, to the south, to the east, but none looks behind him, where lies his fatherland.

"Ye resemble the solitary rock, ocean-girt, the tree which displays its verdure far from the forest, the solitary swallow, whose notes are lost in the azure of the heavens.

"Unite, ye solitary rocks! Gather together, ye solitary swallows! Trees proud of your lonely grandeur, mingle your branches, and multiply your roots!

"Together let us form a chain of impregnable rocks, which may withstand the waves of an ignorant crowd!

"Let us unite in a forest where the trees, from their proximity, appear more verdant; and then, let the storm come, it shall not bow our interlaced crests!

"Let us swallows sing in chorus; our voices will be not less sweet, and their tones united in one harmonious hymn, shall ascend to heaven itself!"

Not even my bad translation could destroy the beauty of this charming little poem. Marcelle and Laura were both struck with the *graceful* idea, I with its *aim*. I admired this appeal to the German muses, who, each occupied in singing in its bower what it felt, or thought it saw in the clouds, never once turned their thoughts and attention to the one great subject of interest—Germany itself. I wished that this call might resound elsewhere, in every corner of the earth where a country existed; that its poets united, might thus form a rampart to defend it; a forest to protect it; and an harmonious chorus to comfort and support it!

Meanwhile Justin sat quietly by, picking a flower to pieces; and on our asking the cause of his silence, he replied:

"Because I am not like you, satisfied with it. Where is the good of merely diverting art from the contemplation of individual egotism to that of another? What is country, but an enlarged personality? If we sing its praise, do we not still praise ourselves? Poesy, which is the gift of God as much as light and heat, should like them benefit mankind in general. Why sing of Germany, England, or France; why not rather of the entire human race! What do your patriotic hymns do, but divide the world into separate factions? each repeats his own, under a standard belonging only to a people, instead of singing it under the glorious sky, which is common to us all. By this means you convert your glorifications into insults, and your patriotic love into cries of hatred. All sympathy with your fellow-men stops at a boundary traced by the chances of war; within, they are your brethren; without, your enemies! and yet they are one and all, men accessible to the same emotions, and subject to the same wants! On merely observing the countenance, you recognize a fellow-creature, but at the sight of the cockade, the hand extended to grasp, is raised to strike!—it is a ferocious rivalry which cherishes and encourages all man's baser instincts, and causes blood to flow like water. Patriotism has been, till now, one of those idols on whose altars France has sacrificed her vanquished. Never, therefore expect me to admire those who sing its praise; I care not to listen to the bard of a *nation*, he whom I would hear, is the poet of all mankind."

I warmly defended the cause of patriotism: "Would you have us then regard the land in which we first beheld the light no more than any other portion of the earth; the spot which has witnessed our birth, from which we receive our first impressions, our language and habits, every thing in fact that makes a man? We might as well say that the mother who bore us is the same to us as any other woman. The Greeks of former times held that they were born of the very earth they cultivated; is not this a precedent for all other nations? May we not say that each nation is born of its own soil, with which it is connected by a thousand invisible roots, and that, to a certain degree, its temperament is influenced by it? Each race is planted in its appropriate soil and climate; each occupies its place, fulfils its appointed part, accomplishes its evolution, gives *its note;* whilst the whole composes, as some one has said, 'The gamut of human feeling.' Attempt to amalgamate the nations, diminish their personality, and you will have false notes, and destroy the gamut; consequently any idea of harmony in the vast concert of nations is impossible. A distinction between nations is as necessary as between individuals, if you wish to preserve to each group of humanity its peculiar instincts and capabilities. Doubtless this distinction induces rivalry, but the multiplicity of social ties, complicated interests, and neighborly kindness, do much to soften this feeling. To attempt to substitute philanthropy for patriotism is to endeavor to replace instinct by pure ideality, and to raise logical speculations above the claims of gratitude and early associations. Were the thing possible, what would you gain? Only a diminution of the faculty of devotion. At present man instinctively and spontaneously attaches himself to his country, he could not so attach himself to humanity, without reflection and a conscientious effort. The greater portion of mankind require simple, visible duties, an involuntary affection, and an aim within reach of the smallest minds and shortest arms. The accomplishment of your wish supposes a world of stoic philosophers versed in the most difficult rules of the algebra of duty, and not the ignorant and impulsive crowd which will always constitute the mass. By endeavoring to stretch the feelings of responsibility and devotion too far, you risk their breaking altogether; let them develop themselves in patriotism, and do not place us between an ideality we cannot grasp and our own personality, or we shall be borne away by the latter, and you will lose the patriots without making men. Believe me, the love of country is still the best teacher of hearts, and it is that which, above all, preserves to us on earth, the traditions of courage, patience, and self-devotion."

"You forget," exclaimed Marcelle, "our first teacher, Home, which instructs us in all those qualities necessary to the existence of larger societies; where else do we learn obedience, industry, self-devotion, responsibility? And what is country but an extended home?"

My father, who had joined us, and listened to the preceding conversation, now smiled.

"Yes," he said, "each of you sees only his own star, and desires that it alone should occupy the heavens; but all three shine at the same time, only in different spheres. Here, nearest to earth, behold Marcelle's star, which is our constant guide, while it illumines our path; without it each step would be a stumble, each action a stain. A little higher and you come to Henri's, which glitters in the regions of storm, a noble planet under whose influence heroes are created. And higher still in the blue vault of heaven, less visible to vulgar eyes, scintillates the star of Justin, worshipped by the wise and gentle. These three lights illumine our firmament. The great point is to decide which it is your duty to follow when they lead you different ways; for in this scale of obligations, beginning with those of home, and ascending successively to those of country and humanity, the usual order should sometimes be inverted."

"And what rule are we to follow in our choice of duty?" we all asked.

"That of justice, not preference," replied my father. "Each time a struggle occurs, let the nation subdue the individual, and the species the nation. Be first a man, to obey the God who gave you that name, then a patriot, to render to your country that you owe to it; the title of head of a family, which is generally paramount, ought only to rank third. When these duties are opposed to each other they must be performed according to the order of their importance, always preferring general to individual duty."

Thursday.—Yesterday Justin and I could not agree upon a point of history. The discussion waxed warm: we spoke loudly, and did not stop to pick our words—for the moment antagonism of opinion silenced friendship. At this juncture we were joined by Marcelle and Laura, and the question, after they had given their opinions upon it, assumed a perfectly different aspect. They shrouded it in grace and playfulness, and where we had launched a Latin quotation, they ventured a smile. Becoming more calm, we discovered that our opinions differed less than we had imagined, and we separated perfectly satisfied with each other.

But this trifling circumstance made me reflect on the advantages that would accrue from the association of women in our intellectual pursuits, as well as practical concerns. Surely our companion for life is our most natural interlocutor: why should any separation exist between our minds? and would not men do well to initiate her into the world of ideas, that she may be fitted to follow them through it? We leave her in ignorance of the greater part of the questions which occupy our thoughts, allowing her to blindly influence and counsel us, yet do not grant her the means of enlightenment. What is there to prevent our raising her to our own level? Interested in all that concerns us, she would then know better how to assist, console, support, and soothe. She would live with us that inner life, be acquainted with our every thought, and know exactly what spring to touch, and what wound to heal. There would, in fact, be but one soul between us, or rather two souls in perfect communion; for there, as elsewhere, the woman would bring her more acute sensations and practical faculties into action, be the question one of art, philosophy, or education; and she would ever be able, like Molière's housekeeper, to enlighten even genius itself, upon the realities of life.

Saturday.—Behind our garden runs a narrow alley, occupied by the poorest class of laborers, and this evening our attention being drawn towards it by the varied sounds which issued from it—children's cries, the shrill tones of women scolding, mingled with men's rougher voices—our conversation turned upon the means of ameliorating the condition of the working people. Each brought forward his own pet scheme, and then proceeded to justify it; at last, when we had exhausted all our theories of reform, my father turned to the, till then, silent Madame Roubert, and asked her what she would do for the poor work-people. "I?" said the old aunt. "Parbleu! that's quickly answered; whilst you build them castles in the air, I knit flannel jackets for their children."

Everybody laughed; but Madame Roubert's answer recurring to me afterwards, I could not help thinking of how much more real use she was to those whose hard lot we had been deploring than any of us. Our dreams of ameliorations were rather themes for the exercise of our imagination than the expression of real sympathy; for what result did they produce? And were it possible to put our plans into practice, should we have the courage and patience to persevere? We resembled the Pharisees, who contented themselves with talking of their charity, whilst Aunt Roubert gave in silence to the needy that cup of cold water, in reward for which Jesus Christ has promised the kingdom of heaven. What is the use of dreaming of a future terrestrial paradise for them, if we do nothing towards lessening the misery of their present life? Can those be called good intentions which result in no good action?

Such thoughts as these had for some time occupied my mind, and I at last communicated them to Marcelle. We both agreed that it was time we put our theories into practice, and, at least, extend a helping hand to the shipwrecked mariner before we thought of subduing the tempest. And we are now in search of some good work to accomplish.

Monday.—It is found!—Our laundress came this morning, and whilst counting the linen, Marcelle noticed her troubled air, and deep sighs. On her questioning her, the woman told her that her husband was in great trouble. Employed by one of the large carrier contractors, and being unable to read or write, he had trusted his memory too far, and become involved in the many details. Pay-time had arrived, without his being able to satisfy his creditors, and those who owed him money disagreed about the amount. The poor fellow, completely lost in this labyrinth of complicated obligations, was becoming desperate, and began to talk of suicide. I promised to take his affairs in hand, and on examination found that with order and patience, he might succeed in extricating himself from his difficulties. Marcelle, on her part, devotes two hours a day to teaching their little Colette, who is very industrious, in reading, writing, and ciphering; so that if they all persevere, in a year's time they will be free from their liabilities, and by that period Colette will be able to keep her father's books.

Saturday—was the second anniversary of our marriage.

I like these fêtes in celebration of a serious act, or important epoch in life; they bring with them, besides the lingering perfume of the past, a fresh access of joy and tenderness; and the heart, grown cold from habit, revives at the warm touch of memory. To Marcelle and myself this day could only bring a warmer glow of gratitude to our hearts whilst mutually attributing to each other the cause of our happiness.

After the first moments of tender congratulation, Marcelle took up Aunt Roubert's housekeeping book, and seated herself at my desk like a book-keeper about to show his accounts.

"Come, be serious," she said, imitating the tone of her old aunt; "loving is very well, but a clear balance-sheet before every thing. Let us see if you are satisfied with your housekeeper."

I laughingly interrupted her, but she obstinately continued to drag me along her columns of figures. When I spoke of all the happiness I owed her, she enumerated what we had spent in confectionery; when I alluded to my wishes accomplished and surpassed, she complained of the dearness of butter or charcoal! I was obliged at last to have recourse to my lawful authority, and taking the book from her hands, declared that if she persisted in going on, I would throw it into the fire.

"Ungrateful creature!" cried Marcelle, mischievously; "ungrateful wretch, who will not take the trouble to understand all I have done for him."

I endeavored to assure her she was mistaken.

"No, no," she continued; "you cannot comprehend a woman's feelings in the management of her household. What is to you a mere account-book, is to her a record of all that conduces to your ease and comfort. What to your eyes is a mere register of figures, recalls to mine a thousand desires conquered, economies realized, and problems solved."

"I know it," I interrupted; "the lord and master acknowledges all he owes to his able minister of finance for presenting him with a balanced budget."

"Balanced!" repeated Marcelle: "do you thank me for that?"

"With bent and uncovered head."

"Down on your knees then, Monsieur; down on your knees, for he brings you a *surplus!*"

As she pronounced these words with majestic triumph, she shook above my head a bank-note; but my look and gesture expressed such utter astonishment that she burst intó a merry laugh.

"Yes," she cried, skipping about for joy, "five hundred francs saved upon these miserable articles, of which you could not bear the mention! Five hundred francs!—or rather, no;—listen, my lord, to what this scrap of paper contains."

And, putting her lips to my ear, like a child telling a fairy-tale, she began:

"First of all, that causeuse you have so long wished for, in which we can both read before the fire in the evenings.

"Then a bookcase for your room, to fill up the ugly gap you complained of.

"Then several beautiful books which your father will not buy for himself, because they are too dear.

"And a roasting-jack for Aunt Roubert."

"And a new toilet-table for Marcelle," I exclaimed.

"And a new secretary for Monseigneur," she added.

"And some Dresden china-ornaments for the mantelpiece.

"And some bronzes for the consoles.

"And a carpet for the salon.

"And four orange-trees for the garden."

Again we both broke into a hearty laugh.

"Decidedly, we shall find the whole world in this bank-note," I said.

"No doubt of it," cried Marcelle: "you have not forgotten Chamisso's tale, in which the devil successively draws from his pocket a tent, a dinner, and a carriage, every thing in fact that he asked for? You know, dear, the Germans consider this a myth; but I think the true Devil's pocket is a bank-note, from which one can produce whatever he chooses; only, as we might be encumbered if we asked too much, let us choose from this chaos of articles."

And then came fresh embarrassments and disputes. Each obstinately objected to what was intended for himself, and was only anxious to secure what would please the other; at last we came to a compromise. We drew up a list of purchases, in which each had his share; and, being now agreed, we determined to finish the business at once. Marcelle hastened to don her bonnet and shawl, I my hat, and off we set on our shopping expedition.

We did not meet with what we wanted at the first places we went to, and Marcelle nearly stamped with impatience; for she was anxious to celebrate the day with her pleasant surprises; and to do that all must be at our house by dinner-time, when my father and Aunt Roubert were to join us. At last she remembered a small upholsterer, who had sometimes served her, and who, if he could not supply us with the required articles, would at least direct us where we might procure them.

Gaubert lived in the old part of the town, and on entering the shop, we found only a little girl of about twelve years of age in attendance, who saluted us with a frightened stare from her large blue eyes, as she tossed her disordered hair aside, and called her father in a trembling voice. But no one answered; and, hearing voices in the back-shop, we took the liberty of entering.

There we found Gaubert standing with drooping head and listless arms against the opposite wall; near him, in an old arm-chair, cowered his invalid wife, her face covered with her handkerchief, sobbing bitterly; whilst near the door stood a great, big man, hat in hand, whom I immediately recognized as the sheriff's officer, Baron.

Just as we made our appearance, he seemed to be giving the couple a last alternative; but seeing us, he stopped short; then recognizing me, he turned round, and taking me aside, exclaimed:

"For God's sake, Monsieur Remi, be so kind as to explain to Maître Gaubert that I cannot defer the execution of a writ; and that if I proceed against a neighbor, it is not my fault, but my employer's."

"But what is the matter?" I asked.

"An execution for the miserable sum of three hundred and thirty francs. I have myself begged old Rigot to wait a little longer for his money, but one might as well preach abstinence to a ravenous wolf! He is determined to seize the goods. Faith, I'm sorry for it, but what am I to do?"

Gaubert, who had been silent until now, began to inform us how the debt had originated; it had been contracted in a moment of difficulty, and increased by usury. He ended by bursting into a towering passion, showering maledictions and menaces upon his creditor. His wife endeavored to soothe him, and added some touching explanations. Nothing had prospered since their marriage; failures, loss of custom, and illness, had followed one upon another. The marriage portion she had brought her husband, had entirely dwindled away, and they were now left without money and without work. Only one resource remained—to remove to a neighboring village, where one of her brothers was established; there, they would have no competition to fear, and, as far as they could judge, there was every probability of their succeeding. It was a door of salvation opened to the poor creatures; but the hardness of old Rigot rendered it of no avail. At the news of the intended seizure of goods, the other creditors, who had before agreed to wait, would flock in to claim their share, and all hopes of a re-establishment would be crushed. For want of three hundred and thirty francs, the entire future of an honest family was clouded, and the only refuge for the dying wife and mother was a garret, or the hospital.

At the mention of this, Marcelle turned her eyes, humid with emotion, upon me, and her hand sought the bank-note hidden in her bosom. On my making a sign in the affirmative, she quickly drew it forth, and, laying it on the woman's knee, said gently:

"Take this, my good Madame Gaubert; pay M. Baron, and make use of the rest to move without delay."

The poor woman, overcome and unable to speak, held out her hands with an inarticulate cry; the upholsterer stammered forth his broken thanks, whilst the sheriff's officer bowed repeatedly and profoundly. But Marcelle took my arm and hurried away.

"Ah!" she exclaimed as soon as we got into the street,

and pressing my arm against her beating heart, "I am so happy! this, our first good action, will be a pleasant commemoration of our happy anniversary! * * * Aunt Roubert, who is a neighbor of the upholsterer, has been speaking of them this morning:

"'I can't think what has come to those Gauberts,' she said. 'I fancied they were badly off, and yet I have just met little Valentine coming from market with a goose fit for an abbess, and the finest carp I have seen this season. But it's just like the Gauberts; they have always eaten what they have not drunk. They are honest folks enough, but never can manage to keep any thing in their pockets; and you know the proverb says, one fault will spoil a house, as one rat will sink a ship.'"

Marcelle and I exchanged glances. The discovery pained us, and I was still unwilling to believe it could be true, when the upholsterer himself made his appearance with the receipt for the five hundred francs we had lent him; but he was no longer the same man as the depressed and wretched creature whose misery had so moved us a few days ago. His sparkling eyes, flushed face, and excited manner, all proved that he had only just left the dinner-table; and in the course of conversation, I discovered that his wife's brother had been dining with him. The former continues to press him to remove to his village, but now Gaubert is again undecided, and hesitates; his wife prefers waiting for better days; he himself hopes to have several orders. I saw, in fact, that our bank-note, in rescuing the poor family from an immediate danger, had only encouraged their natural improvidence. I told Maître Gaubert my mind, but he received my observations with so bad a grace, that we parted angrily.

Marcelle, from whom I conceal nothing, is quite depressed at the unfortunate result of our first effort. Is it then so difficult to confer a benefit rightly? And is that really true which has been so often said, that all disasters, and even ruin itself, are but punishments justly merited by those on whom they fall? After a review of our own experiences, and the recent conduct of Gaubert, we are almost inclined to believe it to be the case.

Whilst leaning over the balcony, and revolving in our minds this painful doubt, we are silent, and our eyes wander over the streets below. Presently we perceive near the crossing, a crowd of children running at full speed, and shouting with all their might at a poor, deformed, tipsy wretch, who struggles on in the midst of the uproar. It is Jacques the idiot, who has scarcely any thing human about him; cruel and cowardly, he strikes a solitary child, but flies with craven fear before his companions; whilst for a glass of brandy he will kiss your feet and lick the very ground you stand on; yet who thinks of blaming or refuses to pity him? I call Marcelle's attention to him, saying—

"Perhaps he whom we have attempted to assist, is like the poor idiot Jacques—a victim to some mental infirmity, or mistaken education; and can we, though we blame, refuse to succor him? A benevolent action is not only an investment for the benefit of the receiver, but the accomplishment of a pleasant duty to the giver, and though lost on the obliged party, who knows not how to value it, need never be so to the benefactor, who may ever find in it a wholesome exercise for his sympathies and self-denial. To become disgusted with doing good, because the object benefited is unworthy, is rendering benevolence a worldly calculation, and not the warm impulse of a grateful heart. That a fellow-creature suffers, is sufficient reason for us to succor him, and the remembrance of that act is ample recompense."

CHAPTER V.

EDUCATIONAL TREATISES IN ANTICIPATION OF THE BIRTH OF A DAUGHTER.

JANUARY 20th.—For some time past our room has been strewed with little embroidered robes, gay leading-strings, fine lawns, flannels, and embroidered counterpanes of diminutive size. Marcelle is occupied in preparing the Layette, or baby-linen, of the child who will complete our family. Its little bassinet already stands in the corner with its pink silk drapery, quilted counterpane, and pillow edged with lace. Nothing seems good enough for the little personage expected. All our lady friends are busy working for us, covering muslin, jaconet, and cashmere with "chefs d'œuvres" of their handiwork, the results of which daily increase Marcelle's treasures.

This morning I found her in ecstasies over a little wadded mantle trimmed with swan's down, which had just arrived; and when, a little later, Aunt Roubert paid us a visit, every thing was displayed for her to admire.

"Most splendid!" she said, after rapidly glancing at the wonders before her; "but I also am anxious to commemorate this happy occasion, and have brought you my present."

"Oh! dear aunt, what is it?" asked Marcelle.

"Guess," she replied, as she plunged her hand into her unfathomable bag.

"Is it nothing that I have already?"

"Nothing!"

Marcelle thought a long time, and mentioned every thing wanting to complete the first set, and then the second:

"Some caps of Berlin lace?"

"No."

"Some knitted socks?"

"No."

"A coral necklace?"

"No."

"A coral with silver bells?"

"No, stuff and nonsense," cried Madame Roubert, impatiently.

"But what is it then?"

"All my old stockings!"

And she drew them triumphantly from her bag, and spread them out with much complacency upon the sofa. They were of all sorts of colors.

Marcelle and I looked at her in amazement.

"Ah! you fancy I am joking!" she replied; "but your laces and embroidered affairs are only for show; the child will be none the better, nor warmer for them all, whilst with four of these stockings, I will make it a *blanket*."

She then proceeded to show Marcelle how it was done: she cut out, and arranged, and very soon the old stockings before her were transformed into little petticoats with bodies and sleeves. I followed this transfiguration with a great deal of interest; and when Aunt Roubert had finished, she arranged on the bed four woollen and cotton *blankets.*

"Now then," she said to Marcelle, "you have merely to sew them together. The child will be none the worse for having been clothed without expense, and your purse will be decidedly the better. Just now, like all other young mothers, you think only of the ornamental; each tries to bedeck her first-born with all that is charming, but when experience comes, so also do thoughts of the necessary—of economy—arise; she enters upon her serious duties, and no longer wears her child like a bouquet. But there is a time for every thing, only at your age, one begins with the embroidered robes, and at mine with the *blankets.*"

Thereupon Madame Roubert collected her cuttings, bid us good-by, and took her departure.

In the evening my father called. Marcelle showed him all her preparations, including, this time, the *blankets*, and entered into minute explanations of all the precautions we mean to take with the child. We are anxious to maintain an equal temperature in the bedroom, and a stove and thermometer have been bought for that purpose. Marcelle has arranged with a neighbor for the milk of a cow, to be milked under her own eyes. She means to set her face against close swaddling-clothes, and rocking in the cradle; and in due time, when the swallows return, the child is to be taken down to the garden, and the Indian mat spread upon the ground for it to roll about on, that its limbs may strengthen in the fresh and health-giving air. Then came details of the cares of each moment, its food and dress, for every thing has been arranged beforehand.

My father listened to all with an indulgent smile, but when we had finished, surprised at his silence, we asked him if there was any thing in our arrangements he disapproved of.

"Nothing whatever," he replied.

"And have you nothing to add, or to suggest, dear father?" said Marcelle.

"Nothing, dear daughter, unless it be a little story that I must have read in days gone by, in some old book. Here it is:

"'Once upon a time, there lived in Persia a dervish, celebrated for his great learning and wisdom, to whose care the prince of the country wished to confide his treasures, before setting out on a distant expedition. Accordingly he caused all his gold to be melted down, and cast into a statue, which he delivered to the dervish, and departed on his journey.

"'The latter, extremely anxious to preserve his precious charge, and return it as he had received it, set a watch over the statue, and never failed to visit it several times a day. With his own eyes he examined all its details, in order to be certain that it was intact, rubbed it with his hands to keep it bright, testing it from time to time with a touchstone, fearful of some fraud.

"'At last the prince returned, and claimed his treasure, and the dervish restored it to him with the proud joy of one who has faithfully fulfilled his trust; but alas! when the golden statue came to be removed, it was found to be so light, that one man sufficed to lift it. On examination it was discovered that some clever thieves had filed away the precious metal from the inside, leaving only the outer shell. All the dervish's care had proved of no avail, for *he had been busied only with the outside*.' "

With this my father pressed my hand, embraced Marcelle, and left us to reflect upon his parable.

We looked at each other with some confusion, and began to perceive that we had indeed imitated the dervish; and like he with the statue, had thought only of the exterior well-being of the child, who was to be confided to our care. And yet, how numerous the robbers, who might deprive us of the treasures within!

In education, each bad example, each fact misunderstood, each imprudent word, are so many strokes of the file which remove from the heart of the child a portion of its treasured purity. How comes it then that we think so little of this, and that our preparations have been of a material nature only? Is the being we expect merely a body to defend—is there not a soul to guard? I see the clothes and cradle, but where are the principles and faith? To be truly prepared to accept the trust of this living life, we must be capable, as far as erring mortals can be, to protect it from evil, as well as from death. We are provided against cold, fatigue, and famine, but we have forgotten corrupting impressions, fatal instincts, and temptations full of peril. Is this all, that He who will confide to you the living treasure will expect? How answer Him, when He again claims His own, if, like the Persian prince, He *finds it wanting.*

Such thoughts as these haunted me all the evening, and after a restless night I communicated them to Marcelle, and we came to the conclusion that it was a subject requiring much grave consideration, and that we must seek for enlightenment from above. I have borrowed from my father several books treating on this difficult subject, and Justin has lent me various others. So here I am, surrounded by volumes. Whilst Marcelle continues her preparations for the body, I will begin mine for the soul. God grant that I also do not forget the *blankets!*

February 15th.—I have read, and re-read at least twenty different treatises on education. What paradoxes I have waded through! In what Egyptian darkness have I groped my way! and yet, for instants, what flashes of illumination! I feel like a traveller returned from a long journey through distant countries. I have visited high mountains covered with perpetual snow, where not a blade of verdure was to be seen; fiery plains, where every thing lay scorched and withered; and wild forests, where, unguided and unrestrained, nature exhausted herself in useless efforts, and was overpowered by her own fertility. There occurred, only at distant intervals, some happy peaceful prospect of calm villages, their humble roofs glistening in the sun, fields of ripening grain waving in the breeze, vines bending under their delicious burdens, and verdant meadows checkered with groups of cattle grazing under the care of young and merry childhood. But now behold me arrived at the end of my journey, like the wise Ulysses, "after having seen the countries of many people," and I rest myself, reflect, and seek instruction.

At last, after a long discussion with myself, I think I have found it.

"Our first duty," I said, yesterday evening, to Marcelle, "is to prepare the child for the position assigned him in the world. All education should resemble that bestowed on Achilles; every thing enervating, either to body or mind, must be avoided, and the infant plunged in the Styx, and fed on lion's marrow."

"But, grant him, at least, you austere Centaur," said Marcelle, laughingly, "like the king of gods, some portion of wild honey, and milk from the goat Amalthea."

"I would have our promised offspring," I continued, following my own train of thoughts, "taste of the cup of life without any attempt on our part to disguise its bitterness, and taught to accustom himself to bear what is; to learn patience, and strengthen himself against sorrow; let his first effort be a struggle, since his whole life can be nothing else. Hercules began his victories whilst yet in his cradle, by strangling the serpents which menaced his life."

"Right," replied Marcelle; "so long as you do not cast a cloud over the young mind, which reflects every thing in such brilliant colors. The joy of innocence is childhood's peculiar charm, it is its privilege. My care shall be to preserve to the sweet being intrusted me by heaven, the happy impressions of its early years; they are the germs that we must cause to blossom and bring forth fruit. Like the father of Montaigne, I would surround my first-born with nothing but sweet sounds and pleasing images."

"Above all," I continued, not attending to what Marcelle was saying, "let him learn to follow the right path, even though it lead over rocks and hanging precipices!"

"Above all," repeated Marcelle, who also listened only to her own voice, "may he walk with a light heart in the steps of good men, unmolested by dangers, and unarrested by obstacles."

"What matter that his brow be covered with sweat, and his feet with dust, if he feel his soul soar above the clouds which envelop him."

"It does not matter how easy his task, so that he accomplishes it in peace and contentedness."

"Let him be rough, loyal, and true! the armor of steel well defends what it covers."

"Let him be kind and gentle! smiles are a welcome we owe to all men."

"And he will become strong and invulnerable as Alcides!"

"And thus he will be loved and loving as Abel!"

At this, my father, who, seated by the fire, had up till now maintained his gravity, laughed outright:

"God grant it all," he said; "but it will be rather difficult. One would make the child a demi-god, and the other a demi-man. Remi christianizes the school of Lycurgus; whilst Marcelle adopts, with improved morals, the school of Châtelaines—the latter dreams of a virtuous page; the former of a Leonidas, who finds his Thermopylæ in himself. To satisfy you both, the child must be a Spartan twanging a Mandoline."

Marcelle smiled at this, but it made me thoughtful. My father is right! What would become of an education conducted on such opposite systems? and on the other side, how were we to combine them? Even if I succeeded in convincing Marcelle, could I substitute a mere opinion in place of nature—transform the child's entire being, and, so to say, change the metal? How convert this sweet gentleness into stoicism, and joyous gayety to sober gravity? Should I really wish it, if I could?

Much as I thought on the subject, I was unable to solve this problem; and was still employed upon it, when our neighbors, the Huberts, arrived to spend the evening with us.

Little Renée accompanied them; and for the first time I remarked their behavior towards the child. They seemed kind and gentle, but firm. Renée enjoyed every liberty suitable to her age, but the command once given, had to be instantly obeyed.

I made an observation to that effect.

"We never interfere in trifles and unimportant matters," replied her father, "but for the rest our experience must prevail, or run the risk of being forever set at naught. We only weaken our authority by employing it too often, but to allow her to resist us is to declare ourselves impotent at once. The best teacher is habit: let the child once feel and understand that there is no help for it, and he will submit without a murmur, and the will once bent, will answer at the first summons. By this means a species of articulation is formed in the mind, similar to that which is always found in limbs destined to be bent."

Once, however, Renée refused to obey, and screamed and burst into a passion of tears; but her mother remained wrapped in impenetrable gentleness: according as the child's voice rose in her passion, so hers became lower and more impressive, till at last Renée's temper was absorbed in the patient serenity of her mother; even as bullets and cannon-balls are lost in the bank of soft earth prepared to receive them.

I asked if this were always the case.

"Always," replied Justin; "the child submits in spite of himself, and his anger falls to the ground for lack of an antagonist. Do you wish to appease a furious person, then never follow his example; in the moment of passion it is not the reflection of our own image that shames us, but the striking contrast which shows us our hideousness; rebuke and impatience succeed no better, they only serve to fan the flame."

"Then in your opinion the surest educator is example."

"You would be nearer the truth if you said that in my opinion there is none other. A child's mind is a sort of camera-obscura, in which is traced whatever strikes his eye, and these ineffaceable impressions form in the end his character. All that is not a part of our primitive nature is the result of this perpetual, though unseen, instruction. Our truest teachers are the facts surrounding us. If therefore you would insure, as far as possible, the moral health of your child, begin by purifying the atmosphere it breathes."

"And how accomplish that?"

"By improving *yourself*. The educator's attention should be first directed, not to the child, but to *himself*, for by far the most important part of his instruction is derived, not from what he says, but what he does. Do you wish to impart a love of industry and usefulness? If so, let it be your habit to honor it, and never bend lower to the idle rich, because they are such, than the poor laborer. Do you desire above all a sincere and honest heart? prove it by your abhorrence of falsehood, and contempt of any one who departs from the truth. Do you admire the loving-kindness which believes in the good and pardons the evil? then banish all bitterness from your judgment of others, and smother your private animosities. Do you believe that self-sacrifice is the source of all that is great and courageous on earth? if so, practise in silence the abnegation of self, and smile on the cross for them you save."

"But is not this exacting too much," I objected, "and ought we to expect so much virtue of man?"

"Then why expect it of a child?" replied Justin, quickly, "can that which is impossible to you, be more easy to him? Think you, you will be able to make him pay respect to that for which you have none yourself? Do you not know that to learn to live, he must imitate?"

"Then according to you," I said, "the education of our children ought to be preceded by a strict examination of ourselves, and a firm determination to improve."

"Can you for a moment doubt it? The promotion of a human being to this supreme magistracy of home, is surely one of the great events, or crisises of our existence! On entering on these new and sovereign duties, ought we not to feel the necessity of purifying and strengthening our minds? All initiations are preceded by a period of solitude devoted to self-examination and meditation; and wherefore should that which confers the holiest mission on earth be less severe? The juryman who is to decide the reputation, liberty, or life of a fellow-creature, withdraws from the world in trembling; what is it then for the head of a family, who must influence, if not decide, the destiny of his child, whose every action, every word, prepares his happiness or misery, his honor or shame. Whosoever undertakes the education of another, must begin by accomplishing his own, for there is in families, a kind of fatal transmission in the moral, as well as physical system: the child inherits as much of the temperament of the mind, as of the body; but because the natural propensities are variously developed, and thus cause it to differ from the being to whom it owes its existence, the careless observer does not perceive the relation. In some instances, what in the father is only a weakness, becomes in the child a vice; in others, what in the former was but a good quality, is in the latter transformed into a virtue! It is the domestic atmosphere which effects these important modifications, in perfecting or depraving the original disposition, and thus the child becomes our just reward, or punishment."

* * * * * *

I reflected much and long on these opinions of my neighbor, and ended by thinking with him. These educational systems, invented in the closet, and put together piece by piece, are far too complicated machines for general use; for they can only be kept in motion by a continual effort. Having nothing in common with us, they constitute an artificial life in the midst of our more positive existence; and we find ourselves, like the kings of former days, subjects of a written etiquette, which regulates our actions, violates our tastes, and dictates our very words. It is impossible not to forget its observance at times, and let that once happen, and farewell to the whole structure! at the first breach made, it totters, and falls. Educational systems are nothing more than certain rules explained by a professor in the chair; the lecture over, and it is no more thought of. It is evident that the only truly fruitful one, is that which arises from our actions, is conveyed by our habits, lives with us in fact; and this can be no other than example.

Henceforth the necessity for a programme in common to Marcelle and myself ceases; each of us is bound to improve his nature, not leave it uncontrolled; to bring forward what there is of good in him, and thus complete what the other may have contributed.

And now all is clear, and I comprehend our separate duties; the gentle lessons, Marcelle's; mine, the more stoical instruction. It was not without design that God thus submitted the child to the double influence of man and woman. Agreeing on the end to be attained, they differ as to the means; whilst the father points out to his son the abysses and precipices which surround the rough path he must traverse, the mother directs his attention to the sweet refreshing shade in the distance, where he may rest his weary limbs; the former arms him with the iron-pointed stick which assists and defends the traveller; the latter embraces him with kisses and tears, which go far to console him; on the one side a firm voice cries—Courage! on the other a gentle tone whispers—Hope!

I have returned the books I borrowed from my father and Justin; henceforth it is my own heart that I must read. I had prepared a memorandum-book for my notes, and had written on the first page in my best style—*Precepts of Education.*

I have since added below, these two words—*Improve thyself.*

Nothing more! the other pages shall remain unsullied.

CHAPTER VI.

THE FIRST CHILD—THE FAMILY OF FORMER TIMES, AND THE PRESENT DAY.

MARCH 20th.—The sun has begun to pierce his way through the thick clouds of winter; and to-day he shed such refreshing rays upon our little garden, that Marcelle and I were attracted into it, and we found the shrubs beginning to bud, whilst the perfume of violets filled the air.

We seated ourselves under the limes, and let little Renée enjoy herself in running about. Every time she came near us, she saluted us with one of those hearty bursts of laughter, without any seeming cause, which are the very song of childhood, and then again darting away among the lilac bushes.

Whilst watching her, a kind of terror seized me as I thought of all the trials our first-born must go through before it reached that happy age; and pointing to the child, I said to Marcelle—

"Would that she were our daughter!"

"Renée!" she exclaimed. "Ah! I trust our daughter will be far more highly gifted."

And when I endeavored to defend our little neighbor, she began a capitulation of all that she was deficient in.

First of all, her eyes were of so light a blue that they

gave a singular harshness to the expression of her face, the mouth wanted delicacy, her complexion was too florid, and her hair of a doubtful color.

Then Renée was capricious, indifferent, and undemonstrative.

Till now I had noticed none of this; but on reflection was obliged to admit it.

Afterwards, Marcelle passed in review the children of our acquaintances, and was not better satisfied with any of them. Now it was mind that was wanting; now some personal grace, and now heart. At each fault discovered in any one of them, she endowed, in imagination, our child with the opposite quality.

"Yes," she said, with passionate confidence, "ours shall be the most beautiful, the most intelligent, the most obedient, most loving of them all!"

"And to make the matter more sure, you deny every thing to all the others," I added, laughingly; "but take care that, whilst imitating the fairy godmothers, in the old stories, who endowed their godchild with a thousand precious gifts, the mothers of the condemned children do not come, like the enraged fairies, to throw in, out of revenge, some fatal gift, which mars all the rest."

"Ah! do not breathe such a thing," exclaimed Marcelle, putting her hand upon my lips.

"Then, dear one," I replied, kissing the hand, "do not raise your hopes so high. Do not allow the chimeras of your girlish romance to gain entrance into the more serious one of the young mother, and do not make your child a hero of *a thousand and one nights*, as you did your 'fiancé.' It is because we always expect too much, that we are discontented with what is accorded us; the dream destroys the flavor of the reality. Prepare yourself thankfully to receive your child such as God bestows it on you; for it is it we must love, and not your illusions."

"You are right, oh you are right!" she exclaimed, hiding her face, crimson with shame, upon my shoulder; "but you speak only of my folly, where you should condemn my pride and self-love. Why have I depreciated the mothers through their children, if it were not to elevate myself through mine? Why did I rejoice in my secret heart at their failings, but because I hope alone to outdo them? Have I then lost all affection for my friends, and all good-will to my neighbors?"

"No," I replied, drawing her to me; "but, as is no uncommon case, you have, for an instant, lost your proper interest in what does not immediately belong to you, and have had eyes only for that spot of earth which supports your own hearth. Let this be a proof of how the holiest affections may become snares, and that the exclusive love of our family is too often but an idolatrous worship of ourselves."

March 30th.—Our hopes are at last accomplished! There lies the long-expected child reposing near its sleeping mother. Two dear and sacred beings, who shall henceforth never be absent from my thoughts; to whom I will, if necessary, sacrifice all, and their happiness will be ample recompense for all such sacrifices!

How is it that the sight of this frail little creature seems to augment my strength, and that life has assumed a graver, yet sweeter aspect since I first beheld her fragile little form! I feel more strongly and clearly my responsibility, and I congratulate myself upon it, whilst experiencing a fresh access of joy and courage. Until now I have lived for myself: henceforth my life shall be devoted to another; and ere I have well received this precious gift, I shall in my turn be able to bestow.

The little girl asleep in her cradle shall owe me all, and that all shall be gratuitously bestowed; she will be a constant and delightful occasion for my devotion. I feel that her mere presence imposes the exercise of fresh virtues, and that she has raised me in the scale of beings. I have to guide and prepare another laborer in the great work of life. I have now confided to my care a mind to form and enlighten, and every day I shall hear within me the solemn voice which called unto Cain, demanding an account of my charge.

But Clara's eyes have opened, and she utters a plaintive cry; Marcelle starts up—the voice of her child has penetrated her slumbers, and she folds it to her bosom.

Oh, who can view unmoved a young mother suckling her first-born? Still pale from recent suffering, she looks on her child, and smiles!

Wherefore that smile, poor woman, whose chain of constant trial and suffering is even now being forged? Dost see clearly the sad path before thee, in which thou hast taken thy first step, and knowest thou what the future has in store for thee?

First, the ever-recurring fears for this fragile existence, long and weary watchings by the cradle, and all the agonies of suspense.

But the child outlives them, and grows up strong and healthy; and anxiety changes its object. It is now the heart that you watch; and oh! what tears are shed, and what anxious hopes and fears prevail! However, your unceasing efforts are successful! Behold your child standing on the threshold of life in its robe of spotless innocence, and the sparkling crown of youth upon its brow! If it be a girl, there soon come causeless melancholy, solitary reveries, and lastly, if it be the will of God, a reciprocated affection. United to the chosen of her heart, your daughter departs to seek another home; and your house is empty, and your hearth desolate.

Is it a boy? What trembling and agonizing fears! Dost hear the cry of awakening passions? Didst feel their burning breath? It is in vain to tremble, to warn him; a potent and invincible charm leads him on. Daniel must enter the lion's den, and thou, poor woman, must kneel on the brink with thy ear to the ground, listening for, and trembling at each stifled groan—each fearful roar.

God grant you another miracle! and may he you watch reappear victorious! But he will no longer be the gentle youth who bore upon his white and rosy brow the reflection of the sun of childhood; his features will be tanned with exposure to the glare of the world; his lips will have tasted the bitter cup described by Byron, "*which but sparkles at the brim;*" already hardened by the struggle, he will have felt the manly instincts of his nature stir within him; and, bidding farewell to his paternal roof, he will depart, to build elsewhere the one destined, ere long, to shelter his own family. There, another woman will take the first place in his heart, his son the second, and then his son's son.

Thus in all cases the end is the same desolation; you will gradually descend the scale of love; but without losing courage, without complaining. Old and weary, and deprived of your sovereignty, you will be content to view their happiness from the lowest place, without asking or expecting more.

Oh, the unceasing devotion of a mother's love! Ye sainted guardians of our youth! too often, alas! unappreciated till too late; and, like the Christian martyrs, not properly honored till after death!

Would that I had, to glorify you, the lyre whose tones softened the hearts of oaks and stones, and drew forth tears from rocks; ye gentle confidents of the severely-tried ones, who soothe the restless spirits, console the afflicted, and atone forever for the fallen ones!

* * * * * * *

I had for some time undertaken the charge of my father's affairs; I saw to the regular payment of his pension, and collected several small rents of his, which were always behindhand. An unexpected legacy left him by a relative in a remote part of Burgundy, if it did not very sensibly increase his income, added, for the time at least, very considerably to the business to be performed. There were about a dozen acres* of land to be divided between a numerous party of legatees. The notary, charged with the execution of the will, required several indispensable documents, which I went to my father's to obtain.

Marcelle and I found him in his little suburban lodging, overlooking a large nursery-ground. From his window he watched the gardeners in their never-ending toil; sowing but to reap, and reaping to sow again. His eye rested on an eternal youthful verdure—the promise of forests, whose shade he never enjoyed; and of orchards, whose fruit he never saw.

I had feared that these constantly unrealized promises must weary him at last, and that he would grow tired of the eternal infancy of nature which surrounded him; but I found I was mistaken. Following in his thoughts each generation of trees, reared in the nursery-grounds, he beheld with his mind's eye, some, help to increase the welcome shade of the dusty highway for the weary pedestrian, bathe with waves of foliage the arid hills, or wind like verdant colonnades along the banks of streams; others enrich with their fruits the rustic gardens, climb the bare walls, or trail their branches, loaded with the luscious grapes, around the cottage-windows; in fact, diffusing everywhere refreshment or abundance.

"It seems to me," he often said, "that I live near one of

* French acres consist of 100 perches square.

the many sources from whence issue into the world the streams of life; I see them rise from the ground, increase, and distribute themselves abroad; every one of these trees, as they depart, are at once messengers of God and of civilization; they carry away with their freshness, fruit, or perfume, a gift of God embellished by human intelligence. Then again, consider the numerous objects, from various climates, which this small spot of earth contains! the courageous efforts and adventurous researches required, before such a collection could be formed!

"This little corner of the earth is an abridgment of one portion of the world's history; almost every plant it contains reminds one of some distant and dangerous expedition, or recalls some deservedly great name. Our forefathers, before they obtained that vine, had to traverse mountains, and watered with their blood the plains of Italy, from whence they bore it. Lucullus penetrated into the wilds of Asia with the Roman eagle; and this lovely flowering cherry-tree, which covers the fresh spring-verdure with a perfumed snow, was the result. Those roses and magnolias would never have ornamented our borders, if that sublime fool called Christopher Columbus, had not persisted in his determination to discover a new world! And besides these mere transplantations, what new and numerous varieties have been acquired by cultivation! what countless productions have been called forth from earth by man! Each day does his perseverance multiply these holy triumphs, to the benefit of the whole human race; and what victory is worthy of being compared to them?—a new root, which appeases the hunger of the multitude; an unknown flower, which eases suffering, are surely more glorious trophies than any a conqueror can boast! Which, does it appear to you, has best fulfilled his mission on earth—the man who does the most good, or he who makes the most noise?"

When we arrived, my father was seated by the window, watching the gardeners at their work. He called our attention to several fresh clearings already sown; and spoke almost enviously of the lot of men who gain their daily bread in the open air, in the midst of sweet odors and the songs of birds.

"Parbleu! 'tis a pity your cousin's acres do not lie here, dear father, for you would then have been able to play Cincinnatus on your part of the inheritance."

"Ah!" he replied, on observing the papers I held in my hand, "I suppose you have come to talk about that affair!"

I communicated the contents of the notary's letter, showing him at the same time the deeds I had been able to collect, and mentioning those still wanting. He went to his secretary, and taking from thence a file of papers, we seated ourselves to look for those required.

The examination took a long time; each paper recalled past times and scenes to my father's mind, and led to some anecdote or history; but at last I found the remaining necessary deed. It was a certificate of birth, written on coarse greenish paper; the ink had faded sadly, and it bore the stamp of the old monarchy. I remarked that, according to the date, it must have been given the day after the birth of the child.

"Yes, yes," said my father with a smile; "it was a precaution of my worthy mother's, who, entirely taken up with her business, and my brothers and sisters being already numerous, had no time to waste on any of us, so the day after his birth the child was delivered into the charge of a country nurse, who carried it off some twenty miles, with a layette for its use if it chose to live, and a certificate of birth, which enabled it to be properly buried if it happened to die. It was a prudential measure, which guarded against all casualties. My mother did the same with all her nine children, which was fortunate, as only five out of the nine returned to her; the others had *availed themselves of their certificate of birth.*"

"Is it possible," cried Marcelle, "that you were all sent away from the paternal home?"

"And did not return till we were nearly three: such was then the custom in our grade of life; the child was not recalled, until it could in some measure attend to itself. At that time the fanaticism did not exist which denominated the cares of paternity as charming.

'Des charmants embarras de la paternité.'

"You can imagine that the return of the nursling was somewhat of an event. The new-comer underwent a general examination; to see how he walked, if he would say good morning, and how far he suspected the existence of forks. The first hour did much towards classing him in the family. A graceful motion might promise well for his future; an awkward action would allot him an inferior position. In either case he was consigned to the kitchen, until old enough to go to school. He never left the society of the servants, except to salute his parents at stated periods, and receive, as occasion required, a reprimand or a cake. In well-regulated families there was a certain degree of solemnity attached to these interviews—the child took off his hat, inquired after the health of Monsieur and Madame (his father and mother), and remained standing till they were pleased to address him."

"And were you brought up in this manner?" asked Marcelle.

"Very nearly," replied my father; "though only a small tradesman's wife, my mother believed in the wholesome traditions of, business and the household first, and then the children! From the nurse's hands we passed to the care of the old servant, whom we called '*ma-mie*,' and who plied us with morals and bread and butter, till we were old enough to enter the school of the Abbé Silard, who undertook to teach us to read, write, cipher, and make the responses of the mass. In all these arrangements my mother took no part, her ministry was confined to grand occasions, such as measuring us for a new habiliment, to be constructed out of some defunct grandfather's old coats; punishing some serious inroad upon our neighbor's fruit-trees; or presenting us, dressed in our best, and with clean faces, to some country relation."

"So that you grew up as uncared for as if you had been orphans?"

"No, not as orphans, dear girl, but as apprentices to life, consigned to the rough school of reality, and early taught to make the best use of things and men."

"That is to say," I remarked, "that instead of sheltering your cradle with curtains in the secluded dwelling-house, they laid you in the open field, on the first sheaf they came to, just like the reapers' wives are obliged to treat their children. Nobody troubled themselves whether the sun were too hot, or the wasps likely to annoy you, or even the adder to reach you among the stubble."

"Doubtless," he replied, "our rough education had its dangers. The weak and unfortunate certainly succumbed; but, how fortifying and strengthening those very dangers are to those who surmount them! We so quickly learn our path of duty to fall into our allotted place, and exercise continually that cardinal virtue—obedience! In society, as it existed formerly, where the various ranks were regulated by birth, and professions by rank, this was the sole part a child could play; its subordination in the family prepared it for its subordinate position in the world; it trained him for the social regiment wherein his rank was already decided, and too much indulgence would have consequently entailed on his part too much exigence."

"Granted," I replied; "but now, when all the barriers which divided ranks have fallen, and every one may, to a certain degree, shape his own destiny, where the first glance of a new-born infant can embrace the whole world as its domain, this stern apprenticeship is no longer required. What we should now aim at, in the education of a child, is to teach him to acquire the respect of others by preserving his own, and worthily fulfilling his part under the law of equality, which now governs modern society."

"And to accomplish that," added Marcelle, "we must replace authority with affection and devotion; and from the masters we were, become their defenders, guardians, and friends. We must bear their soul in our soul, even as we bore them in our bosoms, surround them with our love, and let them grow and strengthen upon it. The breath of the world is poison to a child: how then can we avoid contagion, but by carefully closing the doors of communication with it! What sweeter or holier mission can there be for those who have given birth to a son, than to guard him in an inaccessible fortress, alike exempt from suffering, and pure from contamination with the world without!"

"Beware, beware, my good daughter," said my father, with a smile; "such citadels too often resemble those built by the princes in fairy tales for their daughters: the first adventurer who passes by needs only a song to make the strong tower crumble to dust, and to capture the lovely prisoner. The pupil too sedulously guarded, becomes incapable of guiding himself, and the child too much cared for, in time, ceases to appreciate what is bestowed on him. Our fathers left too great a part of our education to external influences; but we go to the other extreme, and inclose it with too many precautions. By intrenching the child too much from the world, and allowing it to view life only through glasses of our own coloring, we give him false ideas of what really is, and enervate, instead of strengthen, him for action. If we accustom him to walk only in our pathways, he becomes terror-stricken and falls, when he has to cross the stream. We must never forget that the object of most importance is, not to hide the existence of evil from him, but to accustom him to distinguish and shun it, and thus pass through it unsullied."

We could not deny the wisdom these warnings contained, and resolved to remember them; but at present Clara was too young for us to require any caution. Without power and reason, she was incapable of doing any thing without us: her will was at present a mere succession of wants, which it was our duty to divine and supply. Marcelle in particular evinced a passionate devotion in their fulfilment. Deeply impressed with a sense of her responsibility, she made herself the willing slave of this frail existence, and every thing was made to give way to it; the child became in fact the pivot around which our entire life was made to revolve.

Fearful of abandoning her for an instant to the care of others, her mother renounced her most cherished habits. There were no more evening readings, no more walks, or moments of happy intercourse. Clara's voice alone presided in the house; it regulated our waking and our sleeping; slaves to her weakness, we had lost all possession of ourselves.

The child was not long in perceiving her power, and,

like all who enjoy absolute authority, she exercised a tyranny which became every day more imperious. I endeavored to warn Marcelle of her danger, but for the first time met with opposition. Distrustful of every thing which might distract her attention from the task to be accomplished, she disregarded my warnings, even accused me of trying to tempt her from her duty, and returned to her servitude with that kind of exalted persistence which women evince in self-sacrifice.

I tried in vain to convince her that her duties as a mother did not release her from those belonging to other ties; that devotion itself has its proper proportion and limits, and that she owed something to herself and others: nothing prevailed against this excess of mistaken tenderness, which made her believe that she could only fulfil her duty at the expense of continual suffering to herself.

This was the first cloud in our heaven, slight at first, and frequently broken by bright rays of sunshine. The first years of childhood are so full of promise, and bring with them so many charming surprises: one day, Clara learned to know us, another, to smile upon us. Every instant forged another link which bound her still more closely to our hearts; and last of all, the mind began to develop itself. The moulded clay was still voiceless, but the flame of thought was beginning to flicker into life, and already its reflection might be traced in its humanizing effects upon the countenance.

CHAPTER VII

WHAT IS DUE TO THE FATHER, AND WHAT TO THE CHILD.

One evening as I mounted the stairs with the rapidity usual to me, after a long absence, I heard Clara's clear ringing laugh, mingled with the gentle tones of my dear Marcelle; both heard, and hastened to meet me.

I took them in my arms, and my kisses descended from the brow of the mother to that of the child.

"Well, thank God," I cried gayly, "this is a happy home!"

"Do you not know the news then?" Marcelle interrupted, her whole face glowing with pleasure.

"No, what is it?"

"The child can speak!"

"No, can she really?"

"Listen!"

And addressing the little girl in her most caressing tone, she entreated her to repeat the syllables which she had uttered before. Clara replied at first only with those confused but charming murmurs belonging to early infancy; but suddenly, seeming to think better of it, she distinctly called "Papa," and held out her little hands to me.

Overjoyed, I clasped her in my arms. This first word lisped forth with difficulty, seemed to me as a second birth. The child had quitted the phalanx of mutes, where until now she had been confounded with the creatures of instinct, to enter that endowed with speech, reserved for the sons of Adam only. She had begun to claim her right to the sovereignty of creation; until now she had been but a living image, henceforth another soul was added to our life.

As might be expected, Marcelle's affection for Clara was redoubled, and she became her sole thought and care. To material wants was now added solicitude about her moral training. .She must watch the awakening mind, protect it from unfavorable influences, and surround it, like Montaigne's cradle, with harmonious sounds and lovely visions! And thus the chain became every day more heavy, each fresh improvement of Clara's, by creating a fresh obligation, added another link; and I beheld it increasing with her growth until it filled the house, and drove me from it.

Marcelle felt it, and as an inevitable consequence suffered; but her maternal instinct, added to her exaggerated ideas of duty, made her struggle against these very natural feelings; and these differences of opinion gave rise, too often, to mutual irritation and annoyance.

One summer's evening I returned home, worn and mentally wearied with a hard day's work. A refreshing breeze was just beginning to rise, after the overpowering heat of the day, and whispered among the leaves, as it bore along the perfume of a thousand flowers; whilst the last rays of the setting sun bathed the white houses in the suburbs with a glittering flood of light. My heart was swelling from the long day's oppression, and feeling as though my feet had wings, I hurried home.

Formerly, Marcelle was on the watch for my return, and hastened to meet me; but since Clara had engrossed her whole time, I had been forced to renounce this sweet custom. I cannot tell why I so particularly regretted its loss this evening, but I longed to see her, and take her out with me, to enjoy the delicious freshness of the evening.

I entered quickly, and asked for her immediately; she was in her own sitting-room, which had for some time been devoted to the child's use; there I found her, her head buried in her hands, whilst Clara, surrounded by her playthings, was seated on the floor at some little distance, pouting and with tears yet wet upon her cheeks.

I saw at the first glance how matters stood; there had been another of the child's outbreaks, which were becoming every day more frequent.

I had returned happy and comforted; but the sight of the two countenances before me was sufficient to dispel all my joy; it came like a cloud to shroud the sunshine of my heart. However, I conquered my first impulse, which had been to turn away, and approaching Marcelle, I begged, with a smile, to be informed of the cause of this grand quarrel; but the mother was indignant at my treating the matter so lightly, and began an enumeration of her troubles.

They were the thousand anxieties of an over-watchful mind. Attentive to the child's smallest actions, and from them deducting the most serious consequences, as if it were the peculiar privilege of infancy to be ever influenced by the profoundest reason, which no man constantly obeys, she gave a meaning to every word and every motion, and imagined an intention to exist in the mere caprice of a moment. I had very often endeavored to warn her against her dangerous habit of drawing inferences, to persuade her to let the seed germinate by itself, always taking care to supply it with water and sunshine, without prejudging the ear which is to result from it; but all my efforts had been unavailing, and they were not more fortunate this time. I was again obliged to listen to what I had so often heard before. Clara was selfish and obstinate; her affection was interested; she was submissive, or disobedient, according to fancy!

And then came, Heaven knows, what consequences and fears for the far-distant future! I listened with ill-restrained impatience, for time was flying, and the rays of the setting sun were rapidly dying away one by one. I took advantage of the first pause made by Marcelle, to try to soothe her, and, as she was about to reply, I rose and took her hand.

"Time enough to be serious to-morrow!" I said gayly; "I want you to go with me to the nursery-grounds. My father expects us, and if we do not hasten, the nightingale will have finished her song."

"Go out!" exclaimed Marcelle, "and the child?"

"We will take her with us," I replied.

"Is it not too far?"

"I will carry her, if necessary."

She went to the window and looked out.

"Good Heavens!" she said, "but it is——I am fearful of the evening air, my dear: see, the mist is already beginning to rise; it will not do for Clara to encounter it."

"Well then!" I exclaimed in the restless manner of a man who stands in need of air and exercise, "we will leave her in Jeanne's care."

"Leave Clara here! impossible," Marcelle hastily replied: "every time I absent myself I feel the grievous consequences of my neglect; and now, more than ever, am I anxious to keep her with me, and constantly watch over her."

"Now listen to me, Marcelle," I answered quickly; "there is, notwithstanding, a limit to all things, and it is not right that our two whole existences should be devoted to this child; she was given us by God to be our consolation, I should think, rather than a jailer."

"Oh pray!" interrupted Marcelle, her eyes filling with tears, "do not bring up that subject again; do you not believe that it pains me to refuse you?"

"But why attempt to accomplish an impossible task?" I cried, out of all patience. "The child must learn some day or other to walk alone, then why accustom her to be always supported? Does woman's sole duty on earth consist in rearing her offspring? Can it be a law of nature, that over each imperfect creature in the cradle, another completed being should stand guard, flaming sword in hand, to ward off the spirit of evil? What necessity can there be for this constant external guardian, when God has planted one in the heart of each of us? Conscience awakes of itself, but requires exercise to strengthen it!"

"I am perfectly aware that our opinions differ on this point," replied Marcelle, in a trembling voice; "but——if I am mistaken, why not be more lenient?"

"Because the error into which you have fallen is dangerous to all three; because Clara's little arms entwined around our necks, ought to bring us closer, rather than separate us; but you place her between us as a wall, you make her a trouble, a restraint; and you hazard in this game, not only our more social pleasures, but the true appreciation of our duties! Are you sure that the child you now make an obstacle will not become less dear? that her faults will not sooner exhaust our patience, and that you will not convert an intended joy into a burden?"

"At least I can answer for myself," said Marcelle, whom the severity of my tone had offended, and who was passing gradually from sorrow to bitterness.

"Then you would insinuate," said I, wounded in my turn, "that I alone am capable of forgetting my duty?"

"Was it I who expressed that fear?"

"At least you exculpated yourself at my expense. But no matter, this thirst for martyrdom is a necessary attribute of your sex; you like to feel the crown of thorns; and if God in his mercy lays it lightly on your brows, you press it down with both your hands: every one of you has more or less of the passion for self-immolation!"

Marcelle started, and the blood rushed to her face. It was the first time, in all our disagreements, that a bitter word had passed my lips; she gave me one sorrowful look, then drawing herself up, said coldly—

"So be it, but what need then of this discussion? The wise do not argue with fools."

And taking Clara by the hand, she passed into the salon.

I made a motion to detain her and offer some excuse, but my pride prevented me; perhaps also I yet felt somewhat aggrieved. I had come home my heart swelling with happy hopes, and I could not yet forgive her for having so suddenly dissipated them.

My feelings were not improved by a burst of laughter from the child, evidently elicited by her mother's efforts to amuse her. Presently I heard the piano; Marcelle was playing her noisiest quadrilles, to the evident great delight of Clara, who shouting with joy, endeavored to keep time with her feet to the music. I forgot that this was mere show to conceal her sorrow; and that this forced gayety was assumed to prevent the ready tears from flowing: I took the gay mask as a defiance, and answered with a bravado.

I sought in the drawers of the bureau for a forgotten cigar, the last vestige of my past extravagances, and having found one, began with the greatest effrontery to fill her little boudoir with clouds of smoke! Marcelle continued to play her giddiest dances, I whistled my liveliest airs, each doing his best to vex the other, as much from regret as spite.

We were surprised by Aunt Roubert in this agreeable occupation; she made her appearance at the door of the little room, just as I finished my cigar.

"Eh! eh! you seem very merry here," she said; "my dear boy, you sing like a lark."

"It's the only way to drown the noise of the piano," said I, throwing a glance of ill-humor towards the salon.

"Ah! the piano tries your nerves, poor thing," said Aunt

gayly, as she opened the window to get rid of the acrid odor of the tobacco.

Marcelle, hearing Madame Roubert's voice, had hastened into the room, and now remarked that my tastes must have suddenly and strangely altered, as it was only a few days ago that I had passed an entire evening in listening to this very music which now seemed so much to annoy me.

"Well, very likely! why are you surprised?" asked Aunt Roubert, as, already established in the easy chair, she was beginning to knit; "do you not know that we weary at last, even of that we like best? there should be moderation in all things, my dear."

I darted a sharp glance at Marcelle, who felt, rather than saw it, and colored slightly.

"Doubtless, dear Aunt, when it concerns our pleasures, and—"

"And even when our duties are concerned," peremptorily added Madame Roubert.

"Hear, hear," said I, almost involuntarily: Marcelle bit her lip.

"It seems to me," she replied, "that on the latter point, negligence is more general than an excess of ardor."

"But not the less to be feared," replied her aunt; "and I have reason to say so, as I have experienced it."

"You!" I cried, "where and how?"

"Ah! it is an old story, my child," said she with a sigh. "You would hardly believe it of me now; but I was once young like the rest of you! Your uncle was the husband of my choice, and I was never happy unless knitting, or working at his elbow; so, when business was over, he used to come and seat himself on the low chair at my feet, and tell me all he had done during the day; enter into all his difficulties, and though I sometimes understood very little about it, I wished for no greater happiness than to listen to him."

She stopped, hesitated, and looked up at us.

"You are laughing at the old woman, are you not?" she said with a timid embarrassment not belonging to her age, and of which I should not have suspected her.

I warmly protested against such an idea, and Marcelle with a kiss entreated her to continue. The old lady shook her head,—"Oh, but 't is the usual way, we cannot believe we shall ever grow old, nor forget that we *have been* young! But no matter—I was saying then, that I had become accustomed to your uncle's society, I had made it, so to say, my daily bread, and prayed that I might never be deprived of it. Unfortunately, I had not taken into consideration M. Roubert's zealous activity in the discharge of his business.

"One fine day, he took into his head to think that the work left to the junior clerks, would be better done by himself, that there was need of reform in the office, and that it concerned his honor to look to it. Immediately there was a grand rummaging of papers, looking over of dusty files, and yellow deeds. Every evening he returned loaded with papers; which he remained till past midnight arranging. It was impossible to find out whether he were too hot or too cold, what dish he would prefer, or to inquire if there was any news in the paper; from the moment he seated himself at the writing-table, he became a nonentity, and I might as well have been alone!

"On Saturdays, at least, I tried to tear him from his work, to take a walk with me along the river, or through the fields; but it was all of no use: there was always some document to look over, or some calculation to prove. First I pouted, then I cried; and last of all I got angry in good earnest. I felt that if matters went on much longer in this manner, he at his pen, and I at my needle, we were in a fair way to become strangers to each other; so one day, grown bold by the sorrow I felt, I said to myself,—This state of things has lasted long enough, and must be put an end to. Never shall I forget that day! It was an afternoon in Whitsuntide, about the middle of the delightful month of May. The sun shone brightly on the tops of the houses, the sparrows chirped in the gutters till they were hoarse, and the bells rang out merrily. I watched my neighbors, in their new clothes, double-locking their doors, and preparing to go a Maying; and as I looked my heart grew sad within me, till at last I made up my mind. I went straight to your uncle, who had seated himself at his writing-table and was mending a pen, laid my hand upon his arm, and resolutely said:

"'To-day is a holiday; we have worked hard all the week, and ought to rest to-day; come, and take a saunter in the fields.'

"'Impossible, dearest,' he said gently: 'I have these accounts to look over, and, "duty first, and pleasure after," you know.'

"'But,' I interrupted, 'there is no duty which has any right to monopolize a man's entire life, or to exempt him from all other obligations. You promised me your love and society: do you already regret that promise?'

"'I!' he said. 'Is it possible you can think such a thing, Jeanne?'

"'Then prove the contrary by giving me your society during the hours that I have a right to it.'

"He still endeavored to raise his conscientious scruples as reasons for denying them, but I interrupted him. I told him there was far more pride than conscientiousness in these pretensions to doing better than the rest of the world; and that if he desired to be just, he must divide his time and attention between his various duties: and as he still resisted, I made a sudden dash at his papers, and seized them in my arms.

"'What are you about?' he cried.

"'Rescuing my husband from his business,' I boldly replied, whilst cramming the papers into my linen-chest, the key of which I turned and put in my pocket."

"And what did M. Roubert do?" I exclaimed.

"He started up angrily enough," she replied, "turned red, and then pale; but I brought him his hat, took his arm and said, come! so sweetly, that he was obliged to smile in spite of himself, and there was peace between us."

"But since?"

"Afterwards," she said, "he moderated his zeal, and never again forgot that he was not merely a business man."

My eyes and Marcelle's met, but only for a moment; she turned away abruptly, and rose to put the child, who had begun to fret, to bed.

I then remembered that my father was expecting me. I had letters of business to consult him upon; and, begging Madame Roubert to excuse me, I set off for his lodgings.

I was in that state of mind when one looks upon the dark side of every thing, and all around me seemed to add to my melancholy feelings; during my whole walk I met nobody but beggars, or drunken people quarrelling. Even my father, generally so calm and serene, was that evening quite overcome. He had just heard of the total ruin of a friend of his youth, who had been suddenly reduced from wealth to poverty, at an age when the mind finds it difficult to change one set of ideas for another.

He proposed that we should walk, as was his custom when he felt the need of motion to calm his mind. We went down to the nursery-ground, and wandered by moonlight through its alleys. The flowering acacias perfumed the air; the sky glittered with innumerable stars, and the sound of our footsteps was lost on the freshly-made paths. In this manner we made the round of the grounds, exchanging only, at long intervals, a few words; whilst the sole sounds which in the still evening met our ears, were the distant rumbling of the market wagons, and the barking of a dog on a neighboring farm. At last, the church-clock struck eleven: my father remembered that I had others expecting me, and bid me good night.

I returned slowly home. This walk under the clear sky of night, had soothed the irregular and quickened pulses of my heart; my head was clear, and I felt a longing for that peace and love which constitutes the charm of home. I was no longer angry with Marcelle; I no longer blamed her; but anxious on my side for a reconciliation, I feared to find her less disposed for it; I doubted what reception I should meet with, whilst a foolish pride counselled me not to be the first to make advances.

I very leisurely mounted the stairs, divided between my desire for a reconciliation and this false and foolish pride. I quietly opened the door; the lamp was extinguished, and all was dark and silent. A sharp pang shot through my heart.

She has not heard me, I thought, and is asleep most likely.

I softly made my way to her room, through the unclosed windows of which the stars sent a feeble light.

On finding myself there again, surrounded by objects, to each of which belonged some sweet remembrance; and as the scent of "vétiver," Marcelle's favorite perfume, saluted me on entering, the flood of bitterness which had again risen in my heart subsided, and I drew near to Clara's cradle, in which I heard her breathing softly. A moonbeam, penetrating the light drapery, fell round her head in an auréole of glory.

As I stood gazing upon that fair and rosy face, as yet untouched by care, my heart swelled with emotion.—The innocent happiness of childhood seems to draw us nearer to

God !—I deeply regretted that this dear child should have been made the cause of dispute and recrimination between Marcelle and myself; and I felt I had been guilty of injustice towards this darling little creature. With some remorse I bent over the child, and pressed my lips upon her chestnut curls. As I did so, a hand seized mine, and from behind the white curtains rose Marcelle's sweet face.

"Ah, then! you do not hate her for having separated us!" she said, smiling through her tears.

"Not if you are happy in that separation," I said with an earnest look.

She laid her hand upon the cradle.

"Oh no," she cried, "I am not, I cannot be: let us rather endeavor to consider each other's happiness, and in doing so we shall make our own. Aunt Roubert has enlightened me, and I have understood, and will profit by her lesson."

At these words her hand crept up to my shoulder, her head bent with mine over her child, and she drew us both together in the same embrace.

CHAPTER VIII.

WHAT IT COSTS TO BE JUST.—REDUCED CIRCUMSTANCES.

Five years have elapsed, leaving scarcely a trace behind them. I find in my journal nothing but mere dates, short statements of facts, and memoranda. As for instance—

April 4th.—Birth of my son Léon. Clara is now two years old; she screams aloud for joy at the sight of her little brother, and laughs as she rocks his cradle.

July 7th.—Received the rents of M. Morel; rendered account of them.

September 12th.—My father advises me to read every evening the life of one of Plutarch's great men, to counterbalance the impression left by the men of the present day.

So it goes on, and I look in vain for some touch of feeling, or a page of detail; the journal contains only indications, mere nails driven in here and there, on which I have hung my remembrances, that I need not for the time think of them, and yet be able to find them if wanted.

And wherefore this scarcity of notes and confidences? It must surely be because these five years have been calm and happy? Happiness, as an habitual state, leaves no trace, we breathe it as we inhale the air, without perceiving or regarding it; to appreciate its value, we must first miss it. So long as no storms disturbed our domestic atmosphere I had nothing to write; paper is our confidant in our hours of grief and trouble.

Thus, I find my journal again taken up at the beginning of the sixth year, when I experienced a severe trial.

From the time of purchasing the practice which supported us, I had been patronized by the old General Rigaud, who, having retired to his estate, continued to wage war against his partridges and hares, as he had formerly done against the enemies of his country. Up at break of day, his game-bag slung behind, and his gun under his arm, he traversed wood, thicket, and heath, careless of wind or rain, and pouncing on his prey with a degree of savage fury scarcely to be imagined. For the six years I had known him, I never saw him otherwise accoutred than in large deep leathern boots, hunting-jacket, and high seal-skin cap. It was in this costume that he came to consult me upon his own, or his neighbors' affairs, or introduce me to some wealthy client, for he alone had done more for me than all my other friends and relations put together. My father had formerly served under the General, who was ever anxious to prove his remembrance of the fact by patronizing the son. Rough and violent by nature, he was as energetic in his affections as in his hatreds: his advice was very near akin to command, which one obeyed chiefly from esteem, and a little from fear; and consequently, his protégé became, as a matter of necessity, everybody's protégé.

Thanks to his recommendation, I had been appointed agent to all the wealthiest proprietors in the surrounding country. At the time I am speaking of, I received a letter from the Comte de Noirtiers, inquiring whether I would undertake the charge of a large amount of property recently purchased. If he accepted the terms I had proposed, our income would be nearly doubled, and Heaven knows what projects were entertained by Marcelle and myself beforehand! There where whispers about a house out of town during the summer months; of a little carriage, into which we squeezed, in imagination, the whole family; and a journey to my distant native place. The door of dreams had been opened by a golden key, and at first they threatened to overwhelm us.

Every morning a new plan was proposed, to be abandoned in the evening for another. Madame Roubert accused us of imitating the hunters in the fable, who disposed of the bear's skin before they killed him; but my father only smiled.

"Leave them alone, dear lady," he said gayly; "hope is the half of possession. When they have exhausted their desires in imaginary projects, they will be less impatient. See you not, that satiety follows the dream, even as it does reality? Each succeeding fancy cures the preceding one. A Greek poet has said that *life is the dream of a shadow;* let them then dream on."

"When they sleep, well and good!" replied Madame Roubert, who never in her life could understand a figure of speech; "but awake, they ought not to lose their time in suppositions, for whilst they are arranging how they can best spend the Comte de Noirtiers' money, he may, mean while, have chosen another agent. I would rather see Remi act than spend his time in laying plans. The General recommended him, then let him go to the General, or write, at least, and keep himself in remembrance. We are told to take time by the forelock; but it is ever too short for the dreamers, who only stretch out their hand when the opportunity is gone by."

"Well here is something to prove the contrary," I interrupted, as I glanced over a letter just brought me by Clara.

"Oh! what is it?" asked Marcelle eagerly.

"A note from the General."

"Which gives you hopes?" asked my father.

"See for yourself."

I gave him the letter, and he read—

"Just received a letter from the Comte de Nortiers; he gives me 'carte blanche' in the choice of an agent; I will see you the day after to-morrow, and make the final arrangements.

RIGAUD."

Madame Roubert and Marcelle uttered an exclamation of joy.

"If it only depend on the General, it is a settled thing," cried the latter.

"If Remi agrees to his conditions," prudently added aunt.

My father, who had turned over the leaf, now called my attention to a *postscriptum* bearing evidence to having been written very hurriedly.

"I open my letter; you will see me to-morrow; you must dismiss the miserable forester, who has just insulted me in the Bois Morel."

This *postscriptum* alarmed me. Robert had been elected by me as guardian of the woods and forests belonging to an estate, of which I was the agent. He was husband to Marcelle's nurse, and I had never had the least fault to find with him; consequently the General's request was a most unpleasant surprise to me. I sent immediately to Robert, to say, I must see him as soon as possible. He came early the next day.

I think I see him now, as he opened the door of my study, with the gentle, yet self-possessed air he ever bore, and stood there hat in hand. I eagerly called him forward, and questioned him as to what had passed in the Bois Morel.

"Nothing but what ought to happen," he replied calmly.

"And yet the General, in writing to me, complains of having been insulted," I exclaimed.

"The General is mistaken," said Robert, in the same tone as before.

"Well, then, what did take place?"

"This, Monsieur:—I had often observed the General shooting in our woods without a license, and I had, at last, respectfully begged him to obtain M. Morel's permission; upon which he flew into a violent passion, called me a rascal, and informed me he should come whenever he chose. And sure enough he did; I heard his gun, almost every day, popping away at our rabbits. The poachers of the neighborhood never met me without taunting me, saying, 'Nobody prevents the General from sporting in the Bois Morel; you only know your duty where poor folks are concerned!' I knew very well that it was spite and jealousy which made them say so, but I also felt that it was true.

"Well?" I asked, anxious and impatient.

"Well, Monsieur," replied Robert, "two days ago I met the General at the entrance of the Upper Garonne; he was in the act of discharging his two barrels upon a quail, that his dog was holding by the throat. 'General!' I said, touching my hat, as was my duty, 'you are shooting again in our woods without a license, and I shall be obliged to prosecute you.' He looked at me fiercely, put the quail into his bag, and advanced towards the gate at which I was standing, to continue his sport in our wood. I told him he could not pass. 'Stand aside! rascal,' he cried; and as I remained where I was, he fell upon me, seized me by my collar, and endeavored to force me aside. I told him to mind what he was about, and threw him off. He stood for a moment, furious at my daring to resist, then seizing his gun, he aimed with the butt-end at my head, and I had but just time to jump aside to avoid the blow and disarm him."

"Ha! what, you disarmed him! do you know what you have done? are you not aware that that is the greatest insult you can possibly offer to a soldier?"

"May be, Monsieur, but even then, I could not allow him quite to finish me."

"What is to be done? The General is coming, and see what he says."

I read Robert the *postscriptum.*

"The General is not just," he said calmly, when I had

finished; "he asks you to punish me for doing my duty; he does not know you."

This speech disturbed me, this confidence in his just right and my equity, and a feeling of embarrassment, not unmingled with shame, came over me! Evidently, I had wished to be able to find Robert guilty, and thus satisfy the General without remorse; his innocence *irritated* me, and I blushed that it should. A prey to these opposite emotions, I began to reproach him for not having sooner informed me of his misunderstanding with the General; but he reminded me that he had twice come to town to call upon me, and each time I could not see him. Then I deplored that he had not shut his eyes to these violations of the law it was his duty to maintain, until I could have interfered; he replied that the threat of prosecution had only been forced from him by his unexpected encounter with the General. And lastly, when, as a last resource, I began to doubt if he were exact in his account, he contented himself with assuring me that the General's account of the affair would confirm his own.

There was so much straightforwardness and good faith in all he said, that I was thoroughly ashamed of all my subterfuges. I was seeking something against the man, that I might avoid the necessity of doing him justice. I was in fact angry with him for having done his duty, as it made mine more difficult to perform.

I was still torn by these contending emotions, when the General was announced. I hurried Robert into the next room, and the moment after the old sportsman entered.

He burst into my quiet little study like a whirlwind; the whip in his hand, and the spurs upon his heels, sufficiently indicating that he had travelled hither on horseback; whilst his face was flushed, and his white curly hair pushed up about his fine head.

I hastened to meet him, shook hands, and bid him welcome.

"Good day," he said abruptly: "you got my letter?"

"Yesterday evening," I replied.

"Then I hope that rascal of a gamekeeper is no longer in the Bois Morel," he added in a tone which made the question sound like a command.

"Excuse me," I replied, with some hesitation; "but you told me you were coming, and I wished first to see you."

"To know what the insult is I complain of," interrupted the General; "ah, all very right! Well, you shall hear; you would not believe it from any one else, I am sure!—the villain actually disarmed me!—Me, General Rigaud, disarmed by a gamekeeper! Unfortunately my two barrels were empty, or I would have shot him like any dog."

The General's voice trembled with rage; I endeavored to calm him, and entreated him to sit down, but he continued to pace up and down the room, refusing to listen to reason.

Robert's act, aggravated by military prejudice, seemed a humiliation he would willingly efface with blood. All the intolerance developed by thirty years' warfare and command in this violent nature now burst forth without control, and his thirst for revenge seemed to overpower every other sentiment. He continued to repeat in an imperious tone that it was impossible Robert could remain in the Bois Morel, and that *he counted* upon finding him gone, on his return.

I pleaded the honesty of the gamekeeper, and the misery his family would be reduced to, if he were dismissed; but I only exasperated him the more.

"The devil!" he cried; "what's all that to me? when I was in the army, and any soldier failed in his respect to his superior, he was shot through the heart without reference to his honesty or family! D—— it! one would think you preferred the villain to me!"

I protested against such an accusation, and assured the General of my devotion; but he interrupted me by returning to his demand with an impassioned and bitter obstinacy that nothing could move. At last I found myself driven to the painful alternative of being unjust, or appearing ungrateful, and with a palpitating heart I stammered through some broken sentences, which plainly betrayed my confusion; the General perceived it, and asked me sternly, why I hesitated.

The tone and look wounded me; and I replied more firmly than before, that I was the most to blame, as I had given Robert most strict orders against poachers on the preserves of the Bois Morel.

"Then you do me the honor of ranking me with poachers?" he said, with a bitter sneer.

"General," I replied, "you know to the contrary, but a gamekeeper is incapable of perceiving the distinction; he follows his orders to the letter."

"And those of that wretch were to insult me?"

"No, General, but to protect the preserves of the Bois Morel. By your own admission he had warned you several times previous to this affair, and even that very day you would have had no reason to complain of him, if you had not attempted to force the fence. You confirm his own account."

"Oh! then you have seen him?"

"Yes, this morning. In fact he is still here, and I am sure, General, you will consent to receive his humble apologies."

"You are mistaken, Monsieur; when I came to demand satisfaction against a mere boor, it was with no expectation that I should have to insist; I expected to be credited at least as much as M. Robert."

"General," I interrupted, "you cannot doubt my desire to satisfy you, but be merciful, and do not ask me to do what is wrong; have pity on the poor wretch! Remember that he believed himself in the performance of his duty, that his wife has been to mine a second mother—if not for his sake, then for ours grant his pardon, be generous enough to allow me to be just."

"So be it, Monsieur," said the General abruptly; "I give you full permission to be so, and ask for nothing more."

He caught up his cap, and left me, not listening to another word.

I hastened to my father and told him all that had passed, for he only could make the General listen to reason, and might perhaps succeed in appeasing him. He went to his hotel, and was told the General had not returned; he went a little later; the General, they said, had gone out again. But, as my father was turning away, he saw a well-known profile behind the half-drawn window-curtain; and it became evident that the General was determined not to see him.

I then decided on writing, and dispatched a long letter, in which I neglected nothing that was calculated to convince, or touch; receiving no reply, I wrote again; the letter was returned unopened.

To persist in such fruitless efforts was evidently worse than useless, and I could no longer doubt that it was the General's intention to cut us entirely.

Of this I very soon had certain proof; he sent for all his papers and deeds that I had in my possession, and placed them in the hands of one of my rivals, and I learned that he had also obtained for the same fortunate individual the post of agent to the Comte de Noirtiers.

CHAPTER IX.

TRIALS.

OUR castles in the air had all fallen to the ground. Marcelle declared in a loud tone that she regretted none of them; but in doing so, her voice trembled a little; Aunt Roubert talked of retrenchments in housekeeping, and my father held his peace.

I was angry and dissatisfied in the midst of these sad thoughtful faces; I had done my duty, and had suffered for it; and yet not a word of praise to reward me, nor a whisper of hope to console me, did I get. I was discouraged at the result of this endeavor to do my duty, and but for my father, the feeling would have degenerated into bitterness.

"Beware," he said, "'t is in life as in war, the commander must bear alone the sad consequences of a defeat: it is his place to give encouragement, not to expect it. The head of a family is the main column which supports the rest of the edifice. Until now nothing has gone wrong with you, and you have become enervated by prosperity; now comes the struggle; gird up your loins, and prepare to meet the trial manfully."

And truly it was time, for our trials were only now beginning. My misunderstanding with M. Rigaud did not long remain a secret, and as I had avoided making the true state of the case known, for fear of appearing to accuse, my very moderation was used against me, and those ill-disposed towards me, seized upon the fact as an unfavorable presumption, and bestowed all the blame on me. Thus I beheld gradually increasing the cloud of blame and suspicion, which little by little obscures the sun of prosperity. The number of my clients diminished, and the tone of those that remained was greatly altered; they seemed to think they did me a favor by remaining—I had become the obliged party.

As a finishing stroke to my disgrace, the officious friends of the family kept me carefully informed of each injurious supposition, and every irritating false report. They sedulously gathered together all the poisoned arrows, and, that I might not fail to know they were intended for me, they drove them one by one into my swelling heart, accompanied with a thousand tender sighs of pity.

Our means diminished more and more; I saw Marcelle daily reducing our expenditure, and looking with an increasing anxiety to to-morrow. Aunt Roubert gave no more advice, but I noticed that her bag always arrived full and went away empty. There was no more music in the evening, and conversation itself languished; each seemed oppressed with a secret care. The most frequent interruptions of these long silent hours, were the remembrance of some forgotten household detail, or a reprimand to a child for some too noisy expression of his mirth. Even if Justin succeeded in diverting my thoughts to some other topic, and I for a time forgot our troubles, a sigh from Marcelle, or a remark of Madame Roubert's, was sure to abruptly recall them again. 'T was in vain that I endeavored to bear up; all my ardor froze before those mournful faces, and I felt weak as a child.

Our "tête-à-têtes" had lost all their charm; Marcelle fell into long reveries, which I resented with a sulky silence. Our fireside was no longer the rendezvous of gayety and affection; and instead of the merry chatty hours, to which I had looked forward as my evening's reward for a hard day of toil, I found only sadness and silence. I attempted from time to time to offer some gentle encouragement, but it almost always degenerated into complaints or reproaches: embittered by the struggle, I wanted the patient indulgence necessary to a consoler.

Oh! the weary winter nights thus passed around the evening lamp, I with my eyes fixed upon a book that I did not read, whilst Marcelle sat with bent head over her sewing! What ebbs and flows of bitterness in my bursting heart! What a growing grudge I began to feel against her, who had only to talk and smile to give me hope! Was this what she had promised? when we agreed to share the task of life, had we not each taken our allotted parts? Mine, the labor which assures the daily bread; hers, the song which gives it flavor. Spite of all fatigue and obstacles, I continued to turn up the ground; why then had the singing bird ceased its song?

Spring arrived without bringing any change for the better in our position.

One evening on my return from business, I found that Marcelle had gone down to the garden with Clara and Léon; I followed her, and sat down on the bench by her side. She looked up from her work, as she made room for me, with one of those vague smiles which seemed only a remembrance of the past; we exchanged a few remarks, and some questions without interest, and then, each according to custom, became thoughtful and silent.

The children soon interrupted our meditations by asking for the games left in the house, but their mother refused to allow them to go and fetch them; this was a dissappointment, but of very short duration. After a complaint, and a few tears, they left us.

Fearing that the gravel of the paths would be injured by the winter rains, I had taken it up, and heaped it around the lime-trees, and soon I saw Léon and Clara hasten to it with a bunch of faded flowers they had picked up from under one of the windows, and begin to transform the yellow heap into a flower-bed. Their grief was already forgotten. Both in ecstasies at their work, screamed and clapped their hands for joy.

Marcelle raised her head.

"What have they got hold of?" she asked.

"What we lack," I replied, "facility in being happy. Just now, deprived of their wished-for toys, you saw them depart in sorrow; a little sand, and a few faded flowers have consoled them."

"Happy age!" replied their mother with a sigh.

I seized her hand.

"Great lesson rather, Marcelle," I said gently: "why have we less wisdom than these little children? If a little dry sand be all that is left us, may we not still make it blossom with the small joys that we now trample under foot? Ah! if it be the will of God, let my labor be still more hard, my home less comfortable, my table more frugal, let me even assume a workman's blouse, and I can bear it all willingly and cheerfully, provided I see the loved faces around me happy, provided I can feast upon their smiles, and strengthen myself with their joy. Oh, holy Contentment with poverty! it is thy presence I invoke! Grant me the cheerful gayety of my wife, the free unrestrained laughter of my children, and take in exchange, if necessary, all else that is yet left me!"

There was doubtless something in the tone of my voice which touched Marcelle's heart, for her head drooped on my shoulder, and she burst into tears; but it was only the clearing shower which precedes the bursting forth of the glorious sun. On her raising her eyes, from which the tears had disappeared, I saw breathing in every feature the peaceful serenity whose absence I had so long deplored.

"Grieve no more, dearest," she said; "I will henceforth remember that thou art by my side, that my children are happy, and nothing will then seem sad to me."

And from that day she became her former self again. Roused from the depression of spirits into which she had sunk, she regained her happy, cheerful activity. All the joyous echoes of home were reawakened; the piano made itself heard again; flowers reappeared in the vases, and the spirit of song reigned around. To each fresh economy, enforced by our increasingly contracted means, Marcelle opposed an extra amount of good-humor; she learned to descend laughingly the ladder of success; to keep our wants subservient to our means; and when misfortune redoubled her blows, Marcelle merely shed over each wound a tear, chased away by a smile and a kiss.

Thus supported, I re-entered the world, but only to a certain extent. I had suffered too much in it not to avoid it as much as possible, and I double-locked the door of the abode in which all my sympathies and joys were concentrated. Beyond the circle around my own fireside, which included Justin, Laura, and their daughter, all else was naught to me. With my growing devotion to my own family, increased my hatred of the rest of the world; like the silkworm, I wove around me the shroud in which I wished to die.

At each fresh check I withdrew more and more into myself, and each added injustice rendered me still more suspicious of human nature. No longer a believer in human kindness, I looked for nothing but from God and myself.

In the mean while, the gentleman who had in my place taken charge of the affairs of the Comte de Noirtiers, died, and Madame Roubert hastened to inform me of the fact, at the same time begging me, as the Comte de Noirtiers was himself coming to town, to promise to see him.

"It is the only sure way of coming to an understanding," said she. "Two men put face to face often know more of each other in ten minutes, than in six months of correspondence."

I felt and expressed great repugnance in thus making fresh advances to M. de Noirtiers after my first rebuff; but Marcelle's aunt shrugged her shoulders.

"For heaven's sake, dear friend, don't try to raise objections that have no existence; it is only your 'amour propre' which stands in the way; do, pray, show it the door. If I understand the question at all, it is a simple matter of offering your legal services to the Comte. Why must one ask you for what you long to offer?"

"But if the Comte be prejudiced against me?"

"Prove to him that he is mistaken."

"If he should misunderstand my motives?"

"Explain them to him."

"If he refuse to believe me?"

"That is scarcely likely, but even then you will have done your duty."

"He may be disdainful or insolent?"

"Well, then, he will be a fool, and you may tell him so."

Marcelle added her entreaties to her aunt's, though she wished me first to apply to several of the Comte's friends with whom I was acquainted, and endeavor to obtain their influence in my favor.

I continued, however, to resist these solicitations with impatient obstinacy. The reverses I had lately experienced had so embittered me that I trusted no man, and had no faith in his sympathy.

I had not consented to act as they wished, when my time for going to the office arrived. I took up my papers, and departed without having given any promise.

My mind, however, was disturbed, not by any return of confidence, but by the fear of incurring Marcelle's and Madame Roubert's reproaches.

If I neglect to make this useless application, I said to myself, when the agency is bestowed on some one else, it will all be laid to my door. It will be proved that the Comte merely waited for my visit to offer me his business; that it was not his fault if he at last decided upon another; that, in fact, it was not the fortunate chance which turned against me, but I who had missed the opportunity.

These reflections for an instant overcame my scruples, and I said to myself:

"I will go." But presently doubt murmured:

"And what good will you do? Have you not yet learned that every one in this world cares only for himself? that if one renders you a service, it is only as so much property lent at a high rate of interest; those whose assistance you propose asking, will care very little whether you succeed or not, for they will gain nothing by it; you will only reap contempt as a reward for your trouble."

And then all my former indecision returned. I slackened my pace, wavering, weak, and disgusted. I longed to give it all up and fly to my study, like Shakspeare's Timon to his desert.

I continued in this hesitating state till I had walked to

nearly the other end of the town, undecided as to what I should do.

I had just come to a crossing, and was waiting for some market carts to pass by, when I felt my coat pulled behind, and looked around.

A little girl, about four years old, stood near me, carrying on her arm a basket filled with fruit and vegetables. She was poorly, though neatly dressed; and, on my looking at her, smiled in my face.

"What do you want, my child?" I asked, as I bent down to hear her answer.

"Please, Monsieur," she said in a little voice as clear and gay as the song of a bird, "I have just come from Madame Richard, who has given me all this for mamma—she is so kind to us!—but I want to get to the other side of the square."

"You live near here then?"

"Yes, but mamma is afraid of the horses and coaches for me; and so she has told me, when I come to this crossing, always to ask some one to carry me over."

"And you want me to do so?"

"If you please, Monsieur," she said, holding out her arms.

I took her hand.

"And you are not afraid to ask the first person you see?"

She opened her large eyes at me.

"Afraid! why, Monsieur?" she asked, astonished.

"That they may refuse you."

"Oh! that's impossible," she said with a smile; "for mamma says the big and strong are always kind to the little."

I looked earnestly at her; confidence and peace were expressed in all her features. Much moved, I took her in my arms, carried her across the square, and did not leave her till we reached the street in which she lived.

She thanked me with a nod, accompanied by a friendly laugh, and kissed her hand as children are taught to do. I watched her down the street, and saw her enter one of the poorest houses in it.

I went on my way troubled and yet softened. The poor mother, thought I, very likely finds it a hard struggle to live, and provide food and clothing for the morrow, and yet she has not lost confidence in her fellow-creatures. Necessity forces her to send her child to a distance to receive an alms; and she commits her to God's care, teaching her to believe in the existence of good, and fearlessly to stretch forth her arms to all who bear the stamp of humanity! And I, blessed with so many more privileges, overwhelmed with unmerited gifts, because I have been deceived in some of my hopes, shut my heart against society, and no longer believe in its kind feeling.

The lesson was plain enough, and I understood it. Turning sharply on my heel, and not stopping to discuss the matter farther with myself, I began the visits Marcelle had advised.

The change in my feelings had its proper effect. I bore an air of calm confidence, which of itself won good-will;

and though I found this or that person more or less warm, they were always sufficiently visible and civil to sustain my courage. It seemed to me that several of those on whom I called were gratified by my confiding in their kindness and influence. Whilst holding myself aloof from men, I had fancied them hard and disdainful; but now, when brought in contact with them, I found them, for the most part, polite and willing to serve me.

The next day but one, I learned that the Comte, though pressed by numerous applicants, again inclined in my favor; upon which I fearlessly presented myself, and our interview was as satisfactory as I could have wished. Matters were arranged, and every thing settled before we parted, and thus I was at last possessed of the agency I had been so anxious to obtain.

All that M. de Noirtiers required was, that I should spend the vacations at Viviers (the name of his estate), to superintend the division of the crops, one half of which belonged to him.

I should have greatly enjoyed this country sojourn had the General's residence been situated elsewhere; but his estate and that of the Comte's were contiguous, and I was thus exposed to more than the risk, the certainty of meeting him.

I felt embarrassed as to what position I should take in such a case, and my fear of a rencontre laid an actual constraint upon my movements. I dared not enter one of the avenues common to both proprietors, without first looking well around, to be sure that I should not suddenly be brought face to face with my former patron. And many a time has the glimpse of a figure among the trees, or the discharge of a gun, made me retrace my steps with the idea that he was in the neighborhood.

This apprehension ended at last in entirely depriving me of my liberty; I had allowed it to influence me, until at last I became perfectly ashamed of it, and on seriously reviewing my conduct, I felt that these cowardly precautions were unworthy of me, and gave me, besides, the appearance of a guilty or suspicious character.

In reality, I knew that all this prudence was but so much weakness; I dreaded the trial, in which I feared to prove myself wanting, either in good grace, or good sense, and I endeavored to avoid it by imposing a restraint upon my actions, at all hours and seasons.

Thus reduced to its true proportions, my timidity appeared very ridiculous, for I was not unaware that real courage consists, not only in braving serious dangers, but the thousand and one petty trials of every-day life; that instead of reserving it for great occasions, which rarely or never occur, we must learn to use it in boldly facing the little wearing contrarieties of our daily existence. I remembered that there are in the world plenty of men ready to meet death itself with courage and firmness, who yet cannot support the petty annoyances of a neighbor. Such may be heroic once in their lives, in some great battle, but are cowards every day in the smaller struggles that fall daily to their lot. I continued to repeat this to myself, until I succeeded in quieting my fears; I ceased to avoid the General, and left our meeting, or not, entirely to chance.

I had not long to wait. One morning as I wandered through the fields, book in hand, I heard a step at the turn of the path, and looking up, beheld the old veteran advancing towards me with his gun, as usual, under his arm. The path was so narrow, that, to allow him to pass, I was obliged to stand aside: as I did so, I raised my hat, and then, urged by some feeling I could not resist, I said—

"God bless you, General! I trust you will have a good day's sport;" in a tone which ought to have proved the heartiness of the wish.

He started, threw me a rapid glance, and then coldly returning my salute, passed on.

The blood rushed to my face, whilst humiliation and vexation kept me immovable on the same spot, as I continued to watch the General, until he disappeared behind a clump of hawthorns. This repulse awoke all my former irritation. I was vexed with myself for having saluted him—for having smiled and spoken, but this was the emotion of the moment. As soon as I was cool I felt I had only done my duty, and it was not for me to regret it.

This rebuff, therefore, in the end only served to strengthen my resolution, and the General's obstinate injustice offered another inducement for my continuing in the line of conduct I had chosen.

For three years I persevered in the task of proving myself an obliging neighbor, and whilst maintaining the

Comte's rights, I did so with a deference to the General, which he could not fail to perceive and understand. This behavior embarrassed him at first, but ended no doubt in softening his feelings towards me, for if by chance we met, he was less distant than formerly.

Still, our intercourse had been confined to the exchange of a few slight civilities, when I received orders from M. de Noirtiers to fell a certain amount of timber, and I was myself required to mark the trees which might be felled, without injury to the general appearance of the landscape. Accordingly I started for the country, and summoned the woodsmen.

The second day after my arrival, I was occupied in making my selection, when the forester, as he went his round, stopped and entered into conversation with me about the intended fall of timber. I indicated the different parts of the wood where the axe was to operate, when he, pointing to the end of a thicket which fringed the field, as it pushed itself out from the rest of the wood, asked—

"Then you are not going to meddle with the horn of Brulais?"

I replied in the negative.

"Well! the General is unlucky," he replied; "I'd lay any thing that he would give a thousand crowns to see those trees down!"

"Why, for what reason?" I asked.

"Pardi! because they intercept his view. In days gone by, he saw the hills and the river for more than two leagues distance; but now the Brulais hides it all. It regularly puts out the eyes of his castle; and the General even went to law with the former possessor of this estate about it, but he lost his cause."

I had been, till now, perfectly ignorant of these circumstances, but they made me alter my arrangements. I proceeded to the thicket of Brulais, and noted in what direction it would be necessary to fell, in order to restore to the General his view, and then I wrote to the Compte to obtain his permission.

Immediately on receiving it I set the men to work, and myself remained near, to direct which trees to fell, and urge them to expedition. By the third day only a few more remained to come down, and I was in the act of marking which they were to be, when a voice behind me said—

"Thanks! Monsieur Remi."

I turned: it was the General.

"This then is your revenge," he added: "well, I submit to it without complaint."

"Pardon me," I stammered, much embarrassed; "I do not understand—"

"Nay! do not attempt to excuse yourself," he replied; "I have had a letter from the Comte, and have seen the forester. I know the reason that the trees of the Brulais are chosen for the axe is, that you have endeavored to restore me my view."

"And may I hope that I have succeeded, General?" I asked.

"You shall judge for yourself," he said in his old friendly tone; "for I came in search of you to ask you to dine with me."

From that day forth the General was again all that he had formerly been to me; and his friendship regained, has amply compensated for any injury his resentment may have done me.

CHAPTER X.

THE COST OF PROSPERITY—HISTORY OF A BADLY FRAMED PORTRAIT.

Fresh acquisitions of property, on the part of the Comte de Noirtiers, and several rich clients obtained through his influence, had year by year increased our means. A cabriolet, in which to make my trips to the country, became necessary, and consequently I was obliged to engage a groom, and hire a stable and coach-house. Not a month passed without some addition to our furniture, or some new ornament; and we began to discover a thousand inconveniences about our abode, until then unperceived. The situation was not good, the house mean in appearance, the staircase dark, and the garden too small. After hesitating for some time, we began to speak seriously of taking a house in the new part of the town.

The matter was discussed in a family council, and Madame Roubert decidedly opposed the plan: she maintained that with the addition of extra rooms to those we now occupied, we ought to find our present abode sufficiently commodious; that two movings were as bad as a fire, and that the old furniture, when once removed, would be transformed, for the most part, into rotten planks and rusty nails.

"In my time," said she, "whatever were the changes of fortune, we were born, we lived, and we died, under the same roof-tree. The money we made or gained was invested in land or commerce; it was not squandered in buying infirmities, under the name of fashion; and no one then was too nice to sleep on the bed his father had occupied before him. Thus generation succeeded generation, and dwellings, instead of being known by numbers, had each their separate name. Every street formed one large family, where every one knew everybody, and towns were not then, what they are now-a-days, mere inns, where the last-comer is unacquainted with even the name of his predecessor."

I endeavored to defend the present age by explaining to Marcelle's aunt the advantages arising from this modern mobility, which aimed at one great unity, and only destroyed private associations when necessary for the good of society in general.

"Prove it as you will," replied Madame Roubert, interrupting my disquisition on mankind, "it is not the less true, that it is no longer the fashion to lay by for a rainy day, but that you eat the game as soon as it is killed. It seems to me, dear friend, as if your generation lived in furnished apartments on this our good Lord's earth: the moment the income of any of you increases, you change your lodging. Yourself, for example, who are one of the most reasonable: yesterday your dwelling was all that you could wish, to-day you cannot stir your elbows. One would almost imagine that prosperity was a complaint of a dropsical nature, for where formerly you were quite at your ease, you can now no longer turn."

And then Marcelle, in her turn, tried to justify the proposed change. She proved to her aunt that our circumstances had altered; that the children, as they grew up, required more accommodation; that my greater amount of business created fresh obligations, but all would be rectified by moving; and that once done, we should not want to change again for our whole lives.

My father, who had taken no share in the discussion, now interrupted her, saying, with a smile,

"You are mistaken, dear girl, in fancying such a thing, for each place has its own peculiar atmosphere, which cannot be transported. Whoever takes up new habits and acquaintances, becomes himself transformed."

"But at least his affections remain unaltered."

"Provided they form a part of his new life."

"What! do you really think, then, that an inequality of position can separate hearts?"

"Even as the difference of language raises a barrier between minds. Wherever the joys and troubles of this life are not shared in common by both, the intercourse of hearts must soon cease. How can friendship continue to exist when you can no longer hope and complain together, when the preoccupation of each moment separates you, when the king dreams of his crown, and the shepherd of his flock? Parity of wants and desires is the first condition for the union of souls. Every one who alters his position, necessarily leaves behind him, with his former habits, his old friendships."

Notwithstanding my respect for my father's wisdom and

judgment, I had no desire to believe in the above predictions, and of one thing I was sure, that wherever my abode might be, I should continue to love and esteem the Hubert family as much as I had ever done. A greater distance might render our intercourse less frequent, but it certainly would continue to be as familiar.

Still, when our intended removal was announced to them, neither Justin nor his wife could restrain an exclamation of pain and grief.

"I have been expecting this," said the first; "but I have ever dismissed the thought as I would the menace of a misfortune it was impossible to avert."

Laura, silent and sad, sat looking at us with tears in her eyes, as she drew her child closer to her side. Marcelle threw her arm round her neck, whilst I seized Justin's hand, and both eagerly repeated all that could possibly render the idea of this separation less painful to them.

They accepted these efforts at consolation with gentle sweetness. Possessed of that enviable serenity of soul, they were enabled, the one through strength, the other by submission, to escape the bitterness of grief.

After the first expression of sorrow, which had escaped them in the surprise of the moment, they evinced neither sadness nor resentment; but entering into all our new plans, they listened with interest to the arrangements, discussed various propositions, and joined freely in the merry and somewhat noisy joy which accompanies all success.

When moving-time arrived, Madame Hubert assisted Marcelle in filling the trunks and making up the packages, whilst Justin undertook the charge of my library, which, thanks to his care, arrived uninjured at our new abode.

This was a newly-built house; the elegance and comfort of which had first taken our fancy, but these very qualities soon became embarrassing to us. Our modest furniture, when placed in this charming residence, produced a similar effect to that of a mole or a wart upon an otherwise lovely face. There was, in truth, so great a discrepancy between the frame and the picture, that even Madame Roubert's eye was struck, and shocked by it.

"Good gracious!" she exclaimed, "your furniture spoils all; it's like a rag hanging from a gilded balcony. My dear friends, if you have the least feeling for the beautiful, you will forthwith send all your movables through the window."

Without precisely following this advice, we saw plainly that we must make some alteration; and after consulting our cash-box, we decided upon selling our present furniture.

The Huberts became purchasers of a part, in order, as they said, that they might have something to remind them of our valued intimacy; for things did not end merely as we had imagined—in a loss of neighborly intercourse. Just as we were taking possession of our new dwelling, Justin was appointed, with a very slight advance of salary, to a fresh post, and was obliged to leave our part of the country, to take up his abode in a little village of no importance, in a distant province, without any hope of being recalled for a long time.

It was a cruel separation, though much softened by the resignation of the two exiles; many tears were shed, and a promise of frequent correspondence made. Truly, I lost, in Justin, a great example, as well as a much-valued friend. His utter indifference to the inferior enjoyments of life, had prevented me from ever indulging in them; for, to be able to converse with him, and enter into his feelings and ideas, it was necessary that I should keep up to his level.

This departure had delayed the purchase and arrangement of our new furniture; but our friends gone, we set about it vigorously. The sale of the old stock did not produce very much; while, on the other hand, the purchase of that which was to replace it cost a great deal; for Marcelle displayed, in every article she chose, the excellent taste which she was well-known to possess. Commenting, in her own way, upon Plato's maxim, *the beautiful is the reflection of the good*, she chose all the most elegant and recherché articles she could find. I was a little startled at the bills presented to me, but she proved that good things were never dear, and made me in fact clearly comprehend how perfectly ruinous economy was!

For the rest, our house was charming; the few pieces of our former furniture that we had retained, were either arranged in the shadiest corners, or hidden behind their more brilliant successors; and everywhere damask, velvet, muslin, and silken cords and tassels met the eye! Marcelle glided through it all with the ready graceful ease which women so soon know how to assume in the midst of luxury. One would have thought, on seeing her, that she had never done aught than rustle in silk, and that her dainty foot had never pressed other than Aubusson carpets.

For myself—I felt singularly embarrassed at the imposing splendor which glittered around me, and by the various directions and prohibitions published by the presiding genius of the palace. It was forbidden to put one's feet upon the rails of the chairs, to lay our hat upon the satin-wood table, to leave a book upon the velvet couch, or to sit down on the causeuse, the springs of which were too weak to bear my manly weight, or even to touch the cords of the curtains, of which I was assured, I, in my reveries, unravelled the tassels. Forbidden this—forbidden that—forbidden the other—I read the word prohibition upon the walls, the furniture, my head, and my feet! Ah, how I regretted my old worn leathern armchair, from which, in my hours of meditation, I could leisurely, and without fear of rebuke, extract the horse-hair through some gaping rent! How I sighed, as I thought of my little deal table, that I freely dug and notched with my pen-knife, when my rebellious thoughts refused to arrange themselves, or answer me! However, I became at last accustomed to these embarrassing luxuries. If I lost somewhat in independence, the eye at least was pleased, as it rested on these charming sumptuosities. The change is very gradual; nevertheless, certain it is, that a kind of mental intoxication takes possession of those surrounded by luxury; one becomes proud of, enjoys being in the midst of, so much velvet and gilt-headed nails, and ends by having a much better opinion of himself, and thinking *rather* worse ot others.

Of course, this does not take place all at once, but gradually, and by imperceptible doses. Vanity resembles the fatal miasmas, whose poison we inhale under a sky as blue as the sapphire, and in a breeze seemingly laden only with perfume.

In the midst of all this pomp, however, some remains of our old household gods appeared too conspicuously among the new. The most so was a portrait of Marcelle, given me by Aunt Roubert, whose plain black frame looked grimly down, from amidst the gay carving and gilding which surrounded it. Banished successively from the salon and bedroom, it had at last found refuge on the wall, with the worst light, of the little boudoir in which we usually sat.

One evening that an oblique ray of the setting sun had by chance lit upon it, and made the contrast greater, I was particularly shocked at its appearance. It was the production of one of those strolling artists, who wander from town to town, preparing whole galleries of ancestors, to be handed down to the posterity of the humblest families. There was nothing but a very slight resemblance to attract attention, there were not even the amusing absurdities generally to be found in the productions of this class of artists; and the canvas, without a morsel of expression, betrayed the more than mediocrity of the hand that had wielded the brush. The face was heavy and spiritless, the drapery stiff, the attitude constrained; altogether it had such a poor and mean appearance, that it formed a striking contrast with its neighbors.

On my making some such remark aloud, Marcelle reminded me that she had already more than once proposed sending it to the lumber-room, there to join other pieces of family canvas, already consigned to oblivion; this time I agreed to her proposal. But then came the question of what was to take its place.

We were hesitating between some gothic hanging bookshelves, a Venetian mirror, or an engraving; and I still held in my hand the condemned portrait which I had taken from the wall, when my father entered.

We informed him of our perplexity, and asked his advice; without answering, he took from my hand the black frame, and began to examine the portrait it surrounded.

"You are endeavoring to find some resemblance, are you not?" I asked with a smile.

"No," he replied, "I am merely looking back to former days."

"Indeed?"

"This painting was given you by Madame Roubert, was it not?"

"Yes, it was," said Marcelle.

"You were at that time only engaged to each other, and Remi had often regretted that he did not possess your portrait, when the arrival of an artist was announced in our little town. It was the time when your aunt's lawsuit, which she has since gained, was pending, and great economy was the order of the day; the expenses of every week, aye, and every day, had to be calculated and kept under, and the price of such a canvas and frame would have destroyed the balance of a whole year."

"Oh! I remember it well."

"And then it was, if I am not mistaken, that Madame Roubert began to knit sailors' woollen shirts; she rose earlier, and sat up later, and the result of that extra labor was this production from the painter's brush."

"Ah! that I never knew," I cried.

"But at all events you must remember your delight, when you found this very portrait hanging on your chamber wall," my father replied; "and I, at least, have not forgotten your transports, when you came to tell me of it; I see you, even now, as you stood before the picture holding me by the arm:—but look, father, there are her very features!—just her calm air, and slightly timid glance; and see, she has chosen my favorite dress, and there, in her hand, is the very book I gave her! You went nearer to the picture, you laughed, and seemed to long to hug it in your arms; in your delight you never even noticed the common black frame; the portrait was embellished with your love, and richly framed in your joy!"

"Yes, and believe me, I have forgotten none of those circumstances," I replied, looking down embarrassed.

"I hope not," he gently answered; "but it is evident that you think this figure is no longer at home; she looks down from her mean-looking frame in astonishment at all that surrounds her, and has come to the conclusion, that as she can no longer recognize any thing, she will be better with her old friends upstairs."

Marcelle and I looked at each other.

"No," I replied after a little hesitation, "it shall never be said that we allow our new luxuries to banish old remembrances.

"Go back to thy place, dear portrait that recallest the past! May Heaven reward me as I deserve, if ever I am ashamed of thee! remain to remind me of the time when our wishes were few and modest, and prevent me from forgetting that I have been young, poor, and happy."

The very next day Marcelle and I collected together in the boudoir all that was left of our former ménage, in order to find company for the portrait, and this room we reserved for our most social meetings. In it each found his or her favorite seat, and fell back into their old habits. Carried away, in spite of myself, during the week-time, in the whirl of the world in which my connections obliged me to mix, I returned there every Sunday to enjoy the simple pleasures which had for so long been all-sufficient for me. I hoped that this retreat, closed as it was to all strangers, would resemble the secret cell of the Persian shepherd, to which, when he was grand vizier, he resorted at various intervals, and thus maintained his primitive habits; so I, in my little room, trusted to find thoughts and reminiscences which would serve me as safeguards in the world without.

CHAPTER XI.

THE ECONOMIES OF THOSE WHO ARE UNWILLING TO DEPRIVE THEMSELVES OF ONE LUXURY.—A LESSON IN FRIENDSHIP.

In spite of our resolutions to the contrary, we were hurried away in the whirl of the world. Obliged frequently to visit the richest residents in the country around, we were led, insensibly, to live in the same style. Our children, from constantly mixing with theirs, were obliged to adopt the same expensive costume; and our table, to which it became necessary to invite them occasionally, grew every day more recherché. I have before mentioned that my frequent visits of business to the various estates under my management, had obliged me to purchase a cabriolet; then when we began to visit at the various country residences, as well as for the winter soirées, a calash was indispensable. Thus we glided on, at the edge of the ominous precipice, our expenses always equalling our increased means; the stream of money which flowed into my cash-box, only passed through it, it never collected there, so that we were not really richer, we merely spent more.

Aunt Roubert often reminded us, that he who does not save is always poor, for he is ever at the mercy of the future; and she never visited us without making some reference or other to the fable of the ant and the grasshopper. We perfectly agreed with her as to the truth of all she said, but we allowed the means of reformation to slip by.

At last, however, we became seriously alarmed at the increasing amount of our expenses, and calling a family counsel, we began to discuss the budget; Marcelle, as minister of finance, brought forward all her accounts, and submitted them to our examination.

The first item which struck us as large, was the rent; and Madame Roubert repeated all her former objections to our present residence, to which Marcelle replied with the doctrine of a *thing once done cannot be undone!* She acknowledged her fault, and did not defend its consequences; they were quite at liberty to condemn the past, provided the present was not touched upon.

Then came the calash and cabriolet, and I, in my turn, proved that the latter was indispensable, and that the former once bought was no longer much expense.

Next came the table; Marcelle observed that it was a business necessity to invite to dinner those to whom I was either the patron or the protégé, as the dinner-table was often the only place where certain persons could meet, and certain matters be arranged; and according to her opinion these dinners ought properly to be included amongst business expenses.

Then we attacked the matter of dress; but here again we found our necks inclosed within the yoke of custom, and, willing slaves, we declared it to be impossible for us to dress differently from those with whom we associated, and that the elegant appearance of Clara and Léon, was dictated not by choice, but by stern necessity. Marcelle assured us that no one deplored more deeply than herself, the extremes to which modern fashions were now carried; that though her daughter did wear silks, it was contrary to what, if she were able, she should choose; and that her son's velvet jacket was a sore trial to her. But then surely this was better than, by dressing otherwise, to make themselves remarkable, and she was very sure that the most certain way of making her children hate simplicity, was to render it a matter of humiliation to them.

We turned to the subject of servants, and I had no difficulty in proving that I required the services of the man-servant, and Marcelle as clearly showed that she could not possibly do with less than two maids. The sole diminution in our expenses that appeared feasible was a reduction in the wages we gave.

The principal items relating to the garden, journeys, interior improvements, evening parties, and correspondence, were all successively examined, and supported as indispensable; and my father came to the conclusion that it was with domestic as with state budgets, they were discussed merely to prove that there was nothing to alter in them; but Marcelle begged to differ with him on this point, and proposed several minor retrenchments.

First, that we should leave off subscribing to two journals, and for the present buy no more new books. We had, till now, employed work-people of standing, whose terms it was impossible to dispute, but, thanks to competition, we might get our work done elsewhere for far less.

Marcelle had already changed her laundress and seamstress, and would, therefore, have courage to continue this reform. Again, we had been at great expense for private masters for our children, and this might be lessened, by sending Clara and Léon to one of the fashionable morning-schools. All these changes would produce a considerable diminution in our expenditure, and would lead to many others it was impossible to enumerate.

Madame Roubert had listened in silence to all this as she sat at her knitting, and at the conclusion said, with an emphatic shrug of her shoulders,

"You'll not save a hundred crowns with all these reforms; take my word for it."

Marcelle loudly declared it would be more.

"Well," replied her aunt, "we will say a thousand francs if you like; what a handsome portion that will make for your daughter, and how greatly it will assist in putting your son forward in the world!"

"Without taking into account," added my father seriously, "that you, who cannot dispense with one of the many superfluities of your table, are determining to deprive your mind of its daily bread. You must have the same amount of luxury to which you have accustomed yourselves, but you mean to exact it at a lower price from those who earn their subsistence by supplying you with it. In fact, you find it easier to economize upon the instructors of your children than upon your horses and carriage!"

Marcelle changed countenance, and would have attempted to defend herself, but my father took her hand, saying, as he kissed her forehead,

"Nay, dear daughter, do not seek excuses; you did not properly reflect: it was, I know, no lack of kindness which made you think of such arrangements; but, alas, how many there are who practise what you propose! Down from the great lady, who during Lent dines herself as usual, but makes the rest of her household fast as a penance for their and her own sins; what numbers there are who would willingly profit by reforms, so long as they themselves are not affected by them! This is one of the consequences of a too highly-flavored prosperity; it deadens to a certain degree our sense of justice, enervates us, and we become gradually accustomed to leave the burden to be borne by others, and are ourselves constantly adding to it, whilst taking no share in the toil. Believe me, dear children, better not attempt to economize at all, than do so upon the hardly earned wages of the laborer, rather than upon your own vanities and pleasures."

We did indeed find that the only way was really to make a firm stand against the expensive habits we had allowed to grow up among us. For the rest, the money spent was not the only evil; the loss of liberty, time, and health, weighed far more heavily upon me. The visits we were obliged to make and receive, left us not a moment to ourselves: we had to renounce our family meetings, and my father and Aunt Roubert only saw us now at rare intervals.

I began to feel we were becoming unfitted for this social

intercourse. In neglecting our duties to satisfy the world, all that we accorded to our acquaintances were so many deprivations to our friends. The, at first, active correspondence with the Huberts had quickly slackened on our side, but Justin, still buried in his meditations, continued to write me long letters, in which he discussed the great problems of life, which formerly had so powerfully interested us. I answered him, however, very cursorily, in the manner of a man too much absorbed in business, to have time to think about his soul, and the good of mankind. Laura, on her side, informed Marcelle of the walks they took, the books they were reading, and her daughter's progress; asking, at the same time, numerous questions about our children, and for details which we never had time to give.

The remembrance of these dear friends was thus gradually disappearing in the whirl of our modern life; and without our being conscious of the change, their continued affection began to embarrass us: we no longer wore it as a crown, but dragged it after us as a chain. Shameful infirmity of the soul, which all continuity fatigues, and where nothing permanently endures! We form the sweetest, the most beautiful attachment, to which we owe all, and receive from it all; it seems to have become an inseparable part of our being; and yet, even at the very moment of its greatest fervor, oblivion is silently weaving her web in a corner of our heart. Let an inevitable separation occur to turn our attention from this holy friendship: when we seek it again, we find it has undergone the fate of those epitaphs over which the moss silently, but surely creeps, and ends by effacing.

Not that it had yet gone so far as this with the Huberts, but we were tending towards it. Neither of them, however, seemed to suspect it, for their letters were as affectionately communicative as ever, and in their eyes our neglect merely proved our servitude; they did not complain, but pitied us.

The only thing they murmured at was our separation, and they constantly recurred to the hope of seeing us again, if it were only for an hour: it was their favorite topic in their letters, their dream in their walks and by their fireside; and an unexpected circumstance seemed likely to realize it.

The Comte de Noirtiers wrote to inform me that he was confined to his chateau by gout; and, as it was therefore impossible for him to meet me as usual at Fresnaies, to arrange the work for the coming year, and would lead to a tedious correspondence, he was anxious to know whether I would, with my family, spend a part of the vacation with him at his chateau.

The Huberts were delighted when they heard of this, for our route to the Chateau de Noirtiers lay within a few leagues of their village, and by making a slight bend we might meet again. Our rooms were already prepared; they spoke of nothing else but our coming from morning to night. Justin left his books, and Laura and Renée neglected their lessons.

This fervor of hope and expectation on their part greatly

perplexed us. The Comte was awaiting us: we had arranged to travel post, and a halt in the middle of our journey would upset all our plans; besides, the village where our friends resided lay some leagues out of our way, and there were rumors of all sorts of cross-roads, and difficulties to surmount; so after consulting together, Marcelle and I agreed that we should excuse ourselves on the plea of being expected on a certain day at the Chateau de Noirtiers, and the visit, if it took place at all, was postponed until our return.

This possibility, which we had advanced as a sort of consolation, Justin and Laura took for a promise; and without inquiring whether our eagerness equalled theirs, incapable, in fact, of suspecting their friends, they deferred the promised pleasure, with the kind, indulgent good grace to which they had so long accustomed us.

We had, however, merely staved off our embarrassment for the time. When the day of our return arrived, the same motives which had formerly determined us against the visit, again presented themselves. This time our pretext was the state of Clara's health, about which we had really been anxious for some days past; and, wishing to compensate as much as possible for our broken promise, we both wrote at greater length, and with more affection than usual.

In reality, however, we were dissatisfied with ourselves. We avoided all mention of Justin's and Laura's names, and I, for my part, was anxious to leave behind us the village at which we ought to have quitted the high-road to visit them. When our postilion pointed it out to us in the distance, I could not repress the accelerated beating of my heart. There was yet time to repent of my resolution; like Cæsar, I was on the bank of the Rubicon, and had not yet crossed it; but I hardened my heart against remorse, and allowed the horses to gallop on.

We had reached the first houses of the place, when we perceived a little uncovered chaise hastening towards us, enveloped in a cloud of dust. All at once the carriage stopped, the dust fell, and we beheld M. and Madame Hubert alighting.

My astonishment prevented me at first from speaking, and Marcelle recovered herself sooner than I. Laura first took her in her arms, then the children, and then again returned for a fresh embrace, both weeping and laughing at the same time, and asking question upon question without waiting for answers; but in time they became calmer, and we could again hear and understand each other.

On receipt of our last letter, M. and Madame Hubert had both agreed that as we could not go to see them, it was for them to come and see us; being determined it should not be their fault that they had missed the happiness of seeing their friends once more. So hiring the grocer's little chaise, they set off, leaving all business behind them; and for the last three hours had been travelling, exposed to the burning heat of a midday sun. They were much exhausted, and covered with dust, but, unmindful of it all, were only too thankful that they had arrived in time to embrace us as we passed.

So much forbearance, and so devoted a friendship, touched me deeply; and with shame I compared their conduct with ours. The fear of some slight annoyances and disagreeables on the road, had been sufficient to deter us from visiting them; and yet they had braved it all, and more, just to catch a glimpse of us. I actually blushed as I compared our brilliant equipage with their dusty little chaise, and, truly ashamed, I exclaimed:

"We do not part here; after the exertion you have made to see us, dear friends, we must not separate with merely a passing embrace. Let Laura take my place in the carriage, I will go with Justin in the chaise, and we will accompany you back."

"And you will stay?" they both exclaimed at once.

"Yes, till to-morrow."

Justin took my hand, whilst Laura said, as she put her arm round Marcelle: "Ah! now my child will be able to embrace you too. Quick, quick, let us start! every minute we linger we are depriving her of so much happiness."

The journey was a delightful one; our way lying through unfrequented roads, where the soft rich grass deadened all sound from the carriage-wheels. Hubert began one of our conversations of days gone by; and, led back by him into his own atmosphere, my soul reawakened to its former higher aspirations, and, by the time we arrived, I had recovered several of my youthful enthusiasms.

Renée received our children as Justin and Laura had met us. The day passed like an hour: we all dined together under the trees in a rural garden, where nothing was to be heard but the hum of bees and the murmur of a rivulet. The evening waned into night, and the stars had been looking down upon us for hours before we thought of separating.

The rooms to which they conducted us were evidently the best in the house; but Clara and Léon, accustomed to the luxuries of town and the Chateau de Noirtiers, were much struck with the poorness of the furniture; and even I felt a kind of oppression, produced by the humbleness of our surroundings, which I remarked to Marcelle. She looked at me with surprise. "Then you do not recognize all about you?" she asked: "this is the furniture of our first home, which Justin purchased before his departure."

I examined it more attentively, and found indeed that what had so shocked my taste, was the very same furniture that had formerly been so dear to us; and that what had struck our children as being merely poor and *mean*, we had once thought beautiful and sumptuous. Such thoughts as these took possession of my mind, and I stood brooding by the window, where I was presently joined by Marcelle, after she had seen the children to bed: she too seemed sadly thoughtful.

"How many lessons we have learned in one day," I said to her in a low tone; and how does the past shame the present! what of the good resolutions of our youth have we retained? Our hearts benumbed, and our wants increased; the independence of our thoughts and sentiments sacrificed to the dependence of things; life transferred from the inner to the outer man; a flashy brilliance and a noisy mirth substituted for intimate communion and reflection. Oh! if it be possible, Marcelle, let us never forget this day; let us endeavor to resist the love of the vanities of this life, and the effeminacy of over-luxuriousness, that when next brought in contact with the scenes of our earlier life, we may not, as to-day we have done, despise them. And let us try henceforth to remember that no road is too long, no vehicle too uneasy, and no weather too bad, when, by encountering these disagreeables, we enjoy the happiness of embracing a true friend!"

CHAPTER XII.

REFORM—EACH REASSUMES HIS FORMER POSITION—CLARA AND LÉON—WHAT CAN BE SEEN THROUGH A HEDGE—EVENING CONVERSATIONS—COURSES OF READING—CHILDREN'S BOOKS.

Our visit to the Huberts was productive of very important results. After having been suddenly transported back into the past, we were better able to feel how great the change had been which had taken place in our mode of life. In reality, our new habits had arisen less from choice than from circumstances; for it was evident that the proper place of one of the workers of the world was not in the midst of sumptuous uselessness, where the heart suffers no less than the purse; and it became necessary to come out from it.

We had thought before that reform in our style of living was difficult, but we only needed to wish it seriously to accomplish it. The world that we had thought it impossible to deprive of our society, was scarcely conscious of our absence; and we then perceived that our presence had been rather endured than desired. From mere politeness it had allowed the business man to glide from the office to the salon, but he was permitted to disappear again without remonstrance or even notice. I had summoned all my strength of mind and resolution to resist the objections and prayers I had expected, and to my chagrin I found I did not in the least require either of them.

This disappointment humiliated me sufficiently to strengthen my former resolution, for when I discovered how little I was cared for or appreciated, my pride came to assist me in making a speedy retreat; whilst Marcelle, who shared in my sentiments and annoyance, did all in her power to encourage me. The calash was sold, our grand dinner-parties discontinued, the servants desired to find other places, and the evening parties given up.

In all these changes we were influenced partly by prudence, and a good deal by wounded pride. On again re-entering the calm of social family intercourse, we experienced at first a kind of weary languor; and therein lies the danger of the pleasures of the world; incapable themselves of satisfying us, they yet render all others distasteful. After becoming accustomed to intoxicating liquids, we no longer perceive any flavor in the pure water from the stream!

It, therefore, took some time to reaccustom us to the simple pleasures of the domestic circle, which in itself had to be formed again. Our recent mode of life had insensibly slackened the ties of relationship in the family. We had met more rarely, and had again, so to say, to renew our acquaintance, and each to seek his former position in the circle.

Aunt Roubert very soon found her way back to her little low chair, and brought forth her knitting; my father again began his walks from the door to the window and back, listening, without the appearance of doing so, to all that was said, and throwing from time to time into the conversation a humorous remark, or a recompensing smile. The children were more difficult to reform.

Having been a little neglected during the period in which we had courted the world, they had sought their amusements apart from us. Taken up by business and visiting engagements, I had merely glanced at, rather than penetrated these two natures; the brother and sister had only appeared before me, at my hours of leisure, with healthy faces beaming with smiles; and I found that to know them, I needed to see them nearer and for a longer time.

At the bottom of our garden was a bower devoted to their use and amusement, and that of the neighbors' children with whom they associated. One day, as my father and I were seated in an arbor separated from their part of the garden by a green hedge, but not thick enough to prevent our overlooking their sport, my father all at once ceased to take any part in the conversation in which we were engaged, and, following his glance, I saw through the hedge that Clara and Léon had separated themselves from their companions, who were calling to them to join them.

"No, no," replied Léon, who had evidently quarrelled with the rest of the group; "I prefer playing by myself."

"Because we wont do as you want?" asked a voice.

"Yes."

There was an indignant murmur.

"Behold the new Cæsar!" said the same voice, "who

would be master of all the world. Obey him, all ye nations! Bow down before the conqueror of the Gauls, and the victorious enemy of Pompey!"

A loud burst of laughter followed this speech. Léon answered with a shrug of his shoulders, and approached the place where we were sitting, twisting the piece of cord he held in his hand.

Clara, who had from habit followed him, now asked what he meant to do.

"Amuse myself," replied Léon, going up to one of the lime-trees.

"But how?"

"You shall see."

As he spoke, he began to fasten his cord to two trees planted in a line with each other.

"You are going to make a swing," exclaimed Clara; "you must not, Léon, you know we are forbidden to do it."

Her brother went on with what he was about without appearing to have heard her; she renewed her opposition, repeating all her mother's reasons for forbidding the amusement.

Léon whistled a favorite quadrille whilst finishing his swing; and seating himself in triumph, began to make it fly among the branches. His sister, alarmed, drew back.

"Léon, come down immediately," she exclaimed; "you will get giddy."

"Why should I come down, if it is my pleasure to remain?" replied the little fellow, swinging himself higher as he spoke.

"Oh, stop!" cried Clara; "the rope may break."

"It's too strong for that, my dear."

"But if you fall?"

"That's my affair."

"No, do not, pray," exclaimed his sister, beginning to cry; "Léon (stamping her foot), come down immediately! leave off! you know mamma has said it was dangerous."

"Well! and what of that?" replied Léon, leaning his weight upon his wrists, and springing upright in the swing. "A little danger does not matter—when it amuses."

"Ah! if mamma only knew! Léon, are you not afraid she may come?"

"If she comes, she will scold—she will punish me," said the boy, whose sentences were cut up by the rapid oscillations of the swing; "but that's better than always obeying; one never enjoys one's self unless one can do as one chooses. See, see, how high I go!"

At each swing he now disappeared among the leaves, and Clara's terror increased in proportion. She passed from warnings to entreaties, and from entreaties to tears; but Léon evidently felt a wicked pleasure in tormenting her. Half from bravado, and half from excitement, he continued to send the swing higher and higher, with a thousand teasing remarks, intermingled with joyous exclamations.

"See, see," he merrily cried; "here I go higher still—up, up, among the little birds! Would you like some of the lime blossoms? Stay, I'll beat them down with my feet"—and immediately down came a shower of perfumed petals upon Clara's head—"there, I touched the large branches—the leaves kiss my cheeks. Ah! if you only knew what a sweet smell, and so fresh—this is better even than riding on horseback."

As he continued describing his sensations, Clara's sobs became less violent, her eyes followed the oscillations of the swing, and insensibly terror was succeeded by interest and curiosity; Léon's perfect freedom from fear at last completely reassured her. She ceased reminding him of her mother's prohibition, and began instead to ask him questions.

"Are you sure that there is no danger?" she asked, wiping her eyes and drawing nearer.

"No, to be sure not, don't you see that the rope is too strong to break," replied her brother, who was now swinging more gently.

"And—is it really as you say—so very pleasant?"

"You feel as if you were flying through the air like a bird."

She crept a little nearer.

"But you can go very gently, if you wish to, can you not?"

"To be sure, you shall see," said Léon, who reseating himself gave a very slight impetus to the swing, and swung gently to and fro.

She stopped him with her hand.

"Promise me that you will not swing me higher than I wish, Léon," she said hesitatingly, as if half ashamed to make the request.

"Ah, ah, so you want to try now," said her brother with a laugh; "well I have had enough."

"Do please."

"No, no, mamma has forbidden it," he continued mockingly, imitating her former tone, and pretending to unfasten the rope.

"Only for one minute, Léon," persisted Clara.

"Impossible," he replied; "it would make you giddy."

"I will go very gently."

"But even then you might fall."

"But you say it is so very pleasant."

"Yes, only you seem to have forgotten that you would be disobeying mamma."

"How disagreeable you are, to be sure, Léon," she cried with vexation; "you never will do what I want, and are always teasing me; you are a very naughty disagreeable boy."

Her eyes filled again with tears, and Léon laughed outright, as he took her hand.

"Come, come, don't cry," he said; "just now you cried because I would make the swing, and now you are crying because I am going to take it down. Oh! this is always the way with you girls; you preach to us about obeying, till you want to disobey yourselves, and then it's all forgotten in a minute. There, are you on?"

"Yes."

"Well, hold tight and the rest will go of itself."

He gave the swing a touch, which sent it off in a curve, large enough to make Clara scream and cling convulsively to the rope. But the first moment of surprise over, she recovered her courage, and her exclamations of terror were changed into laughter. Soon, excited by the pleasing sensation of a peril that she felt she had courage to brave, she begged Léon to swing her higher, and with the swing rose her bravery. With sparkling eyes, heightened color, and hair floating disorderly in the breeze, she continued to scream for joy, crying, "Higher! higher!" until I, alarmed myself at her hardihood, thought it time to interfere.

The two children were all the more disconcerted at being caught in the very heat of disobedience. I contented myself, however, with giving them a short, though severe, reprimand, and sent them into the house to Marcelle. But when I found myself alone with my father, I turned towards him with an anxious inquiring face, to which he replied with a shrug of his shoulders, saying—

"It has become very necessary that you should know the real character of those children better than you have done till now; and you may thank God for having been pleased to grant you a sign, which it is for you now to understand."

"Alas! it is too plain to allow of any doubt," I replied. "The sign, as you call it, has been a double one: it has revealed in Léon, not only the love of tyranny, which imposes the yoke upon others, but the audacity to throw it off himself; whilst with Clara, an innate sense of right is rendered naught by her instability of character. The former seems in a fair way to become a despot or a rebel; and the latter is an excellent example of a weak and fickle mind.

What is to be done to render these two natures fit for the struggle of life, when one of them yields to every impulse, whether right or wrong, whilst the other is inaccessible to neither, and is bent only on making others yield to him? 'Tis like endeavoring to harness to the chariot of stern necessity two animals that will never pull together—the capricious goat, which wanders wherever it is attracted by a tuft of grass or inviting herbage, and the wild boar, which follows in a straight line the object of its desires through bogs, hedges, ditches, whatever, in fact, lies in its way."

"Study and observe, and you will learn," replied my father. "Absorbed as you have been in the busy world of fashion, you have had time neither to see nor hear; but now, having again returned to your domestic circle, you will soon learn how to rule and regulate it. What has occurred to you is the history of the larger portion of mankind, who, from being entirely taken up with the things of the outer world, are strangers to all their species. The beings with whom they live are so many closed books, the form and title of which are all they are acquainted with. How can we be surprised at the impossibility of knowing the different characters of which our family circle is composed, when we are often so perfectly ignorant of our own natures!"

I did my best to remember, and turn these words to account. The time had arrived when Léon and Clara required constant care and attention. The new light in which they had appeared to me that day, was my first step towards sounding the depths of these characters, and I was soon able to form a better estimate of what my duties were, and what difficulties I should encounter in their fulfilment.

Marcelle, whom I consulted, shared in my apprehensions. We decided that the children should be brought into more familiar intercourse with us; that a greater community of sentiments, occupations, and pleasures, ought to exist between us. Accordingly they were admitted into the family circle, where not only a place was reserved for them, but they were allowed a voice in the conversation.

Our evenings were divided into two parts, the first of which was almost entirely devoted to them. Until the moment when they came to receive their evening kiss, Marcelle and I became children again, in order to understand and be better understood, and all proper freedom was permitted in the conversation. Becoming their interlocutors, we endeavored to regain in this hour of companionship all that we had lost of their confidence during the day, whilst exercising the necessary authority of master; and then, whilst their hearts were opened, they were at full liberty to say all that during the preceding hours had occupied their minds; and thus the two children gave us an opportunity of seeing their real characters, whilst freely expressing all their little hopes and wishes. It was highly important, however, never to make use of these involuntary confidences against them afterwards, but strictly to observe the sanctity of the truce between the two eternal enemies, the pupil and the educator.

This we were particularly careful to observe, and consequently admitted without fear into the confidence of brother and sister, we were gradually enabled to penetrate into the mysteries of these as yet unformed natures, watch the dark spot which might in after years increase to a storm, and anticipate such a calamity by dissipating the menacing cloud.

To accomplish this, besides the indirect instruction conveyed by conversation, we called to our aid the more decided kind, which results from reading.

Much has been said and written upon the importance of these intellectual family repasts, as calculated to create, by community of emotions, the same moral temperament. But the choice of the viands which are to form them, requires peculiar care. Of all diets, that of the mind is the most important, and at the same time the most difficult; for unless nature be assisted, it suffers: all that does not strengthen, enervates; all that does not insure health, induces disease. The smallest thing is of consequence in this delicate culture, where a single hurtful seed, dropped in the most obscure corner, will quickly take root, spring up, increase, and choke the harvest of good.

Unfortunately, we lacked books to assist us in our task. I sought in vain in my own library and that of my father, for suitable subjects. In all I found the same great fault—that talent, when not directly inimical to morality, is scarcely ever to be found combined with it. Art is an exclusive lover of *beauty,* and, like Phidias, it is occupied merely with the form, sculpturing indifferently vice or virtue; delighting in the most splendid imagery, seeking what pleases rather than what is right, and aiming less at improvement than fascination.

Did I succeed in finding here and there a few pages unstained with evil, Clara and Léon were unable to comprehend them, without my explanation of what they could not read. I was obliged to assist them in their ignorance, and lead them by the hand through a thousand illusions or intricacies, and thus, in spite of all I could do, the intended amusement was transformed into a lesson.

Warned by their wearied looks and distracted attention, I gave up the higher classes of works, where the range of prospect was too extended for them to take in, and returned to the narrow-limited horizon of books, written expressly for children.

Then it became my turn to grow impatient. Wearied with going over the same ground, again and again, where every event is known beforehand, with the certainty of its all coming right in the end, in the most approved and orthodox style; I at last stopped the reading, angry with the book, and vexed and annoyed at the evident pleasure the children took in it. Before, their little necks had ached with looking too high, and now I was angry at their looking so low.

It was in vain that I questioned all whom I thought might enlighten me, and even our friends the Huberts were only able to name one or two volumes. "'Tis useless seeking a library for childhood, or even for youth," wrote Justin, "for, saving a few rare and brilliant exceptions, writers of any worth have despised the glory of assisting in the formation of men. The intellectual, like the domestic world, has its *nursery maids*, to whose care the minds of the young are abandoned; and it is absurd to require of such the perspicacity to divine, the skill to direct, and the nobleness of mind to elevate the various instincts displayed by different children. Prejudice is their guide, and custom their principle, and they teach morality as a dancing-master teaches elegance. For the rest, there is much excuse to be made for them, for in many cases they are ignorant of the existence of what they destroy. Doubtless a day will come, when guides and counsellors more worthy of the trust reposed in them, will be given to future rising generations. We shall in time comprehend, I hope, that for the first nourishment administered to the mind, as for the body, no nurse can be too strong, too healthy, nor too diligent; and our noble hearts and great minds will not deem it any degradation to become the foster-fathers of the future."

When at last, by dint of much search, I succeeded in forming a little collection of volumes that I could confidently place in the children's hands, as sure and pure friends, a fresh scruple arose in my mind.

These books consisted of two classes; the first conveyed instruction in a positive and direct form, the second contained adventures and tales, in which instruction was secondary to amusement; the latter addressed the feelings through the imagination, the former appealed to the conscience, with reason and good sense. Both had their advantages and inconveniences. The first class were difficult to read and understand, and the fatigue experienced in their perusal, was liable to annul the good result intended; and in the second, the charming medium through which the instruction was conveyed, very often caused the end to be forgotten. If the children were allowed the liberty of choice, it was evident that each would reject the less attractive volumes, to feast upon those which better pleased their taste; and thus reading, instead of acting as a sedative, would become an excitement, and exaggerate what it should rather balance.

By addressing themselves to the different faculties, these books each formed the complement of the other, and could not be separated with impunity. The difficulty lay in getting the children to accept them, if not with the same pleasure, at least with some amount of interest; and I found that the only means of accomplishing this was by making the evening readings a reward, and not a matter of course.

I was fortunate enough to succeed in this, and, thanks to this rational arrangement, Marcelle and I were enabled to prolong the winter amusements; and we did more. In the variety of moral lessons contained in our collection, it was almost always easy to select one appropriate to the need of the moment, and every serious fault committed during the day, received its covert reprimand, and the precept or example conveyed, was felt all the more from coming at the moment of trouble, which precedes repentance.

As was to be expected, the grief and remorse experienced

by the brother and sister was as different as their characters. With Léon, sorrow for his fault, struggling with his pride, always preserved the appearance of revolt; he disputed every inch before he gave way, and never but half admitted that he was in the wrong, remained angry with the cause of his fault, and bore for some time a grudge against those he had offended. In reality, however, all this bad temper proved how keenly he felt his culpability; and had he been less dissatisfied with himself, he would have been more easily reconciled with those he had injured. Thus, though the obstinacy of his character deprived his repentance of its charm, it secured to him all its advantages; he never fully admitted his fault, but he also carefully avoided a recurrence of the same.

Clara, on the contrary, was so ready to accuse herself, and repented with such fervor, that rebukes with her generally ended in efforts at consolation; it was impossible to remain long angry with her, the humility and sincerity of her repentance disarmed you, she knelt so humbly and so low, that your only thought was how to raise and comfort her. All quickly ended in supplicating promises and a ready pardon; but the same mobility of temperament which enabled her so readily to own her fault, made her as readily err again; the error once repented, was forgotten, to be again committed, and again sorrowed and wept for. Thus the ungracious roughness of her brother troubled me less than her ever ready submission; for with him, the faults that made him suffer, and, for the time, alienated the affections of others, gave far more promise of a victorious result, sooner or later, than those of Clara, which merely produced a sudden storm, and left her better loved and more happy than before, yet as likely as ever to fall into the same error at the very next temptation.

CHAPTER XIII.

AUNT ROUBERT'S PRACTICAL LESSONS—STORY OF M. LE MARQUIS DE NIHIL AND HIS SISTER MADEMOISELLE NIHILETTE—WINTER WALKS.

As I have before stated, our new mode of life had brought back to our family circle my father and Madame Roubert, who both resumed their different parts, which greatly resembled the chorus in the ancient tragedies, my father's being the poetic voice of wisdom, and Madame Roubert's the cheerful tone of good sense.

One day, the latter found Marcelle occupied in reading to Léon and Clara a tale filled with the details of a country life, all of which she did her best to explain to them; the old lady allowed her to go on uninterrupted, but after the book was closed, and the children gone, letting her knitting fall, she asked abruptly—

"Are you desirous of teaching your children every thing?"

"Certainly not," Marcelle replied; "still, I am anxious that the world should not be to them a series of hieroglyphics, which they seek in vain to understand without assistance. They must learn to know something of what goes on in the world in which they are to live, and the various positions that exist, that they may feel the use and value of the meanest laborer, and esteem him accordingly."

"Very good," replied Madame Roubert; "but excuse my saying so, it strikes me that you set about it as a man without hands would stick peas."

"Pray what resemblance can there be?"

"Why, that you are making a great fuss about nothing! What is the use of all that long story you told them about a plough, the making of soft cheeses, and the preparation of flax? Take my word for it, they have not understood a syllable of it all, in spite of your plates, sketches, and caricatures!"

"They will comprehend it better the second time of reading."

"All mere waste of time; I will undertake to teach them all that sort of thing, as well and better than any book-writer ever succeeded in doing."

"How, by explanation?"

"No, by showing them the things themselves! You know very well *my* reading has been little enough. In my time a sensible woman's library was considered complete, when it contained "*The Whole Duty of Man*," "*The Complete Housewife*," and "*The Little Warbler*." We learned, however, what all the printed books will never teach: to have our eyes about us! Now-a-days you expect a number of books, and little boxes, to contain every thing; you put the world under a glass-case, for children's especial use, and teach them to play with the creation, as they would at a baby-house! How much better it would be to encourage them to look and examine for themselves! Show them the plough in the furrow, the flax in soak, and the milker in the cowhouse; it would be much more simple, and, to my mind, more christianlike, for books are but the work of men's hands and brains, whilst the productions of nature are fresh from the hands of our gracious and Almighty God!"

True to her promise, the next holiday that occurred, Madame Roubert carried off the children to the farm which supplied her with butter, eggs, and milk.

We were able to judge that very evening, from all that the children told us, of the beneficial result of this first excursion into the practical world. Léon had tried his hand at the plough, under the superintendence of the farmer; Clara had taken her first lesson in milking, and both had seen the process of stacking wheat and thrashing oats. Their aunt succeeded in fixing what they had seen in their memory by a tale, which, by dint of repeating several times, and correcting each other when in fault, they never forgot.

This was the history of M. le Marquis de Nihil and his sister, who were educated in a truly aristocratic style, if such consisted in knowing only the arts of embroidery and making sword-knots.

Now when M. le Marquis de Nihil and Mademoiselle Nihilette were respectively fifteen and fourteen, they went to reside at a distance from Paris, at the chateau of their guardian, for they were orphans. This being the first time they had ever been in the country, they were very much surprised to see the roads unpaved; fields, in which other things besides tulips were cultivated; sheep, that were not led by rose-colored ribbons; and trees in other forms than imitations of birds and wigs.

But their astonishment increased when, on arriving at their guardian's, they learned that before French rolls can be made, corn must grow and be ground; that for us to have milk, cows must have grass; and that wine does not run from the vine on the turning of a key, as it does from the cask; and both wandered, in a state bordering on stupefaction, in large fields uninclosed in iron fences, and along a lovely river, where there were neither shops nor quays.

One morning, as they were chatting and sauntering along, they came to a small creek, in which lay a little green boat, the bow of which ended in the form of a swan's head and neck. The Marquis de Nihil, remembering that he had crossed the Seine above St. Cloud in one nearly similar, immediately jumped in, and Mademoiselle Nihilette, out of respect for her elder, followed; but the skiff had not been securely fastened; the shock of their jumping in had detached the rope, and behold them borne by the current down the river.

The terror and consternation of M. de Nihil and Mademoiselle de Nihilette may be imagined. The latter began to cry, as she invariably did when any thing happened which did not particularly please her; and the Marquis laid his hand on his sword, as he had been told every gentleman at all put out should do; but, finding that this procedure did not the less prevent the boat from being carried on by the stream, he let go his sword, and seized an oar instead.

Now it happened, unfortunately, that though M. le Marquis de Nihil was perfectly acquainted with heraldry, and could dance the minuet to perfection, he did not know which end of the oar to handle; so that all his efforts were useless, and he only succeeded in turning the boat quite round two or three times, and forcing it into the very middle of the stream, which carried them on so rapidly, that, as the river continued to widen, they soon lost all hope of assistance from either bank.

M. le Marquis gave it up, and, putting down his oar, went and seated himself in the fore-part of the boat, very much disconcerted and confounded, whilst Mademoiselle Nihilette continued to cry in the stern for want of something better to do. At last they came to an island, which divided the stream into two arms, and, the boat becoming entangled among the rushes, ran aground on the island, and both leaped out highly delighted.

After taking the precaution to fasten the rope to a tree, they set off round the island, in hopes of finding a post-office, where they could write and dispatch a letter, requesting their guardian to come to their assistance; but they made the circuit without meeting with any thing but flocks of sheep, herds of cattle, and fowls, contentedly seeking their food, and an uninhabited house.

They were now both persuaded that they had been cast upon a desert island, similar to those visited by Captain Cook, and that they were condemned to remain, and live upon their own resources and ingenuity.

Such a prospect greatly alarmed Mademoiselle Nihilette,

but M. le Marquis, anxious to sustain the honor of his name, showed more courage, and attempted to reassure her.

"You must not despair, my sister," he said gravely, addressing the young school-girl, "for I think that, with patience and industry, we may find wherewithal to subsist upon. These cows ought to produce milk in abundance, and probably the fowls of this island lay eggs somewhat in the same manner as those of more civilized countries; whilst in the forsaken hut I observed a sack of that white flour with which our guardian's housekeeper pretends you can make bread. So come, and let us see what we can do with these miserable materials; and, as our valets and maids are left at the chateau, we must not hesitate about helping ourselves."

Mademoiselle Nihilette agreed with him that it was the only thing to be done; but when they came into the actual execution of their plan, they met with a few difficulties. In the first place, they found that they could not get the milk without first milking the cows; and, besides that, neither knew in the least how to set about it; the great-horned beasts completely frightened them. However, M. le Marquis found his courage increase with the occasion for it, and, resolutely drawing his sword, he advanced towards the nearest cow, threatening her with immediate death unless she then and there delivered up her milk; but, at this alarming announcement, the cow turned such a gentle ruminating glance upon him, that M. de Nihil was perforce obliged to put up his sword.

He was not more fortunate with the fowls, who fled, making a loud clucking on his approach.

Meanwhile, Mademoiselle Nihilette, who had gone to the house, wandered from door to window and back again, in a most disconsolate state. She had certainly found the bag of flour discovered by her brother, but she had not the least idea how it was to be converted into bread; she saw a large side of bacon hanging in the chimney, and spent some time in conjecturing what it could be. The fire, too, had gone out, and she knew no other way of relighting it than by calling her maid Catherine.

And thus hours ran by, until hunger began to call aloud. M. le Marquis began to wear a very wry face, which did not add to his dignity, whilst Mademoiselle Nihilette began again to cry and blow her nose, which was, as before stated, her ordinary resource under difficulties. At last, as evening began to fall, they both left the house, as the wolf leaves the wood, and recommenced their search for something to eat.

They saw plenty of hazel and chestnut trees bearing their fruit, but the chestnuts were hidden in their prickly coverings, and the nuts in their green husks, so that they did not recognize the fruit they had been accustomed to see only on the dessert table; all they could find were a few miserable windfalls of wild cherries, and even these the poultry disputed with them.

They had just completed this truly anchorite's repast, when an exclamation from behind made them turn round, and to their astonishment, they beheld a party of men and women who had just landed from a boat close by, and proved to be the farmers of the island, who had been spending the day in the fields bordering the river, making hay.

M. le Marquis de Nihil related his adventures, and not all the respect they really felt could restrain the hearty laughter which burst forth several times during the narration; however, they soon atoned for their lack of reverence by conducting the brother and sister to the house, where the good wife served them an excellent meal, composed solely of the productions of the island; thus proving, that unless we possess the knowledge necessary to avail ourselves of the means within our reach, we might as well be without them.

This little tale, told at much greater length by their great-aunt, and interspersed with numerous absurdities committed by M. de Nihil and Mademoiselle Nihilette, roused the children to observe, and desire to understand all that passed around; and they were fully determined that, should they ever find themselves in the predicament of M. le Marquis and his sister, they would at least know better how to help themselves; and they did not let us rest until they had seen and had explained to them all the different varieties of farm labor.

This single excursion had taught them more than all the little practical treatises with which, until now, we had wearied them. I felt extremely obliged to Madame Roubert, who, on her part, promised that it should not be the last.

She was desirous of taking them to the wind and water mills of the valley, the smithies in the suburbs, to the paper manufactory belonging to a relation of ours; everywhere, in fact, where any of those transformations and adaptations of matter were in action, which are at once the task, encouragement, and glory of man. She instinctively felt, without attempting to explain the feeling, that there alone was the true school for children; there, in the midst of the grand and holy battle of human industry with the brute force of nature. Destined by God to become a soldier in this great work, man must, even in childhood, be inured to accustom himself to action, march in time with the rest of mankind, and take his share in the never-completed conquest of Adam's heritage.

The impression produced by the tale of the Marquis de Nihil, had proved the beneficial effects produced by such anecdotes told during the daily walks, or evenings, and what useful auxiliaries they might become to the evening readings. Their more familiar forms rendered them peculiarly adapted as vehicles for the indirect hints and reproofs we might wish to convey; they admitted more easily of interruption from comments, or questions, and led more easily to the desired deductions. Then we were better able to consult the dispositions of our auditory, and the tone of the story, grave or gay, was made to agree with our listener's condition of mind. In fact, the dish was prepared according to the appetite of the eater, as Madame Roubert used to say.

Whilst Madame Roubert was thus developing the children's intelligence with her practical lessons, I endeavored to awaken in their minds a sense of the source from whence flowed all that we enjoyed; and when their eyes had rested for a time upon the productions of human ingenuity, I tried to fix them on the far higher works of a Divine Hand.

In our walks I continually found opportunities for directing their attention to the beauties of the creation; the verdant meadows bespangled with flowers, the golden harvests, the flocks and herds, all eternal sources of life flowing constantly, yet never exhausted; I made them feel for themselves the pulsations which vibrate throughout all nature, so plainly indicating the presence of an unseen power, and implanted in their hearts that unspeakable gratitude which rises at the sight of all the goodness and mercy of the great Creator.

But both at present, only half comprehended me. Still prisoners in the bonds of infancy, where intelligence is glimmering into dawn, and where the soul is yet only partially separated from mere matter, they resembled a rough statue block, the chiselled head of which begins to reflect a soul, whilst all the rest is as yet a mere shapeless mass; and it was only slowly, and with much care and patience, that the thick veil would fall, piece by piece, and leave, in the end, the blocks converted into complete beings.

We were in the depth of a cold, gloomy winter, which had for several weeks confined Clara and Léon to the house; at last, one morning on perceiving that the snow had ceased to fall, and that there were a few glimpses of blue sky to be seen between the heavy leaden clouds, I determined to sally forth with the children.

We hastened through the wet and sloppy streets to the whole country beyond, where the snow-buried houses rose here and there in the valley, and would scarcely have been distinguished as such, but for light curls of smoke rising from them. The paths were hard and slippery with the frost, a sharp piercing mountain wind cut our faces, and the bright patches I had seen in the sky were again quickly overcast, and the heavens resumed their former dull leaden aspect.

The children suffering from the cold, and slipping at every step, followed me sadly enough; wherever they turned their eyes nothing was to be seen but barrenness and solitude. The trees extended their branches over our heads like withered arms, sharp points of rock were the only things that pierced the white shroud in which the earth was enveloped, and not a sound was to be heard in the dead and frozen landscape!

In this manner, having scarcely spoken, we arrived at a deserted quarry; the rain with long dripping had in some places worn away the stones, and now stood frozen in the cavities, forming a rough and uneven mirror, on which lay the carcass of a horse, half-devoured by the dogs and birds. His emaciated sides allowed the light to pass through, the cavities of his eyes were filled with snow, and his bare teeth seemed still to grind convulsively.

Clara started back with a shudder, Léon did not advance,

but stood with his eyes fixed on the remains of the noble animal with a mixture of pity and horror.

"Oh, come away," said Clara, seizing her brother's hand, and endeavoring to drag him away.

But Léon resisted; it was evident that the hideousness of the spectacle, though it disturbed, at the same time attracted him, and his curiosity struggled with disgust.

After questioning me as to the probable cause of the horse's death, and the reason of the carcass having been conveyed to the quarry, he threw a last look at the half-devoured animal, and slowly turned away, walking off with his head bent down as if in meditation.

Some sad thoughts evidently occupied his mind, and after a long silence I asked him what they were.

"I was thinking about death," he replied, raising his eyes; "if God loves us as you say he does, why did he make death, or winter? See how sad every thing looks about us—those black leafless trees—that poor horse which is food for the crows; I cannot help wondering what good these sad things can do."

"That is to say, you are tempted to judge the designs of the Supreme," I gently replied; "alas, it is an infirmity which belongs to all men, great and little; but do you not perceive that you allow the first cause to escape you? We are surrounded by mysteries which we cannot penetrate, and it is not for us to judge our God, but humbly to accept the lot assigned us. Do you know why things live, any more than die? Are you even sure that they do die? The world, which to you appears merely as a vast cemetery containing the dust of successive generations heaped one upon another, is in reality only a divine laboratory, where incessant changes and renewals are taking place. The fallen leaves of that tree, the flesh torn from that carcass, are not annihilated; they merely form part of a new life; the former are transformed into the sap which nourishes the plants, the latter into the blood which circulates through the birds of prey. Nothing that is the work of God can perish; but every thing undergoes changes of form, and is carried on by the vast stream of life, of which we are mere imperceptible atoms. You have seen in the warm summer days the water rising in vapor from the lake, which shrinks more and more within its banks; to the fish that inhabit its half-dried bed, the water no longer exists, it has perished; but to you, who can see further, it is merely changed from its form of water to vapor, and these clouds, borne away by the wind, spread themselves in refreshing showers over the thirsty earth, and then, sinking into the hidden reservoirs and streams which communicate with the lake, the water, which for the time the sun had borrowed, returns again to its parent lake.

"This is but an example, and the history of the lake is that of the creation. There every thing obeys the laws of transformation, established by the sovereign Master, and all that heaven and earth contain become agents of his will. We stand before this immense machine as you, the other day, stood in the spinning manufactory, before the engine which gave motion to all around. We are incapable of understanding its construction, but our eyes see the result, which gives such overwhelming proof of the supreme intelligence which presides over all. Hereafter, when every fresh observation made by yourself serves to confirm my words, you will better understand the importance of the subject. Your horror of death will diminish, for you will learn to understand that it is only an appearance, a separation of that which belongs to the visible world from that which belongs to God.

"Then, also, the sight of the great works of the Creator will no longer sadden you with their details, but will soothe and console you. You will allow yourself to be borne on unresistingly by the stream of life; you will lose your personality in the midst of its immensity; and better convinced of the transitory nature of your existence, you will accept, with more tranquillity, its trials.—But, I see, I had forgotten to whom I was addressing myself. However, try to remember what you understand of our conversation, and upon the rest you will be enlightened hereafter. Ideas resemble seeds, many of which fall on barren rocks, incapable of affording nourishment; but with time soil collects around them, and then, though dormant for years, the germs burst their bonds, and springing up, produce an abundant harvest."

CHAPTER XIV.

TWO PAGES FROM THE JOURNAL—VISIT TO NURSE NANETTE—WHAT BECOMES OF THE PURSE WHEN IMAGINATION HOLDS THE STRINGS—THE PRODIGALITY OF POOR PEOPLE.

Years pass on, and I find nothing on the pages of the Family Journal but short notes relative to daily events of no moment, and leaving no trace: money losses, coldness of friends, complaints of the children, anxiety for the future, and passing misunderstandings with Marcelle. Our general life continues without any serious changes, the same sorrows succeeded by the same joys, and "vice versa." 'Tis in vain we seek to be on our guard; the clouds arise from the same point in the horizon, and each grows old and strengthens in his infirmity. Clara blooms like a rose, Léon grows like a young palm-tree; but the latter still continues to defy wind, storm, and rain, whilst the former bends to every passing breeze. I find among my notes twenty anecdotes which distinctly indicate their different characters; suffice it to select two, chosen at hazard, from the pages of my Journal.

May 6th.—"Quick, quick, Félicité, come and help me to dress! Mamma says I may choose my own dress to-day; for we are going to see my nurse, who lives in the country. Dear Nanette! how pleased she will be! How I shall hug and kiss her! Oh, what a beautiful day!

See, Félicité, the sun is coming out again, and the darling birds are singing me a song."

I am sitting with my elbows on my desk, in my own room, whilst Clara is thus chattering away to her mother's maid. We are merely separated by a little court, and her voice sounds clear and distinct through the open window. I hear her laugh, sing, and reiterate to Félicité, "Quicker, quicker!" and then stop her to discuss again the question of what she shall wear.

I can make allowances for this very turbulent joy; for nearly a year this visit has been promised and constantly put off, to the great vexation of everybody. But this time Nanette is expecting us, and "la petite," her little one, as she calls Clara.

Though Nanette was not her wet-nurse, she has been a second mother to her: in her arms she learned to speak, and night and day she watched over her unceasingly, answering her tears with caresses, and soothing her childish sufferings with merriment and songs. Even after her marriage with a poor country laborer, the devoted affection of this excellent woman for Clara did not lessen; she is still the same "Servante de tendresse," as they used anciently to be called. She cannot speak of "la petite" without tears, and, like the rest of her good-hearted class, is more thankful for what she has been able to bestow than what she has received.

I never think of her without being struck with our ingratitude and exaction towards the people we employ. We are irritated and annoyed at their slightest faults, whilst we expect them to bear unmurmuringly with ours; we condemn their vices without pity, and are highly indignant if they even seem to dream of our having any; and we receive their daily services without remarking the kindly feeling with which they are performed, forgetting that this at least is a *gratuitous gift.*

Whilst I was thus meditating upon Nanette, and the thanks we too often refuse to our fellow-creatures, Clara and Félicité were continuing their discussions on dress.

The former, to whom, as before mentioned, the choice of her toilette had been left, began by asking for a simple colored muslin. She should be, she said, more at her ease, and need neither fear the dust, damp, grass, nor bad weather, with that on. But her intentions altered at the sight of the drawers opened by Félicité. Catching sight of a lace mantle she had worn only once, she thought this was an excellent opportunity to sport it, the weather was so warm, and the mantle so pretty. When she had tried it on, she could not make up her mind to lay it by again, and declared that, *upon reflection,* she would keep it.

Félicité observed that, if she did so, she must give up the muslin dress; and then I heard fresh drawers opened, and renewed discussions about their contents. Clara went into raptures at each dress displayed, and found some excellent reason for preferring it to the preceding. She decided at last upon a silk pelisse, a present from Madame Roubert; and when Félicité very properly objected that it was a winter dress, she remarked that the month of May did not belong to any particular season—that though the mornings were warm enough to admit of a lace mantle, the evenings were sufficiently fresh to make a pelisse acceptable. Her bonnet, boots, and ribbons were each separately discussed; and the result was, that whatever Clara fancied was sure to be suitable to the season; and I beheld her at last issue from her room a mass of silk, ribbons, and festoons, as varied in color as a rainbow.

Marcelle, on joining us, could not repress a movement of surprise, but Clara excused herself, saying she was anxious to look nice in honor of Nanette. Like all those who act on the impulse of the moment, she had an excuse for every weakness, and it was always found that, *upon reflection*, her caprices were the dictates of the profoundest reason.

Neither Marcelle nor I took any notice of this innocent self-deception, but mounting the "char à bancs," set off in the mild spring sunshine, so consoling to ourselves and nature after the dreary winter weather, yet exciting no alarm lest it should become too oppressive.

Léon found it impossible to sit still; he performed all sorts of gymnastical feats upon his seat, the shafts, and the very backs of the horses, and neither the terror nor entreaties of his mother could prevail upon him to cease. As for Clara, her splendid toilette seemed almost too much for her; and her self-satisfaction only occasionally escaped in a sudden burst of causeless laughter. But the sight of the waving meadows brilliant with flowers, the action of the fresh and invigorating breeze, the wide horizon and lovely prospect, at length set her tongue loose, and broke her well-ordered silence. She began by talking of Nanette, whom she knew to be poor, with the cares of a large family; and informed us she was taking her all her savings in a little purse she had knitted for her herself. From want of economy the sum was very trifling, but she had made a resolute determination to be more careful in future.

Whilst she was informing her mother of all her intended plans of saving, a poor woman approached the "char à bancs," which I had stopped for a minute or so, to give the horses a little breathing time. She was bent with age, and begged in that absent, piteous manner habitual to those accustomed to refusals. Clara interrupted herself with a lively expression of pity, and, hastily opening her purse, presented her with a small piece of silver.

A little farther on we met an infirm old man, then some ragged orphans, and each time she wanted to add her mite to our alms, saying, as she looked at her mother, that she was sure Nanette was too good to mind her gift being a small one.

Soon after, on reaching the village where the horses were to rest, we found the green covered with bright-looking little booths, the annual fair of the town being in process of celebration. Spiced gingerbread, colored prints, and gay toys abounded.

Of course, Clara and Léon were to be conducted through narrow alleys lined with tempting booths on either side. The latter made a dead-stop at an archery stand, where I allowed him to test his awkwardness in handling the bow; whilst his sister was attracted by a lottery, whose prizes of colored glasses and gilded china charmed the eyes of the rustic multitude.

The proprietor, mounted on a stool, shook his bag full of tickets over the heads of the gaping crowd, announcing that by purchasing only one of them, the owner might gain the richest prize in his shop.

"Oh, mamma, how delightful! if I could only take Nanette one of those beautiful vases!" she said, turning towards her mother.

The latter reminded her of the little probability of such a chance.

"Well, I can but try," she replied, more and more fascinated: "it costs so little!"

And, without waiting an answer, she bought a ticket.

Fortune seemed to favor the trial; one of her numbers turned up, and, though not a vase, she got a child's glass drinking-mug with a gold edge. She received it with great satisfaction, and, darting a look of triumph at her mother, she immediately purchased several more tickets.

But the fickle goddess had already deserted her, and all her numbers turned up blanks. Still, as she saw that several prizes were gained by others, her covetousness was excited, and she did not hesitate first to double and then to triple her stake. In vain her mother tried in a low voice to caution her: drawn on by the mirage of desired gain, she went on till her fingers felt only one more piece of money in her purse. She half drew it out, but from very shame let it drop in again, and, hiding her empty purse, she rejoined her mother.

An hour afterwards we arrived at Nanette's cottage, and found her dressed for the occasion in shoes (sabots, or wooden clogs, being generally worn by the French peasantry), white cap, and short petticoat, like La Fontaine's Baucis, when she received the gods. I shall not attempt to describe the exclamations of joy, and embraces that followed. Nanette seemed unable to relinquish her "petite;" she eyed her with wondering admiration, scanned her from head to foot, was delighted with her for having grown, and drank in every word she uttered; she brought forth the best of every thing in the house, and wept tears of gratitude to see her deign to eat and drink, in fact make an excellent meal on the good things before her. This artless idolatry touched whilst it annoyed me. I had not the courage to protest against the good woman's exaggerated sentiments, and deprive her of the pleasure of freely expressing her devoted tenderness.

Besides, Clara's grateful manner of accepting this homage reassured me she evidently felt the true affection which dictated all this sincere praise, far more than the flattery it contained.

Nanette, having been informed of our intended visit, had exerted herself to her utmost to provide for our refreshment. She had remembered our various tastes, and each found his favorite dish included in the luncheon she had prepared for us. For a whole year she had been expecting the announcement of the present visit, and all her powers had been exerted to render her reception worthy of the guests she entertained. The best fruits her garden afforded had been carefully stored up, and the purest honey and finest flour had been reserved for the same happy occasion. At each fresh delicacy offered, she recalled with a triumphant laugh the many precautions taken during the long time she had looked forward to this event. When she brought us the latest winter pears, decaying from the cold they had endured, and the apples wrinkled from the same cause, she told us how she had deplored the impossibility of preserving from the frost the fine chestnuts she had picked out for us. Her husband had, however, been fortunate enough to succeed in *forcing* a few strawberry-plants in pots, and she now brought them in, adorned with their pale rose-colored fruit.

All this abundance was interspersed with involuntary revelations, which enhanced its value a hundred-fold. To our questions about the means possessed by the poor little household, she replied with the ingenuous recital of their struggles. Now it was some piece of work for which her husband could not obtain payment, or their little crop of barley ruined whilst yet in flower; now the loss of a brood of chickens, or the passing of the cottage from the hands of one proprietor to another, and a consequent increase of rent. Nanette was perfectly unconscious of the contrast between the importance given to these trifling losses, which betrayed the narrowness of their means, and the profusion of good things prepared for our reception, but we were moved by it almost to tears. Their penury brought out into stronger relief their heart's prodigality.

We fancied that Clara felt it also, for she redoubled her

caresses and attentions to Nanette, following her everywhere, often interrupting her for a kiss, questioning her about their smallest details; and the nurse, unable to comprehend that the girl was merely discharging a debt, was in an ecstasy of delight at the affection of her "little one."

When the hour of our departure arrived, Nanette took her aside to the large press which filled one side of the cottage, and opening a drawer which contained all the important family-deeds, such as the receipts for the year's rent, schoolmaster's bills, etc., she took out a little packet, carefully wrapped in paper, and bestowing a hearty kiss on each of Clara's cheeks—

"Take this, dear," she said in a low tone; "it is all that I could buy with what was left of the money I had earned by my spinning. I had hoped it would be more, but we were obliged to pay for the doctoring of the last little one." As she spoke she removed the paper, and displayed a handsome gold and white china cup, with a pretty motto in gilt letters round the bottom. Clara at first was full of surprise and thanks for so pretty a gift, but presently the color rushed to her face, and turning to her mother she burst into tears. The contrast between her conduct and that of Nanette, now struck her with all its force, and sent a sharp pang of remorse to her heart.

Her nurse hurriedly asked her what was the matter.

"Nothing that need disturb you, nurse," said Marcelle, who saw how it was; "you have only taught her what perseverance can accomplish, when to attain a desired end we try to overcome our own fancies and whims. It has been by depriving yourself, for a long time, of every little enjoyment, that you have been able to receive her with the generous hospitality you have shown to-day; whilst every thing around speaks of wants silenced and desires overcome. She will now *know* that to be able to give to others, we must first learn to deny ourselves."

"Good gracious! why that is easy enough," replied Nanette; "one has only to think of where you intend to give, and the joyful hope of doing so laughs so pleasantly in the heart, that you can listen to nothing else; I'll be bound that the 'little one' has known the feeling often."

Clara threw herself into her arms.

"Oh, no, no!" she cried, with an explosion of tears; "I have been ungrateful and forgetful; forgive me, oh, forgive me!"

The bewildered nurse returned the child's caresses, and endeavored to console her, though unable to understand the cause of her grief; at last the latter was able to explain. She told her the history of the green silk purse, but lightly filled at first, and then emptied on the road, for want of power to resist temptation. She bitterly reproached herself for being unable to keep a resolution, and with many a hug entreated Nanette's pardon, promising better for the future.

Clara's sorrow was so evidently genuine and sincere that it was impossible to resist it; even though we knew by experience how more than probable a relapse was, we could not avoid being touched by the depth of her repentance.

No matter how often the prodigal son might stray, the fatted calf was killed at each return.

Nanette, in particular, was eager to pardon the fault she scarcely saw, and when Clara, with many sobs and sighs, slid under the blue apron her little purse, containing the single coin which remained of her savings, she received it with the same pleasure and gratitude as if the treasure had been what it was at first.

I trusted that the lesson would not be entirely lost upon Clara, who parted from Nanette unaware that, before leaving, Marcelle had amply compensated her for all her trouble

CHAPTER XV.

LÉON'S ACCIDENT—THE ADVANTAGES TO BE DERIVED FROM THE ILLNESS OF THOSE WE LOVE—THE HUBERT FAMILY RETURN—RENÉE THE BLUE, AND MADAME ROUBERT.

FEBRUARY 14th.—On returning home this morning I heard Léon's voice raised high in angry dispute with Marcelle. I hastened up stairs and found him standing in the middle of the salon, his clothes torn, his face bloody, and his hair covered with dust and mud. His mother, who stood opposite, was regarding him with a mixture of grief and indignation; on my appearance she hastened to meet me.

"Come here!" she exclaimed; "come and see how well your son understands and practises the duty of obedience."

And she proceeded to inform me how, instead of going to his tutor's as he had been desired, he had joined a party of his companions by the river-side, and embarked in a boat that they had succeeded in detaching from its fastenings; and that the boatman had been obliged to use main force to dislodge them: the results of the struggle I saw before me.

Whilst Marcelle was relating these circumstances, the culprit, whom my arrival seemed to have disconcerted, hung his head, and kept turning his cap round and round; but his embarrassment and silence seemed to arise more from anger than from shame.

His offence was a grave one, and the more so that it was not the first time it had occurred; he had already been thrice punished for the same fault, and as I had, only a few days before, expressly commanded him never to let it recur again, his disobedience was the more audacious.

Marcelle was again attacking him with merited, but useless reproaches, when I interrupted her by ordering Léon to his own room, for I was fully sensible of the danger of immediate reprimands, given and received in the first heat of anger; as they almost always exceed their proper limit, compromising authority and lessening respect. I also disapproved of, and feared, the spontaneity of these rebukes, which obliged one to improvise the punishment before reflection had enabled us, either to make its severity agree with the fault, or calculate its result. I was aware that, in education especially, the master must be always right, or the pupil will believe him always wrong; and therefore as often as it was possible I adjourned the decision, until both culprit and judge should be cool.

When left alone, I began to pace up and down the room, endeavoring, for a time, to think of something else, but in spite of my efforts to become calm, I felt my grief and indignation increase, as the thought of these repeated revolts against my authority arose in my mind.

First, I heard Severity's voice warning me to be on my guard against the evils arising from impatience of family discipline and paternal rule; that education ought to resemble the Christmas trees so common in Germany, where above the gifts intended to please the children, rises the *rod of example*, destined to punish defaulters!

Then gentler voices murmured the plea, that we should pardon the ignorance and violence of the child; that his revolts are often caused merely by a greater rush of sap through the young frame, or a giddiness of the mind, as yet unable to command itself; and that we should no more judge the man in the scholar, than measure the oak in the acorn!

Tossed about and disturbed by these contrary pleadings, I continued to pace the salon in a state of great perplexity and agitation, when my hesitations were suddenly brought to a termination by alarming cries, among which I recognized those of Marcelle and Madame Roubert. I rushed to the stairs, where I met the terrified servant.

"What's the matter?" I quickly asked.

"It's—it's M. Léon!" she stammered.

"M. Léon! what of him?"

"Monsieur ought to be told—he had gone up stairs—and Madame followed to lock him in—he screamed and begged her not to lock the door; and, as Madame turned the key, he got out of the window and tried to let himself down upon the roof of the little stable."

"And then!" I interrupted with a palpitating heart.

"And then, I am afraid, he fell."

I did not stop to hear more, but hurried down to the court, where I found Marcelle and her aunt hanging over the nearly unconscious boy. I raised him in my arms and carried him to the couch in the drawing-room, whilst the servant was dispatched for the doctor. Fortunately she met him close by, and returned with him immediately.

After a careful examination, he said that there was no fracture, but that the violence of the fall had occasioned such a determination of blood to the head as might prove fatal. However, after bleeding him copiously, the child opened his eyes and seemed to recognize us, which the medical man assured us was a favorable symptom. He assisted us in getting him to bed, and after writing a prescription, he left us, promising to look in again in the evening.

When he returned, Léon had quite recovered his consciousness, but complained of extreme pain. By midnight brain fever had declared itself; he no longer recognized those around, and his delirium soon became alarmingly violent, and amounted almost to phrensy.

The energetic means employed by the physician succeeded in allaying the fever for a time, but it reappeared again, and for hours and days he lay tossing in the dreadful struggle between life and death! Each fresh effort of art to assist the former seemed to produce for a moment a lull in the disease, but again and again it recovered its strength, and raged as fiercely as before.

In this manner, we alternated between hope and despair for the space of eight days. Oh! the hours of cruel suspense passed beside that bed, where this sad problem was being solved before our eyes! How slowly the heavy hours crept on! How the slightest noise from without made us start and tremble with alarm, lest it should disturb the patient! With what anguish did we watch the countenance and eye of the physician! How small and unimportant all other matters appeared, when compared with our present anxiety! And how the world and its interests seemed to recede before the danger of our child! Fortune, pleasure, fame, what would we not have given to see him restored to us?

I have often since thought of the agonies endured during that anxious period, and as often I have asked myself why we have not better profited by their remembrance. When our tempers have been tried, and have yielded before the smaller contrarieties of life, why have we not recalled to mind those far greater trials? Why have we not invoked those terrible hours of suspense, when, leaning over the dying, our heart has trembled with each faint respiration, or ached with anxiety at the continued wakefulness, terrors of delirium, and agony that we could not relieve! How frivolous and slight, when compared with such scars, appear the pricks and scratches of daily life! Having been tried, and proven soldiers in the great struggle of mortality, is it possible we can be disturbed by the sting of a passing gnat? Oh! all ye whom wounded pride, or pecuniary losses may prevent from sleeping, recall to mind the nights of anguish passed by the death-bed of one ye loved, then look on your present annoyances and say, are they worthy to ruffle minds which can and have endured trials so infinitely greater?

One evening, that we were both seated at the foot of Léon's bed, Marcelle was seized with these thoughts:

"How ungrateful I have been to God!" she murmured;

"when all around me were enjoying the blessing of health, instead of being thankful, I complained, and found fault with my happiness. Now, I would willingly welcome the worst hours of the past!"

"Remember that wish hereafter," gently said my father, who was standing behind us.

But at the mention of futurity Marcelle shook her head, and her eyes, sunken with continued watching, turned towards Léon, whose form could be dimly traced in the darkened bed.

"Ah!" she exclaimed, clasping her hands, and bursting into a flood of tears, "it is my fault!—my fault! If I had not locked him in, he would never have attempted to fly! Why did I thwart him? Better have borne all than that this should happen! Authority blinded and rendered me tyrannical; I expected him to feel as I felt, to desire what I desired. I was endeavoring to improve, where I should have thought only of preserving him! Oh, my God! restore him to me, and I renounce all right to guide him; let him only live, and I leave all else to Thee!"

She sank upon her knees by her son's sick-bed, burying her head between her hands. My father took her by the arm, and forced her to rise.

"God listens to no such prayers," he said with grave firmness; "for sorrow and grief do not exempt us from duty; and God gave you a son not merely to love, but to make a man. It is of less consequence to him to live, than that he should be worthy of life. Our almighty Master has never authorized us to renounce the exercise of the power he has confided to us. Jesus Christ, our Lord, bore the Saviour's crown without a murmur; then bear with courage the mother's, even though it tear thy brow. Stand up, my daughter; dry those eyes and strengthen thy heart; our claim to victory depends upon our manner of struggling for it."

His voice, though gentle, was imperative, and impelled obedience. Marcelle commanded her grief, and approached Léon's pillow. He lay with his eyes wide open, the purple flush of fever had faded from his face, and a feeble smile played upon his thin lips.

His mother uttered a cry, and bent over him.

"Do not weep, dear mother!" he said, putting his arms round her neck; "I feel I shall get well, and will never attempt again to disobey you."

The crisis expected by the physician had occurred; the child, restored to his senses, had heard all, and for the first time in his life he freely acknowledged his fault, and declared his determination to improve.

That day was the commencement of efforts often interrupted and sometimes fruitless, but still real. Marcelle became more patient, and Léon more affectionate: this fiery trial had drawn them closer together.

My thoughts have often recurred to this result of domestic afflictions: they not only give occasion for the exercise of devotion, but more fully develop the affections. The heart receives a sudden shock, which shakes off the petty bitterness accumulated in our daily differences, for we can no longer reproach the being for whose life we tremble, and illness rehabilitates him.

Still, the change of which I speak was a very gradual one, and not the work of that or many other days. Sudden and complete conversions are more than human powers can accomplish. Pauls cannot be made saints without the aid of the glory, and the mysterious voice seen and heard on the road to Damascus! The action of man on man is slow and uncertain: he often excites good resolutions without the power of maintaining them. We may for the instant succeed in bending nature to our will, but she soon asserts herself, and returns to her former attitude. We must await the intermittings of the disease we had imagined cured, and content ourselves with less frequent relapses, leaving it to time to weaken the power of the venom of Adam! One of the most dangerous errors is to fancy that the faults of a child can be corrected by prescription, as you would cure a fever. We put too much faith in those tales, where a single lesson suffices to change the character of a man. Education still lingers in the regions of romance: we are ever expecting the wave of some potent fairy's wand, and thence arise never-ending disappointments, and even despair.

Marcelle and I were still exposed to both. Spite of the real efforts made by both children to improve, many clouds yet obscured our sky; but when our dissatisfaction and vexation were greatest, I always endeavored to recall to mind the hours passed by Léon's bedside; and the comparison of past and present soothed us by reducing our trouble to its just proportions, and we united in thanking God that he had thought fit to inflict on us only ordinary family trials, and had spared us those which are *irreparable.*

June 21st.—Our friends, the Huberts, are here. Justin has been appointed to a neighboring town, with an advance of salary, and they wished, on their way to their new residence, to spend a few days with us.

This long separation seems to have produced no change in Justin and myself, or rather we have advanced at an equal rate, so that now we have again met, we find ourselves at the same point. It is the great privilege of friendships, that are based, not on similarity of interests, but on community of sentiments and principles, to have nothing to fear from separation nor time. It matters not how distant from each other two fields may be, if their soil be the same, and the same seed be sown in each, they will produce simultaneously the same harvest. Thus on all questions there is the same good understanding of former times. What Justin desires I wish for; what he demands I also ask. We resemble two magnetized needles, which everywhere point to the same pole.

Each time that this becomes evident to us, it is a fresh joy: the further we see into each other's minds the more grateful we become.

Our children are delighted with Justin and Laura, for they find in them the judicious indulgence which we lack. Clara, who is becoming the young girl, will spend whole hours seated under the trees with Madame Hubert, confiding to her her girlish sorrows and dreams for the future. Marcelle is surprised, and almost inclined to be pained, at this confidence in another, which she has vainly endeavored to obtain; and I have tried to make her comprehend that the mother's necessary authority is opposed to it. Authority is irksome and out of place in a "confidente;" an equal, or at least a disinterested party, is preferred: to confess to a master is to lose one's own identity.

"Let the childish friendship continue, then, content to be her strength and comfort. What does it matter that she pours out to another her passing emotion, when at the first wound or sorrow she hastens to your protecting arms? She may confide in others, but she trusts only in you."

Renée has accompanied her parents: her first appearance gives a painful impression. She is small, thin, and very sallow, almost ugly. Laura and Justin presented her to me without a word, and during the first two days I took scarcely any notice of her; but the other morning I heard her conversing in German with her father, and I know that she is acquainted with the English and Spanish languages. Marcelle obliged her to seat herself at the piano, and we soon perceived that she has already far out-stripped her mother. She has also learned all that can be taught to one of her age—of geography, natural and political history. Clara is in a state of bewilderment at such an amount of learning, and I am still more surprised at so much modesty.

The latter, however, does not soften Aunt Roubert, who, when she was informed of the number of Renée's acquirements, only shook her head. Aunt Roubert's prejudices on that point are not to be overcome. She is suspicious, almost to hostility, of all those who are, what she styles, learned women. According to her, literary studies are perfectly irreconcilable with household duties. No one can understand orthography and back-stitch too, or speak any other language but our mother tongue, and superintend a roast.

"Oh, yes! I have seen your little miracles before," she said to Marcelle yesterday, "who talk about revolutions in China with their stockings in holes; who read poetry, and yet cannot understand the receipt of a pudding; who will describe with accuracy the costume of the African savages, and do not know how to trim a baby's cap! Don't talk to me of such women, my dear girl; the very best they are good for is to be lodge-keepers to the Académie Française."

Notwithstanding these strong prejudices, she treats Renée like everybody else; that is to say, with her usual rude familiar kindness, for Madame Roubert compares herself to a thorny gooseberry bush; to get at the fruit, people must not mind a few scratches.

For the rest, these peculiarities do not seem to disturb the young girl in the least: she laughs at the old lady's whims, and is the first to offer to carry her bag, or fetch her a footstool. At bottom, I believe the good aunt is very fond of her. "After all," she said the other day, "there really is good in the child, and it is not her fault if she has been taught more grammar than cookery."

Consequently she has been very anxious to make her feel the inconveniences of her education. Yesterday she invited us to dine with the Huberts at her house, and begged Renée to come early, and assist her in her preparations. Spite of the ironical manner in which the latter invitation was given, it was accepted.

Madame Roubert was determined to display before the eyes of the little blue-stocking all the splendor of her housekeeping royalty; and Renée found her enveloped in a large apron with an ample bib, her sleeves turned up above her elbows, busy concocting a "tôt fait."

Now, in the opinion of the greatest connoisseurs, the "tôt fait" was the pinnacle of glory in Madame Roubert's culinary art—it was her Austerlitz.

She beckoned to Renée to approach, and after explaining to her the particular merits and difficulties of her favorite dish, proceeded with her cookery.

"You see, my dear," she said, mixing in her motherly way moral precepts and practical explanations, "one of the chief duties of a woman is to make the most of every thing—keep the whites of the eggs for another occasion. Life is made for something more than learning to conjugate the verbs of *I walk*, or *I talk;* to assure to those around us health and comfort—don't put in too much lemon-juice—when one makes it a principle to be useful—the crust is beginning to rise—it is sufficient to keep peace and a good conscience—we put the whole into a mould—and we live happily—in the Dutch oven."

Renée smilingly looked on, not a little bewildered by this odd mixture of philosophy and cookery; and this time, alas! the first most certainly injured the second; for, a thing unheard of before, just when Aunt Roubert, being of opinion that it was done enough, with serene confidence opened the oven-door, intending to display before her pupil's eyes her sparkling pyramid, she found nothing but a crumbled ruin blackened by the fire! Her Austerlitz had become her Waterloo!

The disappointment was the greater because completely unexpected. Besides, dinner-time was drawing near, and, notwithstanding its deceptive name, the "tôt fait" (quickly made), would have taken more time to make again than she could spare.

Madame Roubert had to go out and make several purchases, to look after the servant, a minister in her novitiate whose experience she more than doubted, in uncovering the drawing-room furniture and laying the cloth. She was speaking with resigned repugnance of resorting to the direful extremity of applying to the neighboring pastry-cook, when Renée quietly proposed to replace the missing dish with a concoction of her own.

Madame Roubert actually started with surprise.

"What, my dear child! do you know what you are saying?" she asked: is it possible that you can make any thing fit to eat? you, who can speak all the languages of the Tower of Babel!"

"It is a family pudding, which always succeeds, and does not take long to make," replied the young girl.

"Pudding!" repeated Madame Roubert a little contemptuously. "Ah! I understand, it is some foreign dish, like what they make in England. Very well, *Miss* Hubert! let us see what you will produce: the servant shall supply you with any ingredients you may require."

But Renée assured her she had all she wanted, and set about it without more delay. Half an hour after, when Madame Roubert returned from making her purchases, she found the pudding ready for the table.

Its appearance was such as to strike the eye of a connoisseur. After examining it well, and inhaling the odor, she gave a little nod of satisfaction.

"There is nothing to be said against its look. I should only like now to see how it tastes, for you know 'that the proof of the pudding lies in the eating.' However, I see, my dear child, you are not without capabilities: now come and help me with the dessert."

But a fresh trouble arose. The servant had broken one of the china baskets, indispensable to the service, and there remained only the broken pieces in the sideboard. Madame Roubert, accustomed to the old-fashioned arrangement, could do nothing without her basket; but Renée, who with her mother was obliged to resort to all sorts of expedients in their humble ménage, where the richness of taste hid the poverty of their means, declared she could arrange it all. She ran to the garden, whence she gathered leaves, flowers, and fruits, with which she dressed the table, and hid the discrepancy occasioned by the missing basket. The fine damask, Aunt Roubert's especial pride, the old-fashioned crystal, the many-colored china, and antique plate, were all most elegantly and tastefully arranged; and then Renée added all the little graceful fancies which add so much to the elegance of a well-arranged table, down from the butter in shells to bouquets of radishes. Aunt Roubert was bewildered; but she was still more so when all the dishes being served at once covered the table, and, as she said, "transformed her homely dinner into a Belshazzar's feast."

"Ah, the sly little puss!" she exclaimed, as, thoroughly conquered, she warmly embraced her; "who would have thought there was all this hidden in you!"

The pudding was unanimously pronounced excellent; and Aunt Roubert did not hesitate to relate the history of her "tôt fait" with the noble candor which proves

"L'accord d'un beau talent et d'un beau caractère."

From that moment her opinion of Renée underwent a striking change. She owned to me in a half-whisper at dessert, that she had been too severe, and that our friends had not neglected the "essentials" as much as she had at first imagined. Still she was strongly opposed to "the gift of tongues," which, she maintained, could be available only to the apostles. At last we rose from the table, and adjourned to the little salon, where, whilst waiting the advent of tea, each lady brought out her sewing or embroidery, and Madame Roubert sought the mittens she was knitting. Unfortunately, they had not escaped the general disturbance; a needle had fallen out, which was one of the little domestic miseries our worthy aunt felt most acutely. She uttered a slight exclamation of despair, and went off in search of her spectacles; but on her return she found her knitting in the hands of Renée.

"Ah! you little puss, what are you about there?" she cried in alarm.

Renée returned her the mittens with a smile, and, on looking at them, she found the stitches taken up, and the pattern continued?

She regarded Renée with a stupefied look, then turning to me, she exclaimed in the tone of the highest admiration:

"She can knit! Ah, my friends, I retract my judgment; there is nothing wanting—her education is complete!"

Yes, complete, for the more we know of Renée the more are we struck with the amount of intellectual culture, joined to so much practical good sense. Thanks to Justin's and Laura's judicious guidance, she has travelled on towards the temple of knowledge, as the humble peasants make their pilgrimages to the holy chapels, on foot and in the unsullied simplicity of her heart. Thus, in my eyes, she is the beau ideal of the woman, which our generation ought to prepare for that which is to come. She has a cultivated understanding, yet is not too proud to learn; she has penetrated beyond the clouds, yet not neglected her feet; though clever, she is humble, and is capable both of giving and receiving advice. Ah! the dream of my life has been to possess such a daughter; but, since that glorious happiness is denied me, I thank God for having bestowed it on a friend.

CHAPTER XVI.

THE THREE RUSTIC SEATS AND THE BED OF MIGNIONETTE—MY FATHER'S HEALTH DECLINES—HIS LAST MOMENTS—THE VOID IN OUR CIRCLE—MY FATHER'S WILL.

For some time past my father has found the distance from his lodging to us too much for him; his strength declines, and there is less activity about him; formerly it was he who came to us, now it is our turn to visit him in his suburban lodging.

Almost every evening our family circle is formed there. Yesterday, Madame Roubert accompanied us; she wished M. Remi to taste her preserves, she said, but on our return she took me aside.

"Do you know," she said, "I find your father greatly altered since I saw him last?"

"He assures me, however, that he does not feel ill," I answered.

She shrugged her shoulders.

"As if such old heroes as he understood any thing about illness! they suffer without taking the trouble to complain; and as long as they do not die, they declare they are well! But you will do well to take my advice, and see your father as often as possible."

This recommendation alarmed me; I could not sleep that night, and the early morning found me at the nursery ground.

My father was already up, not in slippers and dressing-gown, but in his usual dress—a coat buttoned up to the throat, strong walking-boots, a black cravat tied rather loosely, and a broad-brimmed felt hat. He still preserved the military habit of making but one toilette in the day, in order that he might be ready for service at any moment.

We went down together into the grounds, but I noticed that his step was slower, and he breathed with difficulty. He stopped when we arrived at a small plantation of young oaks, and we seated ourselves on a bench which I had not before noticed, and I made the remark to my father.

"It is an attention of M. Germain," he replied, "and is the third seat he has had made for my accommodation. In days gone by, I used to make the round of the nursery, and did not stop till I reached the four lime-trees down below there; then, as years increased, I limited my walks to the large pond; and now I cannot accomplish further than to the oak grove. These are all so many warnings; the old soldier is weary, and as he nears the end of his march, he shortens the stages."

I endeavored to turn my father's thoughts from this sad theme, but he purposely continued the same subject.

"Why should I be surprised at sharing the common lot," he said; "think you then that sixty years have not sufficed to teach me how to die? On the brink of the grave I look behind me, and see my career completed. My blood has been spent in the service of the great national family to which I belong; I have been united to the chosen of my heart; I have eaten the bread of honor in peace, and I leave my name stainless to a son who will in his turn transmit it unsullied to his descendants. What is there to detain me, and what more has earth to offer me? No, my soul turns with an inexpressible longing to the unknown world, where my Master awaits me."

As he saw how deeply I was moved, he ceased, and we returned slowly to his lodgings; as we passed in at the door, he pointed to his beds of mignionette, which were beginning to flower.

"You see," he said with a smile, "I have not renounced all harvests, only formerly I planted for centuries, and now I sow for the season."

* * * * * *

My father's health is rapidly declining, and 't is vain for me to attempt to deceive myself. Marcelle has also become aware of the approaching change, but seems unable to speak of it. When we return from my father's, the walk is made in silence, we avoid meeting each other's eyes, we fear to let the other see what occupies our thoughts, and that very fear betrays us.

That which most sensibly warns us that the end approaches, is not only the increasing languor and more marked want of interest in the concerns of daily life, but more especially the lingering sweetness of his tones, the ineffable tenderness of his glance; it seems almost as if the soul prepared for flight were already purified from its earthly tenement, and spoke to us in the language of heaven.

Even Clara and Léon are struck with the change—I was nearly saying transfiguration—and restrain their boisterous youthful spirits; they spend much of their time with the old man, listening with sad respectful gravity, whilst he seems to profit by their attention to engrave more deeply in their hearts the Tables of the Law.

"They will remember the last words of one whom they will never hear speak again," he said to me the other day; "his advice will ever remain connected with the unavoidable sadness of the eternal farewell, and the mind the most rebellious in life will yet make some concession to the dead."

After such a warning, I listen to all that he says to Léon and Clara, with an inexpressibly painful tightening at my heart; each instructive lesson seems a mournful announcement, it appears as if he were dictating his own epitaph.

He alone seems undisturbed in his peaceful serenity; he continues to console us while dying, even as he has devoted himself to our happiness while living.

* * * * * *

For some days past his feet have refused to support him, his hands tremble, and his voice is much weaker; but his mind seems illuminated with a celestial light. He speaks often, and at length, upon the great interests of life, of conscience and happiness, and when he ceases his eyes close, and by the movement of his lips, we see that he is enjoying communion with his God

* * * * * *

This morning, as usual, found us all at my father's. He was seized with a sudden desire to be carried down to the arbor, which is covered with jasmine entwined with the

Bengal rose and rampant vine. We wheeled him in his chair to the desired spot; the rays of the rising sun came flickering through the leaves, and fell in a sparkling shower upon his emaciated features. I stationed myself behind him with Marcelle, who held my hand, and at his feet, leaning on the arms of his chair, knelt the children, their eyes raised to the dying man!

He seemed to perceive the terror expressed in their frightened troubled gaze, for a smile lighted up his pale face, as letting a hand fall on Clara's shoulder, he asked her why she looked at him thus.

The child hesitated, the tears starting to her eyes; and the answer she endeavored to stammer forth was lost in a sob.

My father drew her to him.

"Peace! peace! dear girl," he whispered tenderly; "you must neither of you allow yourselves to be terrified or astonished at what will soon take place; it is but the accomplishment of laws established by the great All-seeing and Almighty One on high. I have not wished to hasten this moment; neither would I delay it. Life, such as it is, and you will know it some day, becomes at last difficult to bear; and for this reason, popular imagination has inflicted it as the greatest punishment for the greatest crime. The Jew who insulted the sufferings of our Saviour, was by it condemned to earthly immortality. Therefore, neither grieve nor be alarmed. Death is the recompense for a life well spent; then, and then only, released from our obligations to our fellow-men, we regain our independence in the bosom of our Lord. We live for others, but our own reward is death!"

He continued in this manner to converse, and bestow his last instructions upon the two young creatures, until his voice becoming visibly weaker, he bent forward, blessed them, and kissed their brows, and then fell heavily back in his chair.

I hurriedly motioned the children away, took their place, and kneeling there with my father's head resting on my shoulder, I awaited the last scene, unable to restrain the tears which rolled down my face.

The struggle was a short one, accompanied by convulsive shudders. Several times he opened his eyes and smiled upon us; at last, just as the neighboring clock struck nine, he raised his head, and murmuring in a low tone "My God," fell forward in my arms, his eyes closing, never again to open in this world.

Marcelle and the children came and knelt by my side, mingling their tears with mine, as I continued still to hold the dear and revered form from which the spirit had forever departed.

Though deeply sorrowing, ours was not the grief akin to despair. The holy calm in which he had died seemed to have communicated itself to our minds; our greatest earthly friend had been called from us, in the midst of the brightest and most sublime sights and sounds of earth. Whilst still engaged in exhorting those who survived him to religion and duty, he had fallen asleep beneath the rays of the rising sun, surrounded by the perfume of flowers, and song of birds!

* * * * *

There is a sensible change perceptible in our home.

Several antique pieces of furniture are added to our more modern stock; several family portraits, some maps, and plans of war, are interspersed among our engravings; and a captain's sword is suspended over my desk.

My eye is pleased, when it falls upon these friends of my childhood, among which I grew up, while my father was yet with us. They bring him more strongly to my remembrance; and his shadow seems to float through our saddened household.

It was many days before I could believe that he had really departed, never again to return. His image had been so impressed upon my heart and habits, that at every opening door, every step that sounded on the stair, I expected to see him enter. It took some time for my mind to grasp the reality of eternal absence; and as it gradually forced itself upon me, my grief, at first restrained, became more poignant as I saw more plainly the void left in our domestic circle. At every doubt, either of reason or conscience, which rose in my mind, my thoughts instinctively turned to him, who had ever been my light and guide, and in place of whom I now found void and darkness.

At first the sublime serenity of this death of the just, had sustained me; admiration had mingled with my regret, and softened it; the vibration of that august voice, which had died away whilst speaking of peace, hope, and virtue, had penetrated my inmost soul, and filled me with a, I know not what, tender resignation; but though for an instant sustained by the wings of the departing soul, I had since insensibly fallen into extreme sorrow.

Marcelle seemed to feel our loss as much as I did. He for whom we mourned, had ever been her stronghold, as he had been my comfort; she had been accustomed to seek support in him when any thing disturbed her at home; he had been the sovereign arbiter in our dissensions, the mute conciliator, the visible divinity of our hearth; and now we had none to depend upon on earth but ourselves; our tender guardian was gone.

We felt the bitterness of these thoughts particularly one evening, as all seated round an autumn fire, Marcelle and I occupied ourselves in putting in order the papers left by my father.

Each of these revealed some interesting point of his grand, though simple, character. There were notes written during the bivouacs and halts of a fifteen years' battle; short notices to himself to keep himself ever "worthy to die;" letters written to my mother during the weary trial of absence, in which the tenderness of the husband struggles manfully with the firm courage of the soldier; receipts and paid bills; betraying many a benevolent action performed, till then unknown to us! Then came his degrees of service; official statements of the principal events in his simple and regular existence, in which there was no act of which he had need to be ashamed; and lastly, his will, written by himself a few months before his death.

I read it again aloud, surrounded by Marcelle, Clara, and Léon, in their mourning garb, none of whom could restrain their tears; and more than once I had to stop during its perusal. I transcribe it here, that my children may find it among the *family records*, and read it in turn to their children!

MY FATHER'S LAST WILL AND TESTAMENT.

I, ANSELME REMI, an old soldier, feeling the hour of eternal repose approaching, with sound mind and submissive heart, write the following, as the expression of my last wishes; not daring, when so near the grave, any longer to speak of my *will*.

Firstly—I thank God that I was born a Christian, that is to say, a *man complete; and I trust to die without losing my title to that name.

Secondly—I render thanks to Heaven for facilitating the performance of my duty, by according me a good name, family love, and daily bread.

God has done yet more for me, he has permitted me to taste all the joys of this life, in granting me a free country, a wife who truly loved me, and a right-minded affectionate son.

To this son and her who can never be separated from him in my love, I leave all that I possess at the time of my death. Both, I know, will care little about the poverty of their inheritance; it will suffice to remind them of him who bequeathed it them.

But I entreat that they will at once remember me with joy, not sorrow. Let them think of me as of a pleasure enjoyed, a fine day ended, a book that one finishes with emotion, but not despair. They ought not to regret my end more than I do; I have lived contentedly, I die happy; resting on God in death as in life.

To Clara I leave the amber necklace and bracelets worn on our marriage day by her who had consented to share my destiny; may they communicate to her grandchild her strength of resolution, and persevering yet resigned spirit in time of trouble.

I leave to Léon my gold watch, which has never gone wrong in twenty years. When he sees the hands constantly obeying the impulse of the wheels, and faithfully recording the hours, he will remember that submission to established law is the first condition of duty.

To my son and Marcelle I bequeath several old companions in arms, whom my pension has assisted to live; they will find inclosed a list of their names and addresses.

* "C'est-à-dire complétement homme." The translator has ventured to retain the literal translation of the above phrase, as conveying better than any other the author's idea.

And more than all, I intrust each to the other's care.

To Marcelle I recommend to restrain Remi's impetuosity, to chase away his gloomy thoughts and feelings, to be the sunbeam of his home, and the singing-bird who charms away sorrow.

I would advise Remi to check Marcelle's over-sensitiveness, gently to bear with her weakness, to shelter and protect her with his strength, and return her strong and abiding love with tenderness and patience.

With respect to my burial, I merely wish a stone in the neighboring cemetery, and the tree which M. Germain will plant at the head of my last resting-place. It will grow nourished by my earthly remains; its branches will one day shelter the children as they sport upon the turf, the birds will build their nests among the leaves; and thus, according to the laws of the Almighty, life will spring out of death.

My hand is tired, my eyes are weary; the setting sun throws only a red glare, almost without light, into my chamber. I cease, and close this testament, with a last embrace of those I love, a last prayer for those who suffer. Oh, God, deal gently with them! Multiply bread to the poor, and heal the broken-hearted!

Written this 12th day of May, at the close of day, in the plentitude of my confidence in Him who gave me life, and will receive me after death!

CHAPTER XVII.

THE CHILDREN GROW UP—LÉON AT PARIS—DEBTS—DEPARTURE FOR PARIS—A YOUNG MAN'S BEDROOM—THE DUEL.

MANY months have elapsed since the last page; the mourning garb has disappeared, but joy is long in returning to our hearts. The spring-time of life is past, and behold autumn, with its toilsome harvests, its falling leaves, and threatening clouds.

What days of rain! with what difficulty the pale sunbeams penetrate the fog! Clara is eighteen: we begin to look with anxiety into the future, and Marcelle asks me, like sister Annie, "If I see the husband coming?" not that she would hasten the moment, for she dreads it at least as much as she wishes it; for the marriage of her child will be the signal doubtless of separation.

Already our family circle is contracted. Léon is gone to Paris, where a cousin of Madame Roubert has promised him an excellent opening to an honorable career. His mother grieves at his absence, and I am anxious about him. What will become of him, so far away from us, surrounded by temptations to which his very character renders him peculiarly susceptible?

His letters are already shorter, less frequent, and it seems to me embarrassed.

Tuesday.—A fresh demand for money from Léon. At first he was timid, and offered the best excuses he could; but now he contents himself with observing that "living is very expensive in Paris." It does not seem to matter to him what we can afford, but names the sum and the day he will require it. A few months ago we were still his parents, now it is evident we are merely his bankers.

I have returned, as my sole answer, an account of what he has already received during the year, compared with really necessary expenses.

* * * * *

Sunday.—Since my refusal to supply him with more money, I had not heard again from Léon; but I suspected him of having written to his mother and sister. I had observed papers hidden on my approach; red eyes, whisperings, and heavy sighs. Through an indiscretion of M. Duplessis, I have discovered all. He came this morning to inform us that the sum forwarded to Léon, through his Paris correspondent, had been taken up. Marcelle endeavored by signs to stop him, but it was too late, I had heard all. After his departure, an explanation necessarily ensued; and the mother and sister acknowledged their weakness. Pressed by Léon's despairing supplications, they had united their savings, and forwarded to him the amount he required, which was a thousand francs!

When I insisted upon knowing how he could be in such urgent want of so large a sum, after much hesitation, they owned the fact—he had played.

I said nothing, but wrote that same evening to Madame Roubert's cousin, determined to know all.

I was totally unprepared for the answer which came like a thunderbolt amongst us. It ran as follows:

"MONSIEUR,

On receipt of your favor of the 8th inst., I hastened to obtain the information you desired, not so much personally, as through my partner, M. Lefort, whose age and habits are more in unison with such matters.

Now it appears from what we can both gather, that the said Léon, your son, of whom we have no reason to complain in business, has, in the indulgence of various tastes, all of an expensive nature, allowed himself to become involved to the amount of 19,643fr. 55c., or approximative thereto, in bills payable at different periods. Inclosed is a detailed account of said sum; and

We remain, Monsieur,

Your Very Obedient Servants,

DUROC, LEFORT, AND CO."

On my reading this letter aloud, Marcelle uttered a shriek, and turning very pale, would have fallen had not Clara caught her in her arms. The sight of her emotion enabled me to restrain my own.

Though the reality far exceeded what I had even feared, I allowed no expression of surprise to escape me; and taking Marcelle's cold hands in mine, I endeavored to encourage her; but she continued to repeat the amount of the debt in a state of stupid bewilderment, asking how Léon could possibly have contracted obligations so far exceeding what he knew our means could satisfy.

I was anxious to avoid all discussion; and, as usual, I postponed taking my final resolution until the next day, in order that we might have time to reflect calmly.

We passed a miserable night, sleep was impossible, and I heard Marcelle continuing to weep till morning. I rose at daybreak, and took a long walk in the fields outside the town. The morning air, exercise, and the joyous tone of nature, all contributed to soothe my perturbed spirits, and I returned home more calm. Marcelle was on the watch for me; when I told her that I should start for Paris in a couple of hours, she exclaimed—

"You are going to find Léon?"

"And pay his debts," I replied.

"Can you possibly do that?"

"Yes, by sacrificing a part of our savings, reducing our expenses, and denying ourselves our accustomed gratifications."

"And you will do all this?"

"I am resolved."

She threw herself into my arms.

"Ah, who could be unhappy with you!" she exclaimed, with an explosion of tears; "for you cause glory to arise out of shame, and sorrow to bring forth joy."

This approval of my determination touched and strengthened me. I spent the morning in arranging my affairs, and, when the diligence left the town, it bore me with it.

The journey resembled a troubled dream. I traversed towns and country, seeing nothing, absorbed in the thought of what I was going to do. The ruinous sacrifices I had determined on to clear Léon were least in my thoughts; my anxiety was, that they might save him not only from present but future ruin. I was going not merely to pay his debts with the fruit of my labor, but to rescue a soul from corruption. Money was all that was required by the world, but untarnished honor alone could satisfy me.

I did not find Léon at home; but, on making myself known, I was permitted to await his return in the little apartment he occupied on the fourth story.

On entering I was struck with its air of disorderly neglect. Not a chair in its place ; the bed unmade ; dirty boots scattered over the floor; a half-smoked pipe thrown down upon an easy-chair; the furniture dusty and soiled; the pendule not going; all evidences that this was not a temporary home, but a mere lodging—a place to sleep and dress in; not where the hours of leisure were spent; no, these were trifled away elsewhere.

This was but too evident by the various tickets for places of amusement thrown upon the mantel-piece, along with cab-numbers, and a black silk mask, such as are worn at masked balls. Faded bouquets of flowers, gloves thrown aside at the first soil, an opera-glass, and riding-whip completed the revelations of this life of false elegance and frivolous dissipation. I approached the little desk strewn with unpaid bills and notes from boon companions, and sought in vain for a book, a letter from his family, or any work begun.

Just as I had concluded this sad inspection, I saw enter a man of about thirty years of age, dressed in the height of bad taste, with an enormous moustache, and a noisy walk. On seeing me he contented himself with touching his hat.

"Monsieur no doubt awaits Remi?" he said.

I replied in the affirmative.

"You have come then about—his affair?" he added, in a lower tone.

"Affair!—what affair?" I asked in astonishment.

The unknown looked hard at me.

"What—oh! you do not know?" he replied, at the same time drawing himself up: "he did not tell you then?"

"I have not yet seen him."

"Ah!—I understand; like me, you only received a note; and the devil, if I should have made it out, but fortunately on my way here I met him in the shooting-gallery, and he explained matters to me, begging me to come on here and meet his other second; and here you are. I will convey you to the spot."

"He is going to fight a duel?" I exclaimed, inexpressibly shocked.

"Most certainly," he tranquilly replied; "in fact, he wished us to promise to make no attempt at any amicable arrangement. You see, this is a first affair, and he must win his colors. A sword wound given or received, gives one a certain weight in the eyes of the world; is a good foundation to begin life upon—provided you survive."

"But where will the duel take place? who is it with? and what can possibly have provoked him to such a step?"

"I will tell you as we go along; my coupé is below, and it is time we started; the rendezvous in the Bois de Boulogne, at noon."

He led the way to the door, and I followed as in a dream—silently, lest some chance word should betray the fortunate mistake which afforded me an opportunity of saving my son.

My conductor assisted me into the remise which awaited him, and, seating himself by my side, drew from his coat-pocket a cigar-case of Russian leather, and offered me a cigar, which I unconsciously accepted; whilst lighting his own, he coolly hummed an opera air; and I, in a state of feverish terror, awaited, till my patience was exhausted, the account he had promised.

"But the duel?" I stammered forth, after a few moments of agonizing expectation.

"Oh! ah! yes, the duel," he tranquilly replied: "well listen. It appears that Remi discovered through one of his creditors, that his employer's partner had, unknown to him and without warning, taken upon himself to inform his family of his irregularities. He naturally enough demanded an explanation of this uncalled-for interference in his affairs; but Lefort carried the matter with a high hand; recriminations rose to high words, and at last Remi, who is hot and easily provoked, ended the discussion with a blow in the face."

A cry of agony escaped me.

"Yes; you see it is not an affair likely to end in a 'déjeuner à la fourchette,'" continued my companion, puffing away at his cigar. "This said partner is a hot-blooded Alsacien, formerly a non-commissioned officer of dragoons, who has chosen the sabre, with which he says he means to trim the insolent young scapegrace. To speak plainly, I rather fear that Remi, in spite of his recent fencing lesson, will feel tolerably uncomfortable when the time comes; I think, too, it would be as well to know the address of his family in case of accident."

I shuddered.

"And you allow a duel to take place between two such unequal opponents!" I exclaimed.

The man with the moustache eyed me from the corner of his eye.

"*I allow;* that's good!" he said with a sneer. "Pray do you happen to know how you can prevent it? Think you a gentleman can receive a box on the ears with the same equanimity as a splash in the street, and that it suffices for him to wipe his cheek with a cambric handkerchief? After what has happened, either Remi or the other must be carried from the field feet foremost."

I closed my eyes without replying. My head whirled, a cold perspiration stood on my brow, and it seemed as if the carriage were sinking beneath me. But I overcame this weakness, and exerted myself to the utmost to regain a calm exterior, and command of my reason. Meanwhile the coupé rolled on, and my companion continued to talk.

As far as I could gather from his broken conversation, he was a Valaque, belonging to the tribe of cosmopolitans, who dissipate their inheritance in the idle luxury of metropolises. Every thing he said more and more clearly showed the abyss into which Léon had fallen. An unfortunate choice of acquaintances, the powerful curiosity of his age, and the boldness of a character which difficulties only encouraged, had all united in drawing him into the dangerous position in which he now stood. Some remaining scruples of conscience had made him continue assiduous in his duties to the house of Duroc and Lefort; reserving his evenings and leisure days for balls, the theatres, and lansquenet. It was a sort of compromise with his conscience: the performance of one single point of duty had sufficed, seemingly in his mind, to cover the infraction of every other.

I had but a confused idea of all these details at the time. My whole mind was taken up with the danger which more immediately threatened Léon, and with endeavoring to find some means of salvation for him. I trembled lest we should arrive too late, and two or three times entreated the Valaque to hasten the driver; but he calmly observed that it was not yet noon, and besides that they could not begin until we arrived.

Never did a foot-pace seem so slow. The trees in the Champs Elysées appeared, as we passed them one by one, to nod with a kind of ironical nonchalance; all the faces we met seemed sad and gloomy, and the usual cries made me start and tremble as at the announcement of some misfortune.

Notwithstanding his absence of mind, my companion noticed my agony, and he thought at first that the participation in a duel alarmed me.

"I see, Monsieur, that you are not accustomed to these affairs," he said, with a half-mocking laugh; "this is perhaps the first time that you have been engaged in one?"

"Yes," I replied, absently.

"In that case, Remi did wrong in requesting you to act in this affair; for it is important that the seconds should have had some experience in such matters, so it is fortunate I shall be there. I have already assisted at a score of affairs of honor, not counting those in which I have been a principal, and they have all gone off admirably. Never in any one of them was a reconciliation attempted. The last was about a mere bagatelle—some dispute about some jockey on the race-course at Chantilly; the pistols were loaded with double shot; our adversary sent us a ball through our right hand, and if it had not been for his seconds we should have continued with the left hand. No, no; if I am to have any thing to do with such matters, they must not be without results. But here we are, and I think I see our men."

I thrust my head out, and saw at about thirty paces off several persons standing at a cross-road; they were M. Lefort and his two seconds, carrying the sabres hidden under their cloaks; Léon stood a little apart, looking in the direction of Paris, with visible impatience; doubtless he recognized the Valaque's coupé, for, his countenance brightening up, he hastened to meet it.

I threw myself back in the carriage, and he came to the opposite door, from which my companion was leaning.

"Quick, quick, Georges!" he said; "these gentlemen have already arrived, and Lefort is playing the bully."

"Ah! very good," said the Valaque, raising his eye-glass to his left eye, and scanning the group awaiting us; "we shall see more about that presently. Tell the driver to move on to the cross-road."

Léon gave the order, and we proceeded slowly to our destination.

I now saw my son's adversary more distinctly; he was a large bony man of about forty years of age, with a countenance expressive of violent passions, and nothing more. He stood waiting our approach, whistling, with his hands in his pockets.

"I beg of you not to hurry yourselves," he cried in a loud harsh voice; "leave us to blow our fingers whilst you finish your virginia in your hired carriage."

"What! my dear Monsieur, are you really so very much pressed for time?" asked M. Georges, without alighting.

"Very much so," replied the ex-dragoon, in a brutal tone, "seeing that I have other business, besides sauntering up the Boulevard de Gand, with my spy-glass in my eye, and my varnished boots glittering in the sun; I must be at Bourse in an hour."

"Ah! indeed, the devil you must!" said Georges, ironically; "but suppose something should happen to prevent your being there; are you quite sure you will be there this afternoon?"

"Get out and you shall soon see," said M. Lefort, evidently out of all patience.

M. Georges coolly opened the door and alighted.

The seconds removed the swords from under their cloaks;

Léon took off his coat and threw it over the arm of a tree.

"Measure the swords and let us finish the business," said his adversary, preparing to do the same.

"Not till you have heard me!" I cried, darting from the vehicle.

At the sound of my voice, Léon turned, and starting back, exclaimed, "My father!" A dead silence followed the first exclamation of surprise.

"What does this mean?" asked M. Lefort at last; "this gentlemen is not a second, then?"

"D——! I thought he was!" replied M. Georges.

In a few words I explained how the mistake had arisen, and how I had profited by it. The ex-dragoon listened in gloomy silence, digging the earth with the point of his sword.

"I understand, I understand!" he cried abruptly, when I had finished; "you came here with the hope of preventing the duel, did you not? Well, you have lost your time; I tell you, were an archangel present, he should not hinder me. I have been insulted, and will have satisfaction."

"And you *shall* have it," Monsieur, I quickly interrupted; I am aware of what has passed, and far from opposing any just reparation, I am here for the purpose of obtaining it for you."

"Well, then, don't let us lose any more time in talking," he said, stepping back, and putting himself on his guard.

"Pardon me," I replied; "but since chance has elected me as a second, I have a right to perform his functions;

and you do not cross your swords before you have heard me out."

"Well, then, thunder! make haste, Monsieur," said Lefort, stamping his foot.

"I am ignorant," I returned, "of the details of this quarrel between you and my son; but this I do know—that I am the first cause of it, having required the information obtained by you, and conveyed to me by M. Duroc."

"Monsieur, your son pretends that I should first have consulted him," said M. Lefort, glancing at Léon with a bitter sneer.

"I can well imagine the anger caused by the exposure of such faults," I said, "when goaded by remorse, and angry with ourselves, we endeavor to revenge the result of our own sins on others."

"But not with impunity," interrupted Lefort, clenching his hands; "come, thousand devils! have you finished?"

"Immediately, Monsieur. You require satisfaction, is it not so? Insulted by your adversary, you are determined that he in his turn shall be humbled; in fact, you wish to have him in your power."

"A pleasure which it will not be long before I obtain," he murmured, bending his sword.

"I hope so," I replied, "but without the aid of violence; for I trust that he who has insulted you will acknowledge his fault, throwing himself on your generosity."

"These excuses come too late," interrupted Lefort; "I will have none of your apologies, I don't want them."

"And I refuse to make any," replied Léon in a firm emphatic tone.

"Then tell your father to leave us alone, or let us go further," said the ex-dragoon, making a movement towards the carriage.

I threw myself into his path.

"No!" I exclaimed, "the offence you have received does not give you an illimitable right to vengeance, and you cannot refuse an atonement. The satisfaction my son owes you is not for the act itself, which might have been the result of accident, and you would then have thought nothing of it; it was the intention, and for that he can atone. Between men possessed of any feeling, a wrong acknowledged is a wrong forgiven; and you know this as well as I do."

Lefort shook his head.

"This is all a useless waste of words," he said, turning away; "in God's name or the devil's, give the sword to M. Remi; we did not come here to prate about forgiveness, but to set to work in good earnest."

One of the seconds now advanced and gave a sword to Léon, who seemed every whit as impatient as Lefort.

"Beware, Monsieur!" I exclaimed, again addressing the latter; "your house required the services of my son, I sent him to you, considering you for the time being his protectors: you accepted the charge; and you are therefore answerable for him to me, and to public opinion in general; and you cannot strike him without dishonor."

These last words seemed to produce some impression upon M. Duroc's partner; he saw at a glance how much ridicule and odium would probably be attached to such a duel between the head of an establishment and a youth of nineteen confided to his care; he changed color, and appeared to hesitate; I did not allow him time to recover himself. "Remember," I added in a lower tone, at the same time seizing his hand, "what a mere child he is; can you possibly take advantage of his youth and inexperience? does not your superiority rather oblige you to use forbearance with him? Perchance you know some other youth of the same age, the son of a relation—of a friend; imagine him in such a situation, on the point of fighting with such a man as yourself! How would you wish him to be treated, and what would you say of the implacable rancor which turned a deaf ear to all attempts at a reconciliation?"

"But, the devil!" interrupted the old soldier, a little softened, "don't you see how the foolish boy continues to brave me? didn't he tell you he would not offer any apology?"

"Well, then," I exclaimed, "if his pride be stronger than his sense of justice, if he prefer nursing his wicked wrath to relieving the minds of those dear to him, I will require nothing from him, but will myself perform his duty!"

Then removing my hat, I made a step forward to M. Lefort, and said in a voice of mingled grief and tenderness—

"I, the father of the offender, who, meriting chastisement, refuses to acknowledge his fault, in his place, and as responsible for the son I have not better taught to respect himself and others, ask pardon for his offence, and this request, Monsieur, I make with joined hands, uncovered head, and on my knees !"

The act followed the words, and doubtless sincerity marked my speech and gesture, for M. Lefort threw away the sword he had held till then, and raising me by the elbows, said in a voice tremulous with emotion :

"Come, to please you, I will accept—I will forgive—though I never before heard of apologies being made by proxy. The devil take me, if you have not saved the life of that young fool, for had you not come I should have slain him like a dog !"

I cut the ex-dragoon short, by tendering my thanks, bowed to the seconds, and taking Léon by the arm entered the vehicle which had brought him there, and drove off.

CHAPTER XVIII.

A MARRIAGEABLE DAUGHTER.

Whether from shame, anger, or remorse, he had not courage to own, my son maintained a profound silence the whole of the way back; and it was only when we reached his lodgings, that he attempted any explanation. I interrupted him before he had said more than a few words.

"We will discuss this matter hereafter," I said; "we are neither of us at present capable of speaking calmly upon it: all I now ask is, that you will immediately supply me with an exact account of all your debts, with the names and addresses of your creditors."

He made no remark, but forthwith seated himself before his desk, whilst I passed into the other room, where I awaited the conclusion of his task. He soon joined me with the required list, where not only was the amount of each debt stated, but with the extreme audacity which marked his character, he had added up the total. The sum was the same, or nearly so, as the amount named in M. Duroc's letter. I asked him if he was sure he had forgotten nothing; and he assured me he had not.

"Now then," I said, "you will accompany me to the addresses mentioned in your list."

The cab was still in waiting, and we proceeded at once to the nearest creditors. I paid them all without a remonstrance on my part to any one of them. Léon evidently could not believe his eyes, and I could perceive that as we advanced on this ruinous pilgrimage, his heart swelled more and more with shame and remorse; at last, when having paid the last bill, we re-entered the vehicle, and I closed my now empty pocket-book, he could contain himself no longer, but falling at my feet, entreated my pardon as well as his convulsive sobs would allow him. I laid my hands upon his head as it rested on my knees, and said—

"I thank you for these tears, Léon, they are the only comfort I could hope for at this sad time; they are, I trust, sincere proofs of repentance. I have now done all that lies in my power to save you, the rest with God's assistance depends on yourself. Collect all your things together, and pack up, while I settle with your landlord; we return to the country this evening, and I take you with me."

He hastened to obey me, and a few hours more saw us on our way home.

The journey was a silent one, but a better understanding existed now between us; I was sad and grave, Léon softened and ashamed. For the first time in his life his proud nature had succumbed, and he condemned himself without any reservation; he had voluntarily descended to the lowest seat, and there remained, like Job on his dunghill, exposed to the eyes of all beholders. His haughty and self-willed nature subdued at last by my gentle treatment, he seemed to perceive that his rehabilitation must begin with sincere repentance; and he thirsted at the moment for some greater humiliation than that he at present endured.

But it was a different matter when Marcelle and his sister received him with loving embraces, mingled however with tears. Not a word was uttered on the all-engrossing subject, but there was a reproach in the long silences, the stifled sighs, even in the tender demonstrations of affection, so sad and entreating, that he felt acutely enough. It was evident that a cloud enshadowed the family, and that in our hearts we mourned.

The day after our return, I obtained a situation for Léon in one of the first houses in our city; his misdeeds remaining a secret, even from Aunt Roubert, who, on her side, asked no questions. But she must have guessed a part at least, from the severe reform apparent in our mode of living. I sold my cabriolet, and travelled in all weathers on horseback; Marcelle dismissed one of her servants; we underlet our garden, whilst Clara became her own and her mother's dressmaker, and endeavored to profit by her excellence in embroidery. Our table was proportionably frugal; we dispensed with coffee, and drank no wine; and all this was done by tacit agreement, without the remotest allusion to the cause; but Léon saw and understood; he alone seemed unable to bear the change with resignation; the more affectionate and forgetful of the past we showed ourselves, the more he drooped his head. He seemed oppressed by our sacrifices.

His obstinacy and impetuosity had given place to a submissive but gloomy docility; and one felt how great was the struggle going on in the effort exerted to conquer his evil nature. His voice was too constrainedly calm to be natural, his submission was too eager not to be the result of a violent effort. A firm determined will to improve had evidently obtained absolute authority over his young soul, and held all other passions in subjection.

I watched with anxious curiosity this mental revolution, the result of which as yet appeared uncertain. The very energy displayed in the effort, evinced the strength of resistance, and the strong curb Léon kept upon his actions, proved how much he yet feared himself. His heart was full of enemies, whom he held mute and motionless, under the iron heel of his *will*, too sure that at the slightest relaxation, they were yet ready to break out into open revolt.

Then came the questions: Would he have the strength to carry out the necessary watchfulness? would his resolution last? Were we witnessing the last efforts of resistance to evil, or the first of self-conquest? Was it the farewell of a conscience for an instant reawakened, or the dawn of serious amendment? These were questions *I* dared not answer. There were yet moments when Léon's old nature returned; they were like mutterings of thunder, quickly silenced, but they proved the existence of the storm, which still slumbered behind the deceptive blue of the peaceful sky.

Time, however, rolled on without realizing our fears. The few last months seemed to have done the work of years with Léon; he entered a youth into the fiery furnace he had just traversed, and left it matured. A slight shade of sadness was the sole visible remains of the severe trial he had experienced, as we might imagine a criminal reprieved from the scaffold would, for some time, retain the palor occasioned by his awful danger.

For the rest, his employer expressed himself much pleased with the intelligence and activity he displayed in business, and had very little doubt he would become a successful and prosperous merchant.

He permitted Léon to become intimate with his nephew, whom he had adopted, and intended one day making his partner.

Raymond had formed a sincere friendship for his fellow-clerk, and soon began to visit us, at first every week, and afterwards every day. Older than Léon by several years, he was attracted to him by the charm of contrast; timid himself, he admired his friend's boldness; irresolute, he leaned upon his strong will; each found in the other the qualities he lacked.

Marcelle and I were pleased with this intimacy, which strengthened the good resolutions of our son, and offered another inducement for him to persevere in them. M. Raymond was, therefore, well received by all, and seemed to become daily more gratefully aware of it. He never quitted Léon, and scarcely ever us, so much so, that our house became his; he formed one in our family meetings in the evening, joining in our readings, and accompanying Clara in her music.

This intimacy had established itself so naturally, we felt so secure, and so happy in it that we had not thought of taking umbrage at it; Aunt Roubert alone seemed to receive M. Raymond with a kind of uneasy impatience.

One evening that we were expecting him and Léon, Clara all at once started up on hearing a footstep on the stairs, declaring it was he!

"And who is *he?*" asked Aunt Roubert.

"Why, M. Raymond," she replied.

"How do you know?"

"I am sure it is he, I know his step; and listen; Médor is silent!"

And to prove that she was right, she ran out to meet the two arrivals.

Madame Roubert shook her head, and looked up at us.

"Have you heard?" she asked.

"Certainly," I replied.

"And you have not understood?"

"What?" asked Marcelle.

"What!" repeated Madame Roubert; "why, my dear, something that you ought to know, which is, that in a house where the daughter is marriageable, it is not wise to allow a young man to visit so frequently that his very step is known, and the dog no longer takes the trouble to bark."

CHAPTER XIX.

THE MERCHANT'S NEPHEW—A SON-IN-LAW REFUSED.

MADAME ROUBERT'S observation had the effect of opening our eyes; and we perceived that M. Raymond's attentions might raise hopes that it would be most imprudent to encourage.

His rich uncle, M. Formon, held large capitals in great esteem, and was desirous that his nephew should form a wealthy marriage, calculating that when he should leave him the concern, the marriage portion ought to be sufficient to cover all the expenses incidental to commercial speculations, and thus leave the capital untouched. Now Clara's portion bore a singular resemblance to that of Molière's Marianne, consisting of industrious habits, easy temper, sober and simple tastes; and M. Formon would not fail, like Harpagon, to find "that all that counted as nothing; and that it was nonsense to pretend to form a portion out of all the expenses she would *not incur* during the coming years."

We communicated our scruples to Léon, who agreed with us, and promised to interrupt his friend's visits.

At first he had recourse to a hundred excuses. One day he took a long walk with M. Raymond; another, he required his advice about something he was doing; and more often, mere caprices of the moment served to break the custom of daily interviews.

M. Raymond submitted for a time. He liked Léon, and was willing at first to let him have his own way; but at last, he seemed to lose patience, and far from becoming gradually accustomed to the loss of his evening visits, as my son had hoped, he declared with much more than his ordinary vivacity, that they had become necessary to him, and he wished to resume them.

Léon answered lightly, that it was too bad his company was not sufficient for him; but no, he continued firm.

"Alone, you are not so completely mine as surrounded by your family," he said; "it is your proper place and fittest frame; all there is in such perfect harmony, that the charm of the whole adds to the charm of each detail. The finest tree standing alone is only a tree, but united to its fellows, it forms part of a glorious forest. Why prevent me from taking a place in your family circle, and breathing its sweet atmosphere of affectionate devotion? Have I intercepted one gentle ray from you, that you wish to withdraw from me your sun?"

And as Léon, embarrassed, knew not what to answer, he continued in a voice trembling with agitation—

"Remember, my friend, that I have been an orphan from my birth, and have known nothing of domestic joys; I passed from the nurse's hands to those of masters, and from the college to the desk. I have ever been surrounded and served by hired attendants, and no one has loved me for my own sake. Till I knew you, the world had been to me as a furnished apartment, and 'table d'hôte;' it was in your home that I first saw and understood what family love really is. If you love me, leave me enjoy my discovery, and do not grudge me the corner from whence I view your happiness."

"God knows I should like nothing better," said Léon, who, though feeling the necessity of coming to an understanding, yet hesitated how to begin; "I trust you do not doubt my sincere friendship; your society has always given us pleasure—but—it may astonish others."

"Have I been intrusive?" exclaimed M. Raymond, interrupting him; "have my visits appeared too frequent to your mother—to your sister? Oh! answer me, I conjure you, Léon, answer me truly."

"Frankly, then, my family have ever been truly pleased to see you."

"Who then has any right to be astonished?"

"Those who look on, yet do not see, who judge without understanding, and condemn without mercy — the world, in fact! Though I have long felt the necessity of saying this to you, I have been extremely unwilling to touch upon the subject, and I do it now with much pain."

"But what is there in our intimacy which can be blamed?"

"Why," said Léon, with a smile, "you surely have not forgotten the infernal regions of mythology, where the dog Cerberus allowed every one to enter, but none to return."

"Well, and what of that?"

"Well, my dear fellow, wise people pretend that this is symbolical of every house inhabited by an unmarried damsel: each disengaged man who appears in it, is supposed to have entered the conjugal inferno: if he remains there, he is considered a victim; and if he escapes, he is looked upon as a victorious Hercules, who has succeeded in tricking old Cerberus."

"And you have no other reason?" said M. Raymond, coloring.

"None other," Léon replied, taking his hand; "but, dear friend, is it not a sufficient one? we may defy the prejudices of the world for ourselves alone, but not when the honor of others is concerned. Forgive me—forgive us all; this has not been done without much pain to all parties; tell me you are not offended at this plain speaking."

"I love and thank you," said Raymond warmly returning Léon's grasp; "but your words have troubled me more than you can imagine; I cannot, I do not choose to reply to them now—give me two days—then—we will speak of this again—and—you shall know all."

With these words he embraced my son, and abruptly left him.

The two days passed: Léon, who had related the conversation to me, by my express command, most carefully avoided doing any thing that might remind M. Raymond of his promise; at last on the evening of the third, he came, but without entering the salon; he asked to see my son, and went up-stairs with him to his room.

He was pale, and seemed very much agitated; Léon took no notice of his manner, however, and asked him if he had come to take a walk with him.

"Yes—get ready—let us go out!" he replied, in a hurried absent manner.

But after taking two or three strides up and down the room, he threw himself into a chair, exclaiming:

"It is not necessary—I can tell you here—I would rather tell you all—and that can be done in one word—Léon—I love your sister!"

My son started, and attempted to speak.

"You need not raise objections," Raymond hastened to add; "I know them all—I care for none but one, and that concerns your sister and family: tell me sincerely, Léon, will they look favorably on my suit? are there other arrangements? have I rivals? In short, can you give me any cause to hope, or to fear?"

"None, and it is their place to answer, and theirs only; but you seem to have forgotten another objection no less important."

"My uncle?"

"Yes."

"I have just told him all!"

He stopped; Léon looked up.

"And what did he say?" he asked.

"Just what one might expect," replied Raymond, bitterly, "and what I was prepared for. What does he know of your sister? and how can he understand the charm of her attractions? In his eyes, marriage is nothing but a business arrangement."

"And he does not approve of this?" I interrupted, entering the room, at the door of which I had been standing for some moments, unperceived by the young men.

M. Raymond started up very pale, but I reassured him by offering him my hand. He understood from what I afterwards said, that I did not consider him responsible for M. Formon's contempt, and encouraged by my evident esteem for him, he declared that his uncle's opposition should not alter his determination.

"Let me only be accepted by Mademoiselle Clara and yourself, and I desire nothing more. No one has any right to influence my choice, and I possess more than sufficient to place the woman who consents to be my wife beyond the reach of poverty."

"But not of regret," I replied: "will she ever be able to forget that she is the cause of your ingratitude? that the tie which unites you can only be formed when those which bound you to your family are broken? For her sake you will live at variance with one who has supplied the place of a father to you: you will have preferred the indulgence of your own will to your duty—surely a dangerous commencement, and sad presage for the future. Can you be sure that she, for whom you would thus renounce your former acquaintances, affections, and remembrances, will sufficiently indemnify you for all these sacrifices? Every time you met the benefactor whom you had forsaken, with averted head, and cold expressionless eye, could you pass him by without feeling a painful tightness at your heart? Believe me, M. Raymond, very few men know themselves well enough to bear such a trial, and still fewer have any right to tempt it. In our social constitution all depends upon the family: it is the centre pivot round which all revolves. To abjure that God gave us, in order to begin another, is like setting fire to your hereditary mansion with the idea of rebuilding on its ruins; very rarely does success justify presumption, and extreme necessity can alone excuse it. For my part, I will give no sanction to such a proceeding: my daughter shall never enter a family unwilling to receive her: she needs sympathy, encouragement, and affection, and I have no desire that her marriage should be the signal for a declaration of war, but rather a treaty of alliance."

All that M. Raymond urged did nothing towards shaking my resolution. I assured him of my esteem and friendship, but I renewed the warning given by Léon: however pleasant his society had been to us, we must henceforth renounce it, and content ourselves with reciprocal wishes for each other's happiness.

At last, when he saw that I remained steadfast in my determination, he ceased to urge me, and retired gravely and sadly. After this we saw him very rarely, only when by chance we met him at the houses of others.

This species of rupture caused us real sorrow; we had become accustomed to one another. The hour of reunion and interchange of sentiments had been an enjoyment to all parties, and formed an agreeable close to the day.

When M. Raymond ceased his visits, there was something wanting; nothing seemed to go on well, and our evenings became very silent.

The change was the most remarkable, and produced the most grievous effect upon Clara. She suddenly lost all her light-hearted gayety, became absent and languid, caring for nothing. It was in vain we endeavored to make her take an interest in what was going on: a vague smile, and thanks, rendered in an absent manner, were all we could obtain.

Aunt Roubert, in particular, was vexed and irritated by this torpor.

"I don't like these sleeping sorrows," she often said; "they are like secret smouldering fires: there is no flame visible, only one fine day the whole edifice falls into cinders."

She several times questioned Clara; but whether she felt too embarrassed to make the avowal, or was really ignorant of the state of her own heart, she always replied that there was nothing the matter with her—she was quite happy.

"So then it is happiness which makes her so thin and pale," said Madame Roubert, out of all patience; "then, Heaven forgive me, but I should like to find some affliction which would wake her up!"

At last she thought she had found one. One evening that Clara was sitting alone in the window, with her elbow resting on the window-sill, her needle hanging idle, whilst her eyes were wandering up the street, she saw her all at once start and bend her head, and then with a blush hurriedly take up her work to conceal her confusion.

Madame Roubert bent forwards, and perceived M. Raymond, who had crossed to the opposite side to obtain a better view of our windows. She shook her head, and slid her spare knitting-needle under her cap—always a necessary preliminary to putting down her work for a time.

"Ah, ah!" she said, continuing to gaze across the square; "that's the nephew of the golden uncle: so, he is still here?"

"Is he going away, then?" asked Clara, suddenly looking up.

"By'r Lady, I suppose so. Have you not heard he is going on a voyage to the Colonies?"

"M. Raymond?"

"Yes; his uncle is desirous of sending him to one of his correspondents—who has a daughter—"

She stopped. Clara was gazing at her with fixed and open eyes.

"Who has a daughter?" she repeated.

"And why not? is that any thing astonishing?" asked Madame Roubert, with a laugh.

"A daughter!—unmarried?" added Clara.

"Exactly so, my dear."

"Then—M. Raymond is going—to marry her?"

"So it seems to be settled."

Clara did not answer, but her respiration became hurried, her needle moved very fast, her lips trembled, and thus she struggled for some moments; at last, overcome, she rose and hastily left the room; scarcely had the door closed upon her, than her sobs burst forth. Marcelle would have followed her, but I detained her.

"Leave her to believe her sorrow a secret," I observed, "that she may endeavor to suppress it before us. Sorrow is at first sustained by the avowal, but when consolation has begun her work of healing, the acknowledgment embarrasses the sufferer."

"But, ah! aunt, why did you tell her this news so abruptly?" cried the tender mother, with tears in her eyes.

"Why?" repeated Madame Roubert, "eh, why truly that I might know for certain what I have suspected before. The little hypocrite would never have confessed that her heart was M. Raymond's, whilst now it is as clear as daylight."

"And what have you gained by the discovery?" I rather sharply inquired; "what need is there to probe wounds that you cannot heal?"

"How do you know that?" she interrupted with bluntness: "M. Raymond and your daughter are of the same mind, I suppose?"

"Certainly."

"But it is the *golden uncle* who is the stumbling-block, is it not? Well, who told you that he is inflexible? that though he may oppose it now, he may not consent in time? Must the poor children give up all hope of happiness, because it is not yet ripe or within their reach? Oh,

Lord! these men! who have neither confidence in God, respect for their fellow-men, nor even patience. Go, Marcelle, go, and console the dear girl; and though you must not *promise* any thing, tell her that even in the cloudiest sky, there is always a little bit of blue to be seen."

I did not approve of these glimmerings of hope being held out to Clara by way of consolation. I always believed it best boldly to face a trial, and bear the whole shock at once. I could not understand these feminine precautions of mixing honey with the cup of gall, and letting despair be tasted drop by drop. But Madame Roubert declared that I was a brute, who rather than see my friends die a natural death, resorted at once to decapitation; that my Stoicism might do very well for the iron nerves of the ancient barbarous philosophers, but that women and children required rather more care and management, and ended by entreating me not to meddle with matters I did not understand.

She left us almost immediately, giving us to understand that she had a plan, the result of which we should hear the next day.

And sure enough she came, but disappointed, and almost furious.

She had seen M. Formon, and had gained nothing by the interview.

I could not hide my annoyance at a proceeding which compromised not only my name, but Clara's also. I felt humiliated and angry, but Madame Roubert cut my complaints short.

"Yes, that's right! *you'd* better attack me too!" she exclaimed. "It's so generous to trample on a fallen friend! Don't you see how provoked I am, and that I should like to fight everybody I come near!"

"But how could you possibly hope to succeed?" I interrupted.

"How?" she replied. "Parbleu! by good arguments! through the heart! If the *golden uncle* had not been such a proud, obstinate, old fellow, I should have convinced him; and even now I am not quite sure that I did not touch him, only of course he did not choose to seem to yield."

"Well, but what could you have said to him?"

"Ah! it's a long story. First, I found him up to the eyes in his American correspondence, and, as a natural consequence, in a bad humor, because, he said, they were trying to dupe him: the agents over there keep the gold, and send him only the purse—that was his expression. I agreed with him in every thing he said, to get him into a good humor; but presently, when he talked of sending his nephew to Buenos Ayres to look after his interests, it was quite a different affair, and I began to object. The *golden uncle*, who is sharp enough under his rough thick shell, saw what I was aiming at; and, getting angry, exclaimed: 'I understand, you want my nephew to remain here, that he may marry your niece's daughter.' So that set me quite at my ease, and I replied, 'You are right.' Then he declared that it should never be with his consent; that if it were persisted in, he would cast his nephew off—that he would disinherit him; in fact, all the absurdities of which a man in the wrong is guilty. I let him go on; till at last he got rather ashamed, and, thinking he had perhaps gone a little too far, tried to improve matters by talking of the great esteem in which he held our family. And there I had him. 'Ah! so you believe us to be worthy people,' I exclaimed, 'and yet refuse to be connected with us; and for what reason, pray?' He dared not say because you have not money enough. He muttered something I could not hear, hesitated, and contradicted himself; so then I took a high tone, and preached away as if I were in the pulpit. He very well knew, I told him, that you would never give your consent to a marriage unsanctioned by him; but did he imagine that such an abuse of authority would endear him to his nephew? Was it wise of him to become an obstacle, where he ought rather to assist? or to set so high a price upon his former benefits as to render them burdensome? Did he think his nephew's love a mere passing fancy?—let him wait and see. Did he think his choice unfortunate?—he ought to make, not avoid, an acquaintance with its object.

"All this greatly embarrassed my man, who is not wanting in common sense; he turned red and then white; he fidgeted, and tried to get into a passion; but I kept to my text of, Give us some reason! till at last he ended by rising and saying: 'The devil! I have but one, and that is, I do not choose it.' This was more than I could stand, and I in my turn got angry. 'True! true!' I cried, 'you have hit the right word ; yes, the real reason is, that you do not choose to be just, you do not choose to act kindly, you do not choose to deserve the love of others! Ah! in that case there is nothing more to be said. But now give good heed to what I say : The day will come when age and infirmity will overtake you, and then, as you have always lived for yourself, you must seek assistance from without. Then go to the rich heiress, whom from ambition and avarice you will have forced your nephew to marry; ask her to nurse you, amuse you, give up her time and pleasure to you ; and, as she will owe you nothing, and as God is just, she will answer in her turn, I do not choose to, I do not choose to!' Thereupon I bowed and took my departure, leaving the hardened old man to petrify amid his self-will and his gold."

Aunt Roubert was mistaken, as I have since discovered : her arguments had startled M. Formon, and her predictions disturbed him. He was, as she had remarked, a man possessed of good sense, but spoiled by long exercise of uncontrolled authority. Absolute in his own house, he expected every thing to submit to him, even reason itself; and that those who associated with him should think and will only as he chose; any thing more was in his opinion open revolt. His nephew's crime in his eyes, was that he should have formed the idea of this marriage himself, that he should have been the first to think of it, and that there should be no real impediment to its accomplishment.

Without clearly acknowledging this to himself, he was

aware that it was so, and something stirred within him, which was perhaps a glimmer of remorse; but he hardened himself against it, taking refuge in his habitual obstinacy, which, whilst feigning passion, only used it as a blind behind which to take his stand more firmly.

CHAPTER XX.

A RENCONTRE AT RICHARD'S—EMBARRASSMENT OF AN UNCLE WHO IS NO LONGER OF HIS OWN OPINION—OUR CHILDREN LEAVE OUR ROOF—THE TWO SWALLOWS.

M. RAYMOND'S melancholy continued to make visible progress, and his uncle became concerned about it in spite of himself. His anxiety was first evinced by a moody silence, only interrupted by abrupt reprimands; but when he found his ill-humor borne with a kind of resigned indifference, with no attempt at rebellion, he became yet more anxious.

After all, he loved his sister's son, and wished to see him happy. Had he met with any opposition, no doubt his determination would have been strengthened by the excitement of the struggle, but this melancholy resignation touched him. Gradually, Madame Roubert's arguments recurred to his mind, as if they had been his own; he pleaded the cause at his own tribunal, not with any idea of changing his decision (that M. Formon declared to be impossible), but from curiosity and by way of amusement. The conclusion of the debate remained always the same :—I do not choose it! but the opposite side had been heard; he had no new nor better reason to offer on the defendant's side: he contented himself with being obstinate.

Thus matters stood, when M. Formon one day had

occasion to call upon our old neighbor Richard, who had now become a carrier by contract. There was some bargain to conclude, and as he was passing in his cabriolet, he stopped and went in.

Richard was absent at the stables, and whilst some one went to call him, M. Formon was shown into the little counting-house belonging to Colette, who, married more than two years before, was now her father's partner.

The room was empty, and M. Formon walked to the open window, which looked upon a garden thickly planted with old trees; almost immediately below was a vine-covered arbor from whence issued the sound of voices, but the speakers were hidden by the foliage.

M. Formon, however, recognized Colette by her accent; she was speaking of her husband's grandmother, who, having just lost her daughter, and being left alone, was anxious to become one of their family; but Colette was rather alarmed at the care and expense such a charge would be to her.

"Think, my dear young lady, of all the trouble!" she said; "the poor creature can scarcely see, and can only walk with the assistance of an arm. She will have to be cared for like an infant."

"Well, then, Colette, you will have an opportunity of repaying all that she has done for your husband's father," replied the unknown speaker.

"Oh! certainly, I should like nothing better," said the former, "but you see old Germone has never behaved kindly to us; for instance! when Baptiste wanted to marry me, Heaven knows what bad things she did not say of me! she pretended I was extravagant, vain, and heartless."

"Then you will have an opportunity of proving the contrary, by receiving her in your comfortable home."

"But you know she will cost us a great deal."

"More than you can afford?"

"Well, I don't say that, exactly."

"Then do not hesitate, Colette, remember that the old woman is poor and infirm, whilst you are strong and young. Your cause is too good, and hers too bad, for you to be otherwise than generous, and to bear her a grudge for her former conduct, is like keeping open a poisoned wound. Oh! if any one endeavored to injure me, I would ask nothing better of Heaven, than to have an opportunity of returning good for evil."

"Oh! who could find it in their hearts to give *you* pain?" cried Colette, with emotion; "but—then you advise me to let the grandmother come?"

"And to be as good to her as you are to everybody else," answered her interlocutor. "The poor woman will not trouble you long, and you will remember for the rest of your life with pleasure and satisfaction, that you did your duty."

Here the arrival of Richard prevented M. Formon from hearing more; he had been surprised and interested, and listened with distracted attention to the contractor's apologies for having kept him waiting, and interrupted him, just when he began to talk about business, to inquire who was conversing in the arbor with Colette.

"In the arbor?"

"Yes!"

"Well, I think—it's Mam'selle Clara."

"And who is Mam'selle Clara?"

"Do you not know? she is M. Remi's daughter."

"Ah! very good," said the merchant, abruptly quitting the window. "Let me see, I came to talk about that affair. Have you made your calculations?"

Richard replied in the affirmative, and began to explain with the tedious verbosity usual to people unaccustomed to accounts. M. Formon tried to give his attention, but in spite of all his efforts, his eye was constantly on the window; and his ear took in, besides Richard's explanations, the voices which continued to murmur in the arbor; at last he distinctly heard Colette bid her guest good-by, and then steps sound on the gravel path.

The merchant could no longer restrain himself, but approaching the window, saw Clara passing through the garden.

He had only once, and that some time ago, seen her, when he had taken scarcely any notice of her, and now she appeared before him in all the splendor of her eighteen years, crowned with her gentle sweetness! The charm operated at first; he felt his heart open beneath the genial rays of youth and beauty; but the sentiment was immediately checked. Struggling against the species of attraction to which he had yielded, be tried to work himself into a passion, and seek some cause of suspicion.

This was evidently the snare in which his nephew had

been caught, and upon the strength of which we trusted to keep him prisoner. It was because we knew our power that we showed so much patience. With such loveliness, a chance meeting, the exchange of a few words were sufficient to sustain the flame already kindled. We might wait fearlessly as long as Clara was present to exercise her fascination !

Whilst thus employed in revenging himself, by unjust suppositions for a moment's benevolent feeling, Colette joined her father, who needed her assistance in the business in hand.

"Is the young lady gone ?" he asked.

"Yes ; she came to bid us good-by : she goes to-morrow," said Colette, her eyes humid from recent emotion.

"Where to ?" interrupted M. Formon.

"To Madame Hubert. It is a sad trial to the family ; but the young lady is not well, and they hope that a few months' change may do her good."

This was such a decidedly negative answer to the merchant's suspicions, that he stood for a moment bewildered. Colette profited by his silence to burst forth in Clara's praise, to which Richard added some grateful acknowledgments of obligations conferred by Marcelle and myself. M. Formon was at last obliged to interrupt them, and asked for the agreement written out by Colette. He rapidly ran it over, signed it, and departed.

But his encounter with Clara, what she had said, and the news of her intended departure, recurred again and again to his mind. Without allowing he had been mistaken, he began to judge us less severely; he still reiterated "I do not choose it!"—but it was now with a kind of pettish spite.

Thus perplexed he spent the day. He found twenty pretexts to enter the counting-house in which his nephew was at work, now to praise and now to scold. He seemed longing to bring about an explanation, either by a quarrel, or in a more kindly manner; but, too sad to notice his uncle's behavior, M. Raymond did not take the hint, and M. Formon, too proud to make the first step, left the office furious.

At last, towards evening, he called his nephew into his private office.

Raymond found him walking up and down the room at a great rate, with his thumbs caught in his braces, as was his custom on great occasions, when, on obeying the summons, he entered, pale, silent, and resigned.

M. Formon stopped and glanced at him, and then with an impatient gesture began his walk again.

"You wished to speak to me, uncle?" said the young man.

"Yes," replied the merchant, continuing to pace up and down; "we have let that affair of Buenos Ayres rest too long—something must be done."

"Léon has been occupied in examining all the books and correspondence."

"I know, I know, but whatever may be the result of his labor, it is very clear that the affair can never be arranged by any correspondence. The house of Formon has been long enough represented at that town, by a set of scamps who defraud us. Now it seems to me that this ought to concern you as well as me, since you will eventually carry on my business. Are you aware that it is the best feather in our wing, and we shall be geese if we allow it to be torn from us ?"

"Very true," said Raymond, coldly; "but do you know a preventive ?"

"Yes, Monsieur, I do—one sure, yet simple—I have mentioned it to you before; and it is, that you embark for Buenos Ayres without delay."

Raymond started.

"I !" he exclaimed; "I leave the country—now !"

"And pray why not ?" replied M. Formon, raising his voice; "what time could be better ? The *Neptune* will be ready to clear out in a month, and which of us two is the fittest to make the voyage ? Would it look well, think you, for the uncle to be ploughing the ocean, whilst the nephew stayed snugly at home ?"

"I did not mean that," stammered Raymond.

"Then pray what do you mean ? Speak, if you please, and let me know, once for all, whether I have a nephew or not. Was not the thing arranged between us some time ago ?"

"It was."

"Then you do not intend fulfilling your part of the engagement; it does not matter to you whether I am deceived, or ruined; in fact, I must not count upon your assistance at all."

"Excuse me, Monsieur," interrupted the young man in a trembling voice, and becoming suddenly very pale; "I am ready to start—whenever you please."

This sudden submission seemed to disconcert M. Formon: he stared at his nephew, coughed a very embarrassed cough, and again began to pace the room, grumbling at the same time,

"Oh yes, it's all very easy to say you'll go, you'll go,—but you must first understand what about, and I'll be bound you don't know a word of it."

"I'll study that part of the business with Léon, Monsieur."

"Ah! yes—Léon—that's your friend? Well, call him here."

Raymond did so, and returned accompanied by my son, who brought with him all the documents connected with the house at Buenos Ayres.

He had carefully examined all the business, and gave so clear a statement of all matters relating to it, that the merchant was evidently quite taken by surprise. He was able to answer every question, to point out the rock on which former speculations had been wrecked, and the means of rendering them successful. The result of his work, short and substantial as it was, was so conclusive, that after well examining every detail, M. Formon could not repress an exclamation of admiration.

"Very good indeed," he said; "now that's what I call understanding business. My dear fellow, you were born to be a merchant.—Have you followed these explanations, Monsieur nephew?"

"Yes, but I think—it seems to me,"—stammered Raymond, awaking from the reverie in which he had been buried.

M. Formon shrugged his shoulders.

"And it seems to me, that you have not heard a single word," said he; "I'll be bound you have understood nothing of the question of exchange, which is the principal point—a splendid idea—and very lucrative—worthy a real merchant.—*You* would never have thought of such a plan—there's nothing of the merchant in your blood, Monsieur! you would never be able to settle matters with these *Guachos* of Buenos Ayres—you are not fit to be sent there, but M. Léon is."

My son bowed at the compliment.

"Especially as you would go unwillingly," added M. Formon—"and consider yourself a victim."

"I have said nothing to give you such an idea," objected Raymond.

"But I can see it—do you think I am ignorant of the attraction which keeps you here?"

"Monsieur—"

"Your obedience is mere resignation."

"I swear—"

"You submit to a misfortune for which you consider me responsible."

"But consider—"

"I have considered, Monsieur, and I do not choose any longer to be made to play the part of a melo-dramatic tyrant; your melancholy fatigues, and your sighs weary me;

I am tired of the sight of that long pale face of yours constantly before me like a spectre; and since you cannot be happy but in your own way, why take it, and I wash my hands of the matter."

"What! uncle! you cannot mean—" Raymond exclaimed, fearing he had misunderstood him; "that you will consent—"

"To your remaining here! Yes, I wish it; but who on earth am I to find to undertake this infernal journey?"

Léon made a step forward.

"Well, what is it?" asked M. Formon, who had his eye upon him.

"Pardon me," he said with some hesitation; "but if that were the only obstacle—"

"Well, what then?"

"I would offer to go myself."

"You would go to Buenos Ayres?"

"In yours and Raymond's service."

"In spite of the danger?"

"Yes."

"And on what conditions?"

"Any that you choose to make."

Raymond seized his hand, declaring it was impossible.

"Hold your tongue!" interrupted M. Formon; "you know nothing at all about it; this is a sensible proposal, consequently one that cannot concern you."

"But remember, uncle—"

"I remember that M. Léon sees clearly, where you don't see at all; and that he will make our fortune, and his own too, where you would only catch the yellow fever. Come with me, my dear sir, and we will talk the matter over more at leisure."

"But, at least allow me—" Raymond interrupted.

"O yes, *I allow you!*" exclaimed the merchant, as he led my son away; "go and ask Mademoiselle Remi not to leave town!"

* * * * *

Two hours after, Léon returned, and related all that had passed. His engagement with M. Formon was dependent on our sanction; but it assured his sister's marriage, and might open the way to fortune for himself. Notwithstanding the grief this double separation cost us, we felt it right to give our consent with thankfulness, seeing that the sacrifice was ours, and did not fall to the lot of those so inexpressibly dear to us.

* * * * * *

To-day our daughter Clara was united to M. Raymond. We could not possibly desire a better assorted union; Marcelle and I feel full of hope and confidence in their happiness, and yet the moment of separation was most cruel, we felt as if our very heart-strings were severing in the effort it cost us to part with our children.—Sublime law, which bereaves declining parents of their offspring, to raise up under other roofs a family of their own; which in its turn is dispersed abroad, thus weaving around mankind a very net-work of alliances—but grievous and bitter trial to those who, having reared their children through the sufferings of childhood, protected them in trouble, and consoled them in sorrow, are now enlivened by their blooming youth.

But why dwell upon such thoughts? let us rather occupy ourselves with their joy!

Just before the departure of the newly-married couple, Aunt Roubert presented Clara with exactly such another housekeeping-book as she had formerly bestowed on Marcelle; to which I added a blank note-book, similar to the one I am now closing. On the first page I had written this heavenly doctrine—

Love ye one another.

Then below, a few earthly counsels and warnings dictated by my own humble experience. The moment of separation arrived. Marcelle held her child long in her arms, then gently pushing her towards Raymond, she said—

"Never give her cause to regret us."

Sad and holy words, which I fervently repeated with heart and lip!

* * * * *

Léon left us yesterday. We accompanied him to the vessel, and watched it as it slowly sailed from our view, till we lost sight of it; then we turned, and slowly and silently regained our deserted home.

We entered the house, and traversed its silent rooms. Arriving at the last, Marcelle threw herself on the couch, and burying her face in her hands, her sobs burst forth. I knelt down on a stool by her side, and leaning my head against hers, said—

"Why this despair?"

She raised her head, and glancing around, exclaimed—

"They are gone, all gone! and we are left alone."

The tears rushed to my eyes, as taking her two hands in mine and pressing them to my heart, I answered—

"Oh! no, not alone, since the remembrance of twenty years of happiness, affection, and self-sacrifice remains to us! To-day, dear Marcelle, we have received our reward for the past! To those who have either neglected their duty, or are not loved, the hour when their hearth is made desolate, when the sunny brightness of their children fades away, and their joyous voices are hushed as the song birds in evening, to such, is indeed a bitter one! How can hearts sundered in the bright dawn of life, approach and comfort each other in its decline? What can these chance associations possess in common, but remorse, bickerings, and 'ennui?' No bright ray from the past embellishing the present, they see themselves as they are—old, sad, declining, and alone; but we, Marcelle—we have a happier lot; we are still possessed of all the richest treasures of the heart—love, esteem, and gratitude! We cannot glance back without encountering some touching or happy reminiscence. We see ourselves young in all our hopes of former times, gay in all the pleasures we have tasted together, and strong in the consciousness of duty fulfilled, to our weak utmost.

"What matter the traces that time has left in your dear face! each one of them reminds me of the many happy years I owe you; the wrinkles on your brow tell of many a hard day's work we have shared together; the silvery threads that streak your soft brown hair, recall your ever-watchful care! and this stooping figure brings before me the many anxious vigils kept beside the cradles of our children! Loved and noble heroine of my home, let me kiss these honorable scars of labor and devotion! No, Marcelle, whilst God in his mercy allows us to each other, I cannot believe ourselves wholly excluded from our earthly paradise. Look up, dearest, look at me; the enjoyments of life cannot be ended so long as we can remember the past, and continue in love one with the other."

With these words I put my arm around her, and gently raised her; she smiled upon me through her tears, as with her head resting on my shoulder, we approached the window. A soft and balmy evening breeze had risen, but not a cloud obscured the autumn sky, and our eyes rested there, their glances lost in the blue expanse. Presently, two swallows appeared winging their way towards the east. I drew Marcelle's attention to them.

"See, dear one," I said, "they also have lived to see their nest deserted, and their young ones scattered; but it has made them neither distrustful of God, nor earth, and on, together, they swiftly fly towards a new and eternal spring."

THE END.

Gems of British Art. 30 Engravings. 1 vol. 4to. morocco, ... 18 00
Gray's Elegy. Illustrated. 8vo. 1 50
Goldsmith's Deserted Village, ... 1 50
The Homes of American Authors. With Illustrations, cloth, ... 4 00
" " " cloth, gilt, 5 00
" " " mor. antqe. 7 00
The Holy Gospels. With 40 Designs by Overbeck. 1 vol. folio. Antique mor. . . . 20 00
The Land of Bondage. By J. M. Wainwright, D. D. Morocco, ... 6 00
The Queens of England. By Agnes Strickland. With 29 Portraits. Antique mor. . . . 10 00
The Ornaments of Memory. With 18 Illustrations. 4to. cloth, gilt, ... 6 00
" " Morocco, . . 10 00
Royal Gems from the Galleries of Europe. 40 Engravings, ... 25 00
The Republican Court; or, American Society in the Days of Washington. 21 Portraits. Antique mor. 12 00
The Vernon Gallery. 67 Engrav'gs. 4to. Ant. 25 00
The Women of the Bible. With 18 Engravings. Mor. antique, ... 10 00
Wilkie Gallery. Containing 60 Splendid Engravings. 4to. Antique mor. 25 00
A Winter Wreath of Summer Flowers. By S. G. Goodrich. Illustrated. Cloth, gilt, . 3 00

Juvenile Books.

A Poetry Book for Children, ... 75
Aunt Fanny's Christmas Stories, ... 50
American Historical Tales, ... 75

UNCLE AMEREL'S STORY BOOKS.

The Little Gift Book. 18mo. cloth, . . . 25
The Child's Story Book. Illust. 18mo. cloth, 25
Summer Holidays. 18mo. cloth, ... 25
Winter Holidays. Illustrated. 18mo. cloth, . 25
George's Adventures in the Country. Illustrated. 18mo. cloth, ... 25
Christmas Stories. Illustrated. 18mo. cloth, . 25

Book of Trades, ... 50
Boys at Home. By the Author of Edgar Clifton, 75
Child's Cheerful Companion, ... 50
Child's Picture and Verse Book. 100 Engs. . 50

COUSIN ALICE'S WORKS.

All's Not Gold that Glitters, ... 75
Contentment Better than Wealth, ... 63
Nothing Venture, Nothing Have, ... 63
No such Word as Fail, ... 63
Patient Waiting No Loss, ... 63

Dashwood Priory. By the Author of Edgar Clifton, ... 75
Edgar Clifton; or Right and Wrong, . . . 75
Fireside Fairies. By Susan Pindar, . . . 63
Good in Every Thing. By Mrs. Barwell, . . 50
Leisure Moments Improved, , ... 75
Life of Punchinello, ... 75

LIBRARY FOR MY YOUNG COUNTRYMEN.

Adventures of Capt. John Smith. By the Author of Uncle Philip, ... 38
Adventures of Daniel Boone. By do. . . 38
Dawnings of Genius. By Anne Pratt, . . 38
Life and Adventures of Henry Hudson. By the Author of Uncle Philip, ... 38
Life and Adventures of Hernan Cortez. By do. 38
Philip Randolph. A Tale of Virginia. By Mary Gertrude, ... 38
Rowan's History of the French Revolution. 2 vols. 75
Southey's Life of Oliver Cromwell, . . . 38

Louis' School-Days. By E. J. May, ... 75
Louise; or, The Beauty of Integrity, . . . 25
Maryatt's Settlers in Canada, ... 62
" Masterman Ready, ... 63
" Scenes in Africa, ... 63
Midsummer Fays. By Susan Pindar, . . . 63

MISS McINTOSH'S WORKS.

Aunt Kitty's Tales, 12mo. 75
Blind Alice; A Tale for Good Children, . . 38
Ellen Leslie; or, The Reward of Self-Control, 38
Florence Arnott; or, Is She Generous? . 38
Grace and Clara; or, Be Just as well as Generous, ... 38
Jessie Graham; or, Friends Dear, but Truth Dearer, ... 38
Emily Herbert; or, The Happy Home, . . 37
Rose and Lillie Stanhope, ... 37

Mamma's Story Book, ... 75
Pebbles from the Sea-Shore, ... 37
Puss in Boots. Illustrated. By Otto Specter, . 25

PETER PARLEY'S WORKS.

Faggots for the Fireside, ... 1 13
Parley's Present for all Seasons, ... 1 00
Wanderers by Sea and Land, ... 1 13
Winter Wreath of Summer Flowers, . . . 3 00

TALES FOR THE PEOPLE AND THEIR CHILDREN.

Alice Franklin. By Mary Howitt, ... 38
Crofton Boys (The). By Harriet Martineau, . 38
Dangers of Dining Out. By Mrs. Ellis, . . 38
Domestic Tales. By Hannah More. 2 vols. . 75
Early Friendship. By Mrs. Copley, . . . 38
Farmer's Daughter (The). By Mrs. Cameron, 38
First Impressions. By Mrs. Ellis, ... 38
Hope On, Hope Ever! By Mary Howitt, . 38
Little Coin, Much Care. By do. 38
Looking-Glass for the Mind. Many plates, . 38
Love and Money. By Mary Howitt, . . . 38
Minister's Family. By Mrs. Ellis, ... 38
My Own Story. By Mary Howitt, ... 38
My Uncle, the Clockmaker. By do. . . . 38
No Sense Like Common Sense. By do. . . 38
Peasant and the Prince. By H. Martineau, . 28
Poplar Grove. By Mrs. Copley, ... 38
Somerville Hall. By Mrs. Ellis, ... 38
Sowing and Reaping. By Mary Howitt, . . 38
Story of a Genius. 38
Strive and Thrive. By do. 38
The Two Apprentices. By do. 38
Tired of Housekeeping. By T. S. Arthur, . 38
Twin Sisters (The). By Mrs. Sandham, . . 38
Which is the Wiser? By Mary Howitt, . . 38
Who Shall be Greatest? By do. 38
Work and Wages. By do. 38

SECOND SERIES.

Chances and Changes. By Charles Burdett, . 38
Goldmaker's Village. By H. Zschokke, . . 38
Never Too Late. By Charles Burdett, . . . 38
Ocean Work, Ancient and Modern. By J. H. Wright, ... 38

Picture Pleasure Book, 1st Series, ... 1 25
" " " 2d Series, ... 1 25
Robinson Crusoe. 300 Plates, ... 1 50
Susan Pindar's Story Book, ... 75
Sunshine of Greystone, ... 75
Travels of Bob the Squirrel, ... 37
Wonderful Story Book, ... 50
Willy's First Present, ... 75
Week's Delight; or, Games and Stories for the Parlor, ... 75
William Tell, the Hero of Switzerland, . . 50
Young Student. By Madame Guizot, . . 75

Miscellaneous and General Literature.

Title	Price
An Attic Philosopher in Paris,	25
Appletons' Library Manual,	1 25
Agnell's Book of Chess,	1 25
Arnold's Miscellaneous Works,	2 00
Arthur. The Successful Merchant,	75
A Book for Summer Time in the Country,	50
Baldwin's Flush Times in Alabama,	1 25
Calhoun (J. C.), Works of. 4 vols. publ., each,	2 00
Clark's (W. G.) Knick-Knacks,	1 25
Cornwall's Music as it Was, and as it Is,	63
Essays from the London Times. 1st & 2d Series, each,	50
Ewbanks' World in a Workshop,	75
Ellis' Women of England,	50
" Hearts and Homes,	1 50
" Prevention Better than Cure,	75
Foster's Essays on Christian Morals,	50
Goldsmith's Vicar of Wakefield,	75
Grant's Memoirs of an American Lady,	75
Gaieties and Gravities. By Horace Smith,	50
Guizot's History of Civilization,	1 00
Hearth-Stone. By Rev. S. Osgood,	1 00
Hobson. My Uncle and I,	75
Ingoldsby Legends,	50
Isham's Mud Cabin,	1 00
Johnson's Meaning of Words,	1 00
Kavanagh's Women of Christianity,	75
Leger's Animal Magnetism,	1 00
Life's Discipline. A Tale of Hungary,	63
Letters from Rome. A. D. 138,	1 90
Margaret Maitland,	75
Maiden and Married Life of Mary Powell,	50
Morton Montague; or a Young Christian's Choice,	75
Macaulay's Miscellanies. 5 vols.	5 00
Maxims of Washington. By J. F. Schroeder,	1 00
Mile Stones in our Life Journey,	1 00

MINIATURE CLASSICAL LIBRARY.

Title	Price
Poetic Lacon; or, Aphorisms from the Poets,	38
Bond's Golden Maxims,	31
Clarke's Scripture Promises. Complete,	38
Elizabeth; or, The Exiles of Siberia,	31
Goldsmith's Vicar of Wakefield,	38
" Essays,	38
Gems from American Poets,	38
Hannah More's Private Devotions,	31
" " Practical Piety. 2 vols.	75
Hemans' Domestic Affections,	31
Hoffman's Lays of the Hudson, &c.	38
Johnson's History of Rasselas,	38
Manual of Matrimony,	31
Moore's Lalla Rookh,	38
" Melodies. Complete,	38
Paul and Virginia,	31
Pollok's Course of Time,	38
Pure Gold from the Rivers of Wisdom,	38
Thomson's Seasons,	38
Token of the Heart. Do. of Affection. Do. of Remembrance. Do. of Friendship. Do. of Love. Each,	31
Useful Letter-Writer,	38
Wilson's Sacra Privata,	31
Young's Night Thoughts,	38

Title	Price
Little Pedlington and the Pedlingtonians,	50
Prismatics. Tales and Poems,	1 25
Papers from the Quarterly Review,	50
Republic of the United States. Its Duties, &c	1 00
Preservation of Health and Prevention of Disease,	75
School for Politics. By Chas. Gayerre,	75
Select Italian Comedies. Translated,	75
Shakespeare's Scholar. By R. G. White,	2 50
Spectator (The). New ed. 6 vols. cloth,	9 00
Swett's Treatise on Diseases of the Chest,	3 00
Stories from Blackwood,	50

THACKERAY'S WORKS.

Title	Price
The Book of Snobs,	50
Mr. Browne's Letters,	50
The Confessions of Fitzboodle,	50
The Fat Contributor,	50
Jeames' Diary. A Legend of the Rhine,	50
The Luck of Barry Lyndon,	1 00
Men's Wives,	50
The Paris Sketch Book. 2 vols.	1 00
The Shabby Genteel Story,	50
The Yellowplush Papers. 1 vol. 16mo.	50
Thackeray's Works. 6 vols. bound in cloth,	6 00

Title	Price
Trescott's Diplomacy of the Revolution,	75
Tuckerman's Artist Life,	75
Up Country Letters,	75
Ward's Letters from Three Continents,	1 00
" English Items,	1 00
Warner's Rudimental Lessons in Music,	50
Woman's Worth,	38

Philosophical Works.

Title	Price
Cousin's Course of Modern Philosophy,	3 00
" Philosophy of the Beautiful,	62
" on the True, Beautiful, and Good,	1 50
Comte's Positive Philosophy. 2 vols.	4 00
Hamilton's Philosophy. 1 vol. 8vo.	1 50

Poetry and the Drama.

Title	Price
Amelia's Poems. 1 vol. 12mo.	1 25
Brownell's Poems. 12mo.	75
Bryant's Poems. 1 vol. 8vo. Illustrated,	3 50
" " Antique mor.	6 00
" " 2 vols. 12mo. cloth,	2 00
" " 1 vol. 18mo.	63
Byron's Poetical Works. 1 vol. cloth,	3 00
" " " Antique mor.	6 00
Burns' Poetical Works. Cloth,	1 00
Butler's Hudibras. Cloth,	1 00
Campbell's Poetical Works. Cloth,	1 00
Coleridge's Poetical Works. Cloth,	1 25
Cowper's Poetical Works,	1 00
Chaucer's Canterbury Tales,	1 00
Dante's Poems. Cloth,	1 00
Dryden's Poetical Works. Cloth,	1 00
Fay (J. S.), Ulric; or, The Voices,	75
Goethe's Iphigenia in Tauris. Translated,	75
Gilfillan's Edition of the British Poets. 12 vols. published. Price per vol. cloth,	1 00
Do. do. Calf, per vol.	2 50
Griffith's (Mattie) Poems,	75
Hemans' Poetical Works. 2 vols. 16mo.	2 00
Herbert's Poetical Works. 16mo. cloth,	1 00
Keats' Poetical Works. Cloth, 12mo.	1 25
Kirke White's Poetical Works. Cloth,	1 00
Lord's Poems. 1 vol. 12mo.	75
" Christ in Hades. 12mo.	75
Milton's Paradise Lost. 18mo.	38
" Complete Poetical Works,	1 00
Moore's Poetical Works. 8vo. Illustrated,	3 00
" " " Mor. extra,	6 00
Montgomery's Sacred Poems. 1 vol. 12mo.	75
Pope's Poetical Works. 1 vol. 16mo.	1 00
Southey's Poetical Works. 1 vol.	3 00
Spenser's Faerie Queene. 1 vol. cloth,	1 00
Scott's Poetical Works. 1 vol.	1 00
" Lady of the Lake. 16mo.	38
" Marmion,	37
" Lay of the Last Minstrel,	25
Shakspeare's Dramatic Works,	2 00
Tasso's Jerusalem Delivered. 1 vol. 16mo.	1 00
Wordsworth (W.). The Prelude,	1 00

Religious Works.

Title	Price
Arnold's Rugby School Sermons,	50
Anthon's Catechism on the Homilies,	06
" Early Catechism for Children,	06
Burnet's History of the Reformation. 3 vols.	2 50
" Thirty-Nine Articles,	2 00

Bradley's Family and Parish Sermons, . . 2 00
Cotter's Mass and Rubrics, ... 38
Coit's Puritanism, ... 1 00
Evans' Rectory of Valehead, ... 50
Grayson's True Theory of Christianity, . . 1 00
Gresley on Preaching, ... 1 25
Griffin's Gospel its Own Advocate, . . . 1 00
Hecker's Book of the Soul, ...
Hooker's Complete Works. 2 vols. . . 4 00
James' Happiness, ... 25
James on the Nature of Evil, ... 1 00
Jarvis' Reply to Milner, ... 75
Kingsley's Sacred Choir, ... 75
Keble's Christian Year, ... 37
Layman's Letters to a Bishop, . . . 25
Logan's Sermons and Expository Lectures, . 1 13
Lyra Apostolica, ... 50
Marshall's Notes on Episcopacy, . . . 1 00
Newman's Sermons and Subjects of the Day, 1 00
" Essay on Christian Doctrine, . . 75
Ogilby on Lay Baptism, ... 50
Pearson on the Creed, ... 2 00
Pulpit Cyclopædia and Ministers' Companion, 2 50
Sewell's Reading Preparatory to Confirmation, 75
Southard's Mystery of Godliness, . . . 75
Sketches and Skeletons of Sermons, . . 2 50
Spencer's Christian Instructed, . . . 1 00
Sherlock's Practical Christian, . . . 75
Sutton's Disce Vivere—Learn to Live, . . 75
Swartz's Letters to my Godchild, . . . 38
Trench's Notes on the Parables, . . . 1 75
" Notes on the Miracles. . . . 1 75
Taylor's Holy Living and Dying, . . . 1 00
" Episcopacy Asserted and Maintained, 75
Tyng's Family Commentary, ... 2 00
Walker's Sermons on Practical Subjects, . 2 00
Watson on Confirmation, ... 06
Wilberforce's Manual for Communicants, . 38
Wilson's Lectures on Colossians, . . . 75
Wyatt's Christian Altar, ... 38

Voyages and Travels.

Africa and the American Flag, . . . 1 25
Appletons' Southern and Western Guide, . 1 00
" Northern and Eastern Guide, . 1 25
" Complete U. S. Guide Book, . . 2 00
" N. Y. City Map, ... 25
Bartlett's New Mexico, &c. 2 vols. Illustrated, 5 00
Burnet's N. Western Territory, . . . 2 00
Bryant's What I Saw in California, . . 1 25
Coggeshall's Voyages. 2 vols. . . . 2 50
Dix's Winter in Madeira, ... 1 00
Huc's Travels in Tartary and Thibet. 2 vols. 1 00
Layard's Nineveh. 1 vol. 8vo. . . . 1 25
Notes of a Theological Student. 12mo. . . 1 00
Oliphant's Journey to Katmundu, . . . 50
Parkyns' Abyssinia. 2 vols. 2 50
Russia as it Is. By Gurowski, ... 1 00
" By Count de Custine, ... 1 25
Squier's Nicaragua. 2 vols. 5 00
Tappan's Step from the New World to the Old, 1 75
Wanderings and Fortunes of Germ. Emigrants, 75
Williams' Isthmus of Tehuantepec. 2 vols. 8vo. 3 50

Works of Fiction.

GRACE AGUILAR'S WORKS.

The Days of Bruce. 2 vols. 12mo. . . . 1 50
Home Scenes and Heart Studies. 12mo. . 75
The Mother's Recompense. 12mo. . . 75
Woman's Friendship. 12mo. 75
Women of Israel. 2 vols. 12mo. . . . 1 50

Basil. A Story of Modern Life. 12mo. . . 75
Brace's Fawn of the Pale Faces. 12mo. . 75
Busy Moments of an Idle Woman, . . . 75
Chestnut Wood. A Tale. 2 vols. . . . 1 75
Don Quixotte, Translated. Illustrated, . . 1 25
Drury (A. H.). Light and Shade, . . . 75
Dupuy (A. E.). The Conspirator, . . . 75
Elten Parry; or, Trials of the Heart, . . 63

MRS. ELLIS' WORKS.

Hearts and Homes; or, Social Distinctions, . 1 50
Prevention Better than Cure, ... 75
Women of England, ... 50

Emmanuel Phillibert. By Dumas, . . . 1 25
Farmingdale. By Caroline Thomas, . . 1 00
Fullerton (Lady G.). Ellen Middleton, . 75
" " Grantley Manor. 1 vol. 12mo. . . . 75
" " Lady Bird. 1 vol. 12mo. 75
The Foresters. By Alex. Dumas, . . . 75
Gore (Mrs.). The Dean's Daughter. 1 vol. 12mo. 75
Goldsmith's Vicar of Wakefield. 12mo. . 75
Gil Blas. With 500 Engravings. Cloth, gt. edg. 2 50
Harry Muir. A Tale of Scottish Life, . . 75
Hearts Unveiled; or, I Knew You Would Like Him, ... 75
Heartsease; or, My Brother's Wife. 2 vols. 1 50
Heir of Redclyffe. 2 vols. cloth, . . . 1 50
Heloise; or, The Unrevealed Secret. 12mo. . 75
Hobson. My Uncle and I. 12mo. . . . 75
Holmes' Tempest and Sunshine. 12mo. . . 1 00
Home is Home. A Domestic Story, . . 75
Howitt (Mary). The Heir of West Wayland, 50
Io. A Tale of the Ancient Fane. 12mo. . 75
The Iron Cousin. By Mary Cowden Clarke, . 1 25
James (G. P. R.). Adrian; or, Clouds of the Mind, ... 75
John; or, Is a Cousin in the Hand Worth Two in the Bush, ... 25

JULIA KAVANAGH'S WORKS.

Nathalie. A Tale. 12mo. 1 00
Madeline. 12mo. 75
Daisy Burns. 12mo. 1 00

Life's Discipline. A Tale of Hungary, . . 63
Lone Dove (The). A Legend, ... 75
Linny Lockwood. By Catherine Crowe, . 50

MISS McINTOSH'S WORKS.

Two Lives; or, To Seem and To Be. 12mo. 75
Aunt Kitty's Tales. 12mo. 75
Charms and Counter-Charms. 12mo. . . 1 00
Evenings at Donaldson Manor, . . . 75
The Lofty and the Lowly. 2 vols. . . . 1 50

Margaret's Home. By Cousin Alice, . .
Marie Louise; or, The Opposite Neighbors, . 50
Maiden Aunt (The). A Story, . . . 75
Manzoni. The Betrothed Lovers. 2 vols. . 1 50
Margaret Cecil; or, I Can Because I Ought, . 75
Morton Montague; or, The Christian's Choice, 75
Norman Leslie. By G. C. H. 75
Prismatics. Tales and Poems. By Haywarde, 1 25
Roe (A. S.). James Montjoy. 12mo. . . 75
" To Love and to Be Loved. 12mo. 75
" Time and Tide. 12mo. . . 75
Reuben Medlicott; or, The Coming Man, . 75
Rose Douglass. By S. R. W. 75

MISS SEWELL'S WORKS.

Amy Herbert. A Tale. 12mo. . . . 75
Experience of Life. 12mo. 75
Gertrude. A Tale. 12mo. 75
Katherine Ashton. 2 vols. 12mo. . . . 1 50
Laneton Parsonage. A Tale. 3 vols. 12mo. . 2 25
Margaret Percival. 2 vols. 1 50
Walter Lorimer, and Other Tales. 12mo. . 75
A Journal Kept for Children of a Village School, 1 00

Sunbeams and Shadows. Cloth, . . . 75
Thorpe's Hive of the Bee Hunter, . . . 1 00
Thackeray's Works. 6 vols. 12mo. . . 6 00
The Virginia Comedians. 2 vols. 12mo. . 1 50
Use of Sunshine. By S. M. 12mo. . . . 75
Wight's Romance of Abelard & Heloise. 12mo. 75

POPULAR NEW LIGHT READING BOOKS.

Just Published

By D. APPLETON & COMPANY,

JOHN;

Or, IS A COUSIN IN HAND WORTH TWO COUNTS IN A BUSH?

BY EMILIE CARLEN.

TRANSLATED FROM THE ORIGINAL SWEDISH.

One Volume, 8vo. Paper cover, price 25 cents.

"A remarkably well-written story, full of pleasant incidents and love scenes, with some light touches of humor, as well as of sentiment."—*American Courier.*

"Full of romantic incidents and admirable sketches, it will no doubt acquire a rapid popularity."—*Arthur's Home Gazette.*

"It will be sought after by all readers of light literature."—*Pennsylvanian.*

"A very pleasant, lively novel—one of the cheerful, chatty kind."—*Evening Post.*

"This volume is one of merit, and one that will please lady readers."—*Daily Times.*

"More animated than Miss Carlen's last novel, while there is the same ingenuity, and sweet pictures of feeling and character."—*Boston Evening Transcript.*

"It is a Swedish story and told with a piquancy that is seldom equalled. Buy and read it." —*Syracuse Daily Journal.*

"While she is Miss Bremer's equal in the portrayal of domestic scenes, she has more vigor of conception and strength of sentiment."—*Palladium.*

LINNY LOCKWOOD.

A TALE.

BY Mrs. CROWE.

AUTHOR OF "NIGHT SIDE OF NATURE," "SUSAN HOPLEY," ETC.

One Volume, 8vo. Paper cover, price 50 cents.

"A perusal of a few pages of this entertaining romance will infallibly enlist the reader for a perusal of its entire contents."—*Norfolk Herald.*

"She is a very clever writer, and Linny Lockwood will have its share of readers."—*Western Literary Messenger.*

"There is a freshness and simplicity in the style of the writer, and human character and manners are well depicted."—*Daily Times.*

"A novel designed to advocate marrying for love and nothing shorter."—*Syracuse Evening Chronicle.*

"The character of the heroine is one of the most delightful creations of modern romance; the story is admirably told.—*Arthur's Home Gazette.*

"It is written with a masculine power and energy, and is full of stirring and rapidly changing incidents, and of refined sentiment."—*Northern Budget.*

THE ATTIC PHILOSOPHER IN PARIS;

Or, A PEEP AT THE WORLD FROM A GARRET,

Being the Journal of a Happy Man.

From the French of EMILE SOUVESTRE.

One Volume, 12mo. Paper cover, 25 cents.

'A greater amount of wisdom, wit, and pathos, it would be almost a sin to expect for twenty-five cents, than is to be found in this truly excellent little volume. It is very much in the style of *Sterne's Sentimental Journey*, and contains passages worthy of Lesage, in his palmiest days."—*U. S. Gazette.*

"This view of the peculiarities of Paris Life from a Garret, has the stamp of true genius upon it. At times it is quaint, and makes you smile; at times rather racy and saucy, and makes you laugh; and at times touching, and makes you inclined to weep."—*Hartford Daily Courant.*

THE GREAT KENTUCKY NOVEL.

D. APPLETON & COMPANY

HAVE JUST PUBLISHED

Tempest and Sunshine; or, Life in Kentucky.

BY MRS. MARY J. HOLMES.

One Volume, 12mo Paper covers, 75 cents; cloth, $1.

These are the most striking and original sketches of American character in the South-western States which have ever been published. The character of Tempest is drawn with all that spirit and energy which characterize the high toned female spirit of the South, while Sunshine possesses the loveliness and gentleness of the sweetest of her sex. The Planter is sketched to the life, and in his strongly marked, passionate, and generous nature, the reader will recognize one of the truest sons of the south-west.

OPINIONS OF THE PRESS.

"The book is well written, and its fame will be more than ephemeral."—*Buffalo Express.*

"The story is interesting and finely developed."—*Daily Times.*

"A lively romance of western life—the style of the writer is smart, intelligent, and winning, and her story is told with spirit and skill."—*U. S. Gazette.*

"An excellent work, and its sale must be extensive."—*Stamford Advocate.*

"The whole is relieved by a generous introduction of incident as well as by an amplitude of love and mystery."—*Express.*

"A delightful, well written book, portraying western life to the letter. The book abounds in an easy humor, with touching sentences of tenderness and pathos scattered through it, and from first to last keeps up a humane interest that very many authors strive in vain to achieve. 'Tempest' and 'Sunshine,' two sisters, are an exemplification of the good that to some comes by nature, and to others is found only through trials, temptation, and tribulation. Mr. Middleton, the father of 'Tempest and 'Sunshine,' is the very soul and spirit of 'Old Kaintuck,' abridged into one man. The book is worth reading. There is a heathy tone of morality pervading it that will make it a suitable work to be placed in the hands of our daughters and sisters."—*New York Day Book.*

MRS. COWDEN CLARKE'S NEW ENGLISH NOVEL.

The Iron Cousin, or Mutual Influence.

BY MARY COWDEN CLARKE,

Author of "THE GIRLHOOD OF SHAKSPEARE'S HEROINES" the COMPLETE CONCORDANCE TO SHAKSPEARE," &c.

One handsomely printed volume, large 12mo. over 500 pages. Price $1.25—cloth.

"Mrs. Clarke has given us one of the most delightful novels we have read for many a day, and one which is destined, we doubt not, to be much longer lived than the majority of books of its class. Its chief beauties are a certain freshness in the style in which the incidents are presented to us—a healthful tone pervading it—a completeness in most of the characters—and a truthful power in the descriptions."—*London Times.*

"We have found the volume deeply interesting—its characters are well drawn, while its tone and sentiments are well calculated to exert a purifying and ennobling influence upon all who read it."—*Savannah Republican.*

"The scene of the book is village life amongst the upper class, with village episodes, which seem to have been sketched from the life—there is a primitive simplicity and greatness of heart about some of the characters which keep up the sympathy and interest to the end."—*London Globe.*

"The reader cannot fail of being both charmed and instructed by the book, and of hoping that a pen so able will not lie idle."—*Pennsylvanian.*

"We fearlessly recommend it as a work of more than ordinary merit."—*Binghampton Daily Republic.*

"The great moral lesson indicated by the title-page of this book runs, as a golden thread, through every part of it, while the reader is constantly kept in contact with the workings of an inventive and brilliant mind."—*Albany Argus.*

"We have read this fascinating story with a good deal of interest. Human nature is well and faithfully portrayed, and we see the counterpart of our story in character and disposition, in every village and district. The book cannot fail of popular reception."—*Albany and Rochester Courier.*

"A work of deep and powerful influence."—*Herald.*

"Mrs. Cowden Clarke, with the delicacy and artistic taste of refined womanhood, has in this work shown great versatility of talent."

"The story is too deeply interesting to allow the reader to lay it down till he has read it to the end."

"The work is skilful in plan, graphic in style, diversified in incident and true to nature."

"The tale is charmingly imagined. The incidents never exceed probability but seem perfectly natural. In the style there is much quaintness, in the sentiment much tenderness."

"It is a spirited, charming story, full of adventure, friendship and love, with characters nicely drawn and carefully discriminated. The clear style and spirit with which the story is presented and the characters developed, will attract a large constituency to the perusal."

"Mrs. Cowden Clarke's story has one of the highest qualities of fiction—it is no flickering shadow, but seems of real growth. It is full of lively truth, and shows nice perception of the early elements of character with which we become acquainted in its wholeness, and in the ripeness of years. The incident is well woven; the color is blood-warm; and there is the presence of a sweet grace and gentle power"

"A WORK WHICH BEARS THE IMPRESS OF GENIUS."

KATHARINE ASHTON.

By the author of "Amy Herbert," "Gertrude," &c.

2 vols. 12mo. Paper covers, $1; cloth, $1 50.

Opinions of the Press.

We know not where we will find purer morals, or more valuable "life-philosophy, than in the pages of Miss Sewell.—*Savannah Georgian.*

The style and character of Miss Sewell's writings are too well known to the reading public to need commendation. The present volume will only add to her reputation as an authoress.—*Albany Transcript.*

This novel is admirably calculated to inculcate refined moral and religious sentiments.—*Boston Herald.*

The interest of the story is well sustained throughout, and it is altogether one of the pleasantest books of the season.—*Syracuse Standard.*

Those who have read the former works of this writer, will welcome the appearance of this; it is equal to the best of her preceding novels.—*Savannah Republican.*

Noble, beautiful, selfish, hard, and ugly characters appear in it, and each is so drawn as to be felt and estimated as it deserves.—*Commonwealth.*

A re-publication of a good English novel. It teaches self-control, charity, and a true estimation of life, by the interesting history of a young girl.—*Hartford Courant.*

Katharine Ashton will enhance the reputation already attained, the story and the moral being equally commendable.—*Buffalo Courier.*

Like all its predecessors, Katharine Ashton bears the impress of genius, consecrated to the noblest purposes, and should find a welcome in every family circle.—*Banner of the Cross.*

No one can be injured by books like this; a great many must be benefited. Few authors have sent so many faultless writings to the press as she has done.—*Worcester Palladium.*

The *self-denial* of the Christian life, in its application to common scenes and circumstances, is happily illustrated in the example of Katharine Ashton, in which there is much to admire and imitate.—*Southern Churchman.*

Her present work is an interesting tale of English country life, is written with her usual ability, and is quite free from any offensive parade of her own theological tenets.—*Boston Traveller.*

The field in which Miss Sewell labors, seems to be exhaustless, and to yield always a beautiful and a valuable harvest.—*Troy Daily Budget.*

D. APPLETON & COMPANY

Have recently published the following interesting works by the same author.

THE EXPERIENCE OF LIFE. 1 vol. 12mo. Paper, 50 cents; cloth, 75 cents.

THE EARL'S DAUGHTER. 1 vol. 12mo. Paper, 50 cents; cloth, 75 cents.

GERTRUDE: a Tale. 1 vol. 12mo. Paper, 50 cts; cloth, 75 cts.

AMY HERBERT: A Tale. 1 vol. 12mo. Paper, 50 cents; cloth 75 cents.

LANETON PARSONAGE. 3 vols. 12mo. Paper, $1 50, cloth, $2 25.

MARGARET PERCIVAL. 2 vols. Paper, $1; cloth, $1 50.

READING FOR A MONTH. 12mo. cloth, 75 cents.

A JOURNAL KEPT DURING A SUMMER TOUR. 1 vol cloth, $1 00.

WALTER LORIMER AND OTHER TALES. Cloth, 75 cents.

THE CHILD'S FIRST HISTORY OF ROME. 50 cents.

THE CHILD'S FIRST HISTORY OF GEEECE. 63 cents.

www.ingramcontent.com/pod-product-compliance
Lightning Source LLC
LaVergne TN
LVHW010216110826
845151LV00004B/1102

9781425527730